THE DEPRAVED

James Raven

© James Raven 2016

James Raven has asserted his rights under the Copyright, Design and Patents Act, 1988, to be identified as the author of this work.

First published by Endeavour Press Ltd in 2016.

Dedicated to my family with love

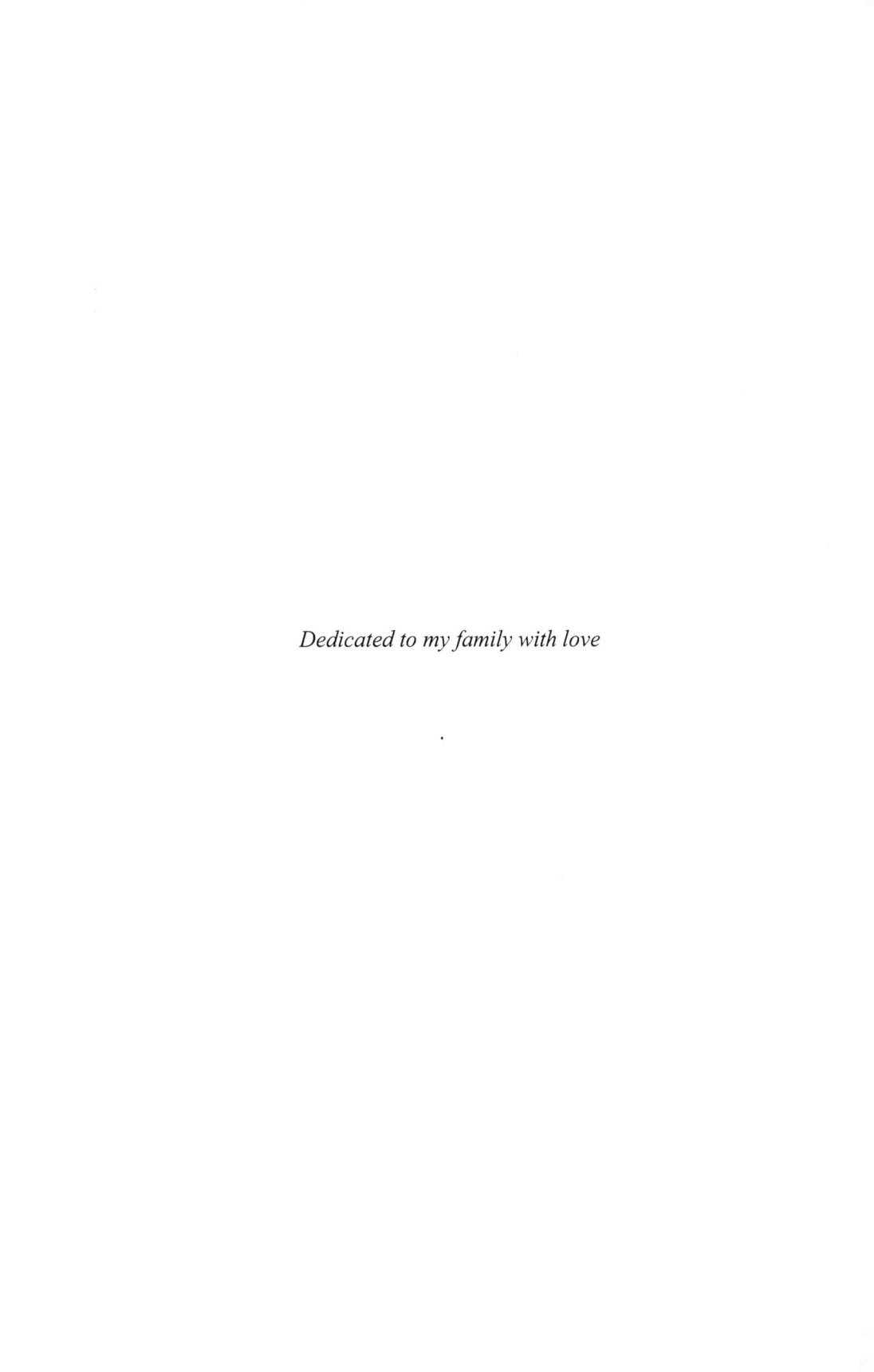

Part 1

Prologue

A crowd maybe 50 strong had gathered outside the Tequila Club – London's hottest new nightspot. It included a bunch of eager paparazzi and a group of screaming teenage girls who didn't look old enough to be on the streets this close to midnight.

Helen Troy smiled through the tinted windows of her stretch limousine as it pulled into the kerb. Her entrance was going to make a great photo opportunity, and with any luck her picture would feature on the front pages of the morning papers. She felt a surge of excitement and anticipation.

Tonight was the latest in a long line of stage-managed appearances to promote her latest album. It was all part of the game, the quest for publicity. She had been playing the game for two years now, ever since her debut album shot straight to number one in the British charts.

Now in the public eye, her every move was monitored by the press and by adoring fans. And she loved it. She loved all the attention and all the pampering. She was living the dream and yet she was still only twenty three.

The limo door was pulled open and she stepped onto the pavement, beaming a seductive smile at the crowd. Flashbulbs popped by the dozen, lighting up the silver sequins in her figure-hugging Jovani party dress. She pouted her lips, waved at the crowd, and as the screams grew louder so her heart began to race.

Helen had never felt so happy. This was her world now and she imagined herself to be a goddess among mortals. Britney and Kylie had had their day. So had Cheryl and Christina. Now it was her turn. Helen Troy was the new kid on the block. The new diva on the world stage. She stopped on the red carpet to pose for the photographers and sparked another blizzard of phosphorous.

'Do a twirl, Helen.'

'Look this way, Helen.'

'Show us some flesh, Helen.'

She responded to every request and took the time to sign a few autographs. The crowd loved her and she loved them back. She was in her element, riding high on a wave of adulation.

Eventually her black-suited driver, who was also her bodyguard, took her elbow and steered her towards the entrance. She slipped into the brightly lit reception area where she was greeted by the manager, a 50-year-old Rod Stewart lookalike named Mike Dennis. She tried not to cringe when he put his wet lips on her left cheek and dug his fingers into her bare arms.

'You look terrific, Helen,' he enthused. 'Absolutely terrific.'

She thanked him and said she was pleased to be here. As she spoke, he gazed openly at the swell of her breasts, a lascivious smile tugging at the corners of his mouth.

'Mr Serova is expecting you in the VIP area,' he said, shifting his eyes back to her face. 'The champagne's on ice and some of your friends have already arrived.'

A door was held open and she stepped into the throbbing darkness of the club. Music boomed, bodies gyrated, and coloured lights flashed to the beat. As she walked across the circular dance floor, Helen could feel the eyes of every man in the room drinking her in.

The VIP area was on a raised deck and cordoned off by rope. Inside it was a bunch of tables, each surrounded by high-backed leather chairs. Most of the chairs were occupied by trendy young things in skimpy dresses and tight, sweat-stained shirts. Helen recognised a few faces. Tasha and Robert from her record label, a flame-haired woman named Babs from her management team, and of course, the Russian billionaire Leon Serova, who blew her a kiss and gave her a wink. He was the man of the moment, having taken over the club this evening to celebrate his fortieth birthday. That was why the place was buzzing at such an early hour. Serova was laying on food, which, along with the booze, was entirely at his expense.

Helen spent the next ten minutes kissing air and saying hi. Then she started on the champagne while feigning interest in the various conversations she got drawn into. These related for the most part to her new album and the world tour she was about to embark on. The champagne, as usual, went straight to her head. But she was too busy enjoying herself to do anything about it. She had no intention of getting plastered, but a little tipsy would be OK.

Eventually she was invited onto the dance floor.

'Time to set this place on fire,' someone said.

She was up for it, as always, but not until she had emptied her swollen bladder.

'I need to pee first,' she said.

Mike Dennis appeared as if my magic, pointing to a door marked private that led to the VIP's exclusive toilets.

Her bodyguard offered to go with her, but she told him not to be silly.

'I'm quite capable of going for a pee by myself,' she giggled.

She went through the door and into a narrow corridor with framed photographs of celebrities on the walls. There were two doors on the right and a much larger door at the far end, which was probably a fire exit or service entrance. The ladies' toilet was adorned with shiny grey tiles and huge round mirrors. There were shelves containing various perfumes and expensive hand creams. Helen slipped into a cubicle to empty her bladder. Then she washed her hands and touched up her face. A dash of lipstick. A smudge of eye shadow. A brush of mascara. Eight minutes after entering the ladies' room she stepped back into the corridor.

And she came face to face with two men wearing black balaclavas.

Before she could scream, the taller of the two lunged forward and clapped a hand over her mouth. She dropped her clutch bag as the other man grabbed her right arm and produced a large knife which he held against her throat.

'If you scream you die,' he said.

Helen was paralysed by fear as she was shoved along the corridor towards the larger door that now stood open. A third man appeared from behind and rushed forward to check that the coast was clear.

Panic exploded inside her as they took her outside. She felt cold air on her face. Tears of fear and frustration shuddered through her.

She was manhandled along a poorly lit alley that was wide enough for a single vehicle. The air was laden with the smell of rotting food and petrol fumes. The moisture in her eyes blurred her vision. It meant she didn't see the white van until it was right there in front of her. The rear door gaped open. The engine was being revved up and smoke was coughing out of the exhaust.

Terror gripped her as she felt herself being lifted off the ground. At the same time the hand covering her mouth fell away from her face. So too did the knife.

She started to scream, but by the time it came out she was already in the back of the van and the door was being slammed shut behind her.

Chapter 1

I was the last person to arrive at the meeting in the small East London community centre. Five other people were already there – three men and two women. There was nothing unusual about any of them. They were sitting on plastic chairs in a circle under a noisy fluorescent light.

They all turned to look at me as I entered the hall, their faces pale and attentive. Only one of them spoke – a tall middle-aged man wearing an open-neck white shirt and brown cords.

'Welcome to Gamblers Anonymous,' he said. 'My name is Jonas and I'm chairing this evening's meeting.'

He gestured with his hand towards an empty chair between a young blonde woman and an elderly man. The woman graced me with a bright, easy smile. Her teeth were white as snow and she had big green eyes. I took off my leather jacket, draped it over the back of the chair, sat down.

'So what shall we call you?' Jonas asked.

I suddenly felt self-conscious. I'd forgotten how hard this was. It had been over six years since I'd last attended a GA meeting and it was no easier now than it was then. I fought down the urge to get up and walk out. I had to remind myself that quitting at this stage wasn't an option. I had to stick with it if I was serious about sorting myself out and keeping my job.

'Name's Sam,' I said.

I knew I didn't have to give my full name or any other personal details about myself if I didn't want to. That suited me. The less they knew the better. I just had to hope that no one recognised me.

'Well it's good to meet you, Sam,' Jonas said. 'I'll let the others introduce themselves.'

One by one the other members told me their names, each one adding the words 'and I'm a compulsive gambler'. Just hearing them say that made me feel more relaxed. At least I wasn't the only schmuck in the room who lacked good sense and self-control.

'So why are you here, Sam?' Jonas said after the introductions.

I'd have thought that was pretty obvious. I was here because I needed to kick the habit. The last couple of years had been tough. Gambling –

especially online poker – had been my only refuge from pain and grief. But over time the bets had got bigger and more risky. The debts had grown like malignant tumours. And it had started to impact on my work.

It was my boss, Detective Chief Superintendent Jason Lattimer, who told me to go to Gamblers Anonymous as part of a recovery programme that included sessions with the Met's own welfare counsellors. I wasn't keen, but he was insistent, said I had to accept whatever help was offered or face the prospect of demotion or even the sack. I was in no position to argue the point.

'In your own time, Sam,' Jonas prompted me. 'We all know how difficult it is to bare your soul to a room full of strangers.'

I drew a long breath and felt my heart beat a little faster. It normally took a lot to rattle my nerves, but now my insides were as tight as a clenched fist.

Then, just as I found my voice, my mobile went off. Luckily I'd switched it to silent before coming into the meeting. It was in my jeans pocket and I could feel it vibrating. It was bad timing and it threw me. I had to pause to gather my thoughts. Whoever was calling could wait. I didn't want to be distracted – not now that I'd taken the plunge.

So I dry-swallowed and started again. I told the meeting just what they expected to hear, that I was a compulsive gambler with big debts and a strong desire to escape from the destructive cycle I was caught up in. I explained that I used to gamble years ago but managed to stop – with the help of GA – when I got married. But then just over two years ago I had a relapse after my life fell apart. I didn't tell them what happened because I didn't want to dredge up the memory and share it with them. Maybe in time I would, when I felt more comfortable and less strung out.

'Gambling helps me to cope,' I said. 'It fills the hours and lets me escape from reality. But at the same time I've created a problem for myself. And it's one that I need to solve.'

My story resonated with the audience. There were nods and grunts of support from around the circle. Jonas thanked me and said he hoped that coming to GA would strengthen my resolve and set me on the road to recovery.

The others took turns then to relate their own tales of woe. One man had lost his life savings on the roulette tables at West End casinos. The young woman next to me had lost her job and her husband through her addiction. Another man owed £30,000 to a loan shark who had made threats against him. I could relate to everything they were saying. I'd been there, done it and had the T-shirt.

After about 30 minutes my phone started to vibrate again and this time I decided I'd better answer it. I was about to get up and retreat to the back of the hall when Jonas announced that it was time for a short coffee break. Half the group got swiftly to their feet and headed for the door, presumably to go outside for a fag.

I checked the caller ID before answering the phone. It was Lattimer.

'I've been trying to reach you,' he said, his voice rough as sandpaper.

'Sorry, guv,' I said. 'What's up?'

He cleared his throat. 'There's been a kidnapping outside a West End nightclub. I want you to get over there and take charge.'

'What's it got to do with us?'

'The victim is Helen Troy, the singer.'

'Blimey.' I felt a twitch in my stomach and took a shallow breath.

The Met had its own specialist kidnap unit, but under an arrangement introduced nine months ago my own team had to join forces with them if the victim was someone famous. It then fell on me to take on the role of Senior Investigating Officer or SIO. It was part of the many changes and efficiencies imposed following the last round of deep budget cuts to the service. The kidnap unit had been scaled back and no longer had the manpower or resources to handle high-profile cases by itself.

'So what happened?' I said.

'I haven't got the details,' Lattimer said. 'All I know is it occurred a short time ago at the Tequila Club on Cromwell Street. DI Crick is already there. She was the officer on call.'

'Okay, I'm on it,' I said. 'I'll call you as soon as I've sussed it out.'

I snapped my phone shut and put it back in my pocket. As I was slipping on my jacket, Jonas approached me.

'Don't tell me you're ducking out already,' he said.

'Something's come up and I have to go.'

He flashed me a knowing grin. 'Police business is it?'

I shot him a quizzical look. 'Excuse me!'

'Don't look so surprised,' he said. 'I know who you are. Recognised you as soon as you started to speak.'

I pressed out a thin smile to conceal my irritation. 'Is that right?'

He nodded. 'You're Detective Chief Inspector Sam Quinn, head of Scotland Yard's Celebrity Crime Squad. I've seen you being interviewed on television. You handle all those cases involving the rich and famous.'

I don't think I'll ever get used to the idea that I'm one of the highest profile detectives in the Met. So it always comes as a bit of a shock when a stranger is able to put a name to the face. Usually it doesn't bother me, but now I was wishing I'd made some small effort to disguise my identity – perhaps with reading glasses and hair gel!

Jonas must have sensed I was a little uncomfortable. He said: 'I won't tell anyone, of course. It's none of my business. Besides, we're from all walks of life here. I'm a teacher. Dave over there is a lawyer. It's therefore in all our interests to be discreet.'

'That's good to hear,' I said.

'So will we see you here next week?'

'Hopefully.'

He held out his hand for me to shake. 'Then good luck with whatever case you're on. Maybe I'll read about it in the papers before we meet up again.'

There was no maybe about it, I thought. The story that was about to break was going to make headlines around the world. It was also going to thrust the squad – and me – right back into the spotlight.

Chapter 2

The abduction of a celebrity like Helen Troy was going to cause a media firestorm. I thought about that as I walked out of the community centre and headed for my car parked across the road.

Helen was a big star with a big following. Not long ago I'd watched her on television singing at the Brit Awards in London. She had long fair hair, a pretty face, and a huge voice. She was a class act and it was easy to see why she was such a sensation.

But A-list stars like her are more vulnerable than ever. The world is obsessed with celebs: they're loved, idolised, hated and ridiculed. And by attracting so much attention they become unwitting targets for unbalanced and jealous individuals.

And for kidnappers.

It's a major downside to being famous. All celebrities are at risk of becoming victims of their own success. That was why the Yard set up the Celebrity Crime Squad, which thankfully had escaped the worst of the cutbacks ... so far.

The squad's brief is to investigate all major crimes involving the rich and famous in and around London. Over the past five years crimes against public figures in the capital had increased dramatically. Before the squad was formed, those high-profile investigations were handled by mainstream detectives. But they often struggled with the relentless pressure and publicity. This led to a series of humiliating cock-ups.

The final straw for the Yard came when a man named Fabian Lamb went on a killing spree and murdered six public figures with a hammer. His victims included a pop singer, a TV sports pundit, and a film star. Lamb had got it into his head that the public's obsession with celebrities was destroying the fabric of society.

I was called in to head up the task force hunting him because the detective in charge couldn't cope. After a few weeks I got lucky and ran him down – but not before he claimed his final victim. She was a 32-year-old British actress named Karen Maxwell who had a promising career ahead of her.

She was also my darling wife.

I still live with the image of her battered body on our living room floor where he murdered her after calling me on my mobile to tell me he was in my house.

*

The image has haunted me for two years, along with the wretched loneliness that I was left to endure. A return to my old gambling vice was how I'd escaped for brief periods from this ugly reality.

And it was how I'd managed – so far – to hold on to my sanity. Karen and I had been married for four years and I'd worshipped the ground she walked on. With her I'd hoped to start a family and have the children I'd always longed for. But it wasn't to be. She was killed for no good reason by a psychopath who was now serving out his life in prison.

The injustice of it torments me still. But at the same time it's what drives me to do my job with passion and vigour.

For me it's personal. I have a grudge against those who stalk, rob, rape and murder people just because they're famous.

I like to think that my beloved wife would be proud of me. I know she'd understand.

Chapter 3

It was a dry Saturday night in May so the West End was packed. A constant stream of tourists and revellers flowed along the pavements while the traffic, consisting mostly of red buses and black cabs, moved at a snail's pace.

The heady mix of sights and sounds never fails to impress me. There's a vibrancy about the centre of London that's almost palpable. No wonder it remains one of the most popular destinations in the world. It's the throbbing heart of the city, a city that is now home to more than eight million people.

It had been my stomping ground for more years than I care to remember, first as an officer in uniform, then as a DCI with the Murder Investigation Team, south of the Thames. Now I'm the front man for the Celebrity Crime Squad.

So it followed that I knew my way around. I was therefore able to bypass the worst of the traffic by nipping in and out of the side streets and steering clear of the usual bottlenecks. But it still took me a good 40 minutes to get to the Tequila Club on Cromwell Street, just west of Piccadilly.

I'd never been here before, but I'd heard about it. It was the capital's trendiest new nightspot, a place where celebs came to be seen and photographed. Taylor Swift had already graced it with her presence and so had Daniel Radcliffe.

From the outside it didn't look much. It was sandwiched between an office block and an antique book shop, and there was a purple awning above the entrance.

Three patrol cars were parked at the kerb in front of the building and crowds of onlookers – including the ubiquitous paparazzi – had gathered on both sides of the street. I wondered how long it would be before hordes of reporters and TV crews descended.

I had to flash my warrant card to a uniformed officer who tried to stop me parking the BMW on double yellow lines. As I climbed out of the car, I said: 'Those people are too close. Can you move them further back along the road?'

For a moment I thought he was going to salute, but much to my relief he nodded and said: 'Sure thing, sir. I'll get right on it.'

I did a quick recce of the area as I approached the club and spotted two CCTV cameras, one above the entrance and one attached to the front of the building opposite. I suspected there were others that weren't so obvious. In this part of town security cameras were more numerous than spots on a Dalmatian.

There were two more uniforms in the reception area. I identified myself and they waved me through to the club's ornate interior. It was bigger than I'd expected and much brighter. That was because all the lights had been turned on, revealing a room the size of a tennis court. There were two bars – one covered with a buffet spread – a raised stage, dance floor and several seating areas. Plus about a hundred clubbers whose night out had been seriously disrupted. They were standing around in groups and sitting at small, glass-topped tables on which stood ice buckets and bottles of expensive champagne. Some of them looked mightily pissed off while others just appeared bemused.

I could see that it was a slow process recording all their names and contact details, and finding out if they had seen anything. The task fell to a dozen uniforms and a few detectives, one of whom I recognised as DI John Taylor of the kidnap unit. He was having a conversation with DI Anna Crick, who was under my command on the CCS. They both spotted me and Anna waved me over.

It was Taylor who spoke first. He held out his hand for me to shake. 'Long time no see, Sam. You're looking good.'

Which was a lie. I'm 41 and most people think I'm a decade older. My face has been ravaged over the past couple of years by lack of sleep and emotional torment, and my hair is thinning at an alarming rate.

Taylor, on the other hand, never seemed to age. He looked the same as he had when I'd first met him ten years ago: late 30s, with a trim physique and a full head of dark, wavy hair.

Bastard.

'So how do you feel about sharing the limelight on this one?' I said.

He grinned. 'No problem at all. At least if it ends badly it'll be you who takes the flak.'

'That's an interesting way to look at it.'

'Just being honest, Sam. Besides, we're already stretched to breaking point. If we lose any more people we won't be fit for purpose.'

The same concerns were being expressed every day across the Met, and across every other force in the country. The austerity cuts were biting hard and had started to seriously impact on frontline services.

'We'll sort out the logistics of a joint operation tomorrow,' I said. 'That's assuming Helen Troy doesn't turn up in the meantime.'

'How much do you know, guv?' Anna said.

Anna was one of my trusted lieutenants on the squad. She'd just turned 30 and had previously worked for the Met's personal protection command where she guarded foreign dignitaries and politicians. She was full-figured and pretty, and with a mind as sharp as a razor blade. She was also a born and bred Londoner, with a broad cockney accent and a dry sense of humour.

'Lattimer only told me that the singer Helen Troy was abducted from here,' I said.

She nodded. 'Happened a couple of hours ago. The kidnappers were captured outside on CCTV, and we've got a witness who actually came face to face with them before they struck.'

That was something I hadn't expected. It was a good start.

'So put me in the picture, Anna,' I said. 'Run through everything that happened tonight from the moment Helen Troy arrived, and then let me see the CCTV footage.'

Chapter 4

I hadn't realised until Anna told me that the entire club had been hired out for the evening by a Russian oligarch named Leon Serova.

His name was familiar to me, as were those of a number of high-profile Russians who were always popping up in the newspapers. He had apparently decided to celebrate his 40th birthday in style. Helen Troy was among those he had invited.

'She arrived just before eight,' Anna said. 'The manager, a guy named Mike Dennis, showed her to the VIP area over there.'

She pointed to a roped-off section on the other side of the dance floor.

'Did she come alone?' I asked.

'She had a minder with her. He's the guy over there in the black suit.'

I followed Anna's gaze and saw a big, broad-shouldered man with a flat nose and shaved head. He was sitting on a chair looking as though he had swallowed acid.

'His name's Simon Nail,' Anna said. 'I haven't spoken to him yet, but he's the one who raised the alarm when he realised something might have happened to Helen.'

'So where was he when she was snatched?'

'In here. Helen had gone to the toilet. We think she was grabbed in the corridor because we found her bag on the floor. Her mobile phone was inside. Follow me and I'll show you.'

I followed her through a door marked 'Private', with access restricted to the VIP area. Beyond it was a narrow corridor, with a uniformed officer stationed at the far end next to a large door or fire exit.

'These loos are used exclusively by the VIP guests,' Anna said.

In the ladies' a forensic officer was already at work checking for clues. He let it be known that there was no sign of a struggle.

'The bodyguard got worried when she didn't emerge after about 15 minutes,' Anna said. 'That's when he collared the manager and together they came through here to find out if there was a problem. The corridor was empty and so was this toilet. But the service door was open and then, to top it off, there was a guy in one of the gents cubicles.'

'Really?'

Anna nodded. 'He's our witness. Name's Bob Adams. He's in the hospitality suite with the manager and Mr Serova waiting for us to speak to him.'

'So who is Bob Adams and why was he hiding in the cubicle?'

'He was one of the guests and he wasn't hiding. The kidnappers walked in on him having a slash. They shoved him in the cubicle at gunpoint and warned him not to come out. So he didn't, and I don't blame him.'

'So can he describe them?'

'He told Taylor they were wearing balaclavas. That's all I know. I was about to talk to him when you arrived.'

We went back into the corridor and then through the large door into the alley. Arc lamps had been set up, and forensic officers were taking pictures and sifting through the rubbish on the ground.

The alley was actually a service road between the buildings and it had been taped off at either end.

'The van was parked here for some 20 minutes with the lights off before the three men suddenly got out and made their way through this door into the club,' Anna said. She flicked her eyes up towards a CCTV camera attached to the wall above them. 'They were picked up going in and coming out.'

'So we must have the van's plate number.'

'We do. Taylor ran a check and it was stolen two days ago from a car park in Greenwich. We've put out an alert for it and a traffic camera search is already underway.'

I frowned. 'So why wasn't this door locked?'

Anna shrugged. 'That's one of the questions we need an answer to – along with how the men knew to enter the building at the exact same time that Helen Troy was using the toilet.'

'Seems obvious to me,' I said. 'They must have been tipped off by someone inside.'

Chapter 5

The digital set-up for the security cameras inside and outside the club was situated in the office. One of Taylor's detectives was copying the relevant footage onto a memory stick when we walked in.

'The gaffer asked me to do this for you, sir,' he said. 'I'll have it ready in a mo.'

I asked him to show us what he had. The footage was in black and white, and despite the night vision capability it wasn't exactly HD quality. Still, the white Ford transit van was clear enough as it drove into the alley, and when the image was enhanced the number plate was easily readable.

When the van was brought to a stop the lights were turned off and nothing happened for about 20 minutes. Then three hooded men climbed out of the front and walked towards the club's service entrance. One of them held the door open and they all marched in like they'd been invited.

A couple of minutes later they emerged, only this time Helen Troy was sandwiched between two of them. One man had a hand over her mouth and the other was holding a knife to her throat.

They wasted no time shoving her into the back of the van. One of them jumped in with her and the others got in the front. Then the van drove slowly out of the alley.

'That was bloody audacious,' I said.

'They were lucky nobody entered the corridor from the VIP area while they were there,' Anna said.

I shrugged. 'One of them probably stood inside the door to make sure that didn't happen.'

'Even so they took a huge risk.'

'Agreed. But having seen how easy it was for them to pull it off, I'm convinced they must have had help.'

'There were over a hundred people in here tonight, guv,' Anna said. 'Any one of them could have sent a text message to the van.'

'I know, which is why we need to check all their mobile phones.'

'But if whoever did it has got any sense he or she would have deleted the message by now.'

'Then we'll have to get hold of all their phone records. It'll take time, I know, but there's no way around it.'

*

The hospitality suite was like a large, sumptuous waiting room: deep-pile carpet, soft leather sofas, even a small bar with enough booze for a week-long party. But the atmosphere was far from party-like. It crackled with tension and despair.

There were seven people in the room – five men, including a police officer, and two women. They were all sitting down and looking extremely anxious. One of the women was sobbing into a handkerchief.

I explained who Anna and I were and asked them to identify themselves. The sobbing woman was a member of Helen Troy's management team. The other woman was employed by her record label, as was one of the men.

The other three guys were our witness Bob Adams, Mike Dennis, the manager, and the Russian oligarch Leon Serova, who had invited Helen to the party.

After giving his name, Serova stood up and said in a deep, heavily accented voice, 'So what is happening, Inspector? Is there any news about Helen?'

He was arrestingly handsome, with high cheekbones and sharp features. He wore a blue silk shirt and tight beige trousers, and he had the tall, confident bearing of a rich and successful man.

'You know as much as I do at this stage,' I said. 'A search for the van is underway across London.'

'Have you found out who it belongs to?' Serova asked.

'Indeed we have, but it doesn't help us much because it was reported stolen several days ago.'

He swallowed hard and sucked in a long breath. I could tell from the look in his eyes that he was struggling to hold his composure.

Mike Dennis piped up at this point, saying: 'I blame her fucking bodyguard. He should have stayed close to her.'

I assumed the bodyguard had already taken some stick, which was why he wasn't part of this gathering.

Mike Dennis reminded me of a younger Rod Stewart. He sported the same shaggy hair style and had the same delicate, raspy voice.

'He reckons that she told him not to go with her to the toilet area,' he went on. 'But that's a pathetic excuse. He should have stayed close to her.'

I turned to Bob Adams and asked him to tell me what had happened.

He was a short man in his 30s, and his face was pale and drained.

'I'd just finished taking a pee,' he said. 'I was doing up my flies when two men wearing balaclavas walked in. One was carrying a handgun. They told me to lock myself in one of the cubicles and not to come out until someone came to tell me it was safe to do so. I tried to say something but the one with the gun pointed it at my face and told me not to speak.'

'Did he have an accent?'

'He did. It sounded Eastern European. Polish maybe.'

'What happened after you shut yourself in the cubicle?'

'Well, I heard them leave the gents' and then I just sat there and waited. It seemed like forever before Mike here and Helen's bodyguard knocked on the door.'

I turned back to Mike Dennis. 'Does the club have its own security personnel?'

He nodded. 'We have a man at the entrance and another inside.'

'So nobody is stationed at the service entrance?'

'Of course not. That door is usually locked and when the club's open only VIP guests are allowed in that area.'

'So how come the kidnappers were able to walk right in?' I said.

He sighed. 'Someone obviously left the door unlocked. Because of the party there's been a constant stream of people passing in and out of there all day – cleaners, caterers, Mr Serova's team.'

'So who has a key?'

'We always leave one in the door, but it's gone missing. There's another one in the office and all the staff have access to it.'

I pondered this for a moment and said: 'Those men knew exactly when to get out of the van and enter the building. That suggests to me that someone tipped them off that Miss Troy had gone into the toilets.'

His body stiffened. 'Well I can assure you it wasn't me or any of my staff. We're all shocked and gutted that this has happened.'

'Then maybe it was one of the guests.'

Serova, who was still standing close to me and smelling strongly of aftershave, said: 'No way, Inspector. I know most of them personally and they would never get involved in a kidnapping. It's ridiculous to even think it.'

'Well someone must have given those men the nod,' I said. 'There's no other way they could have timed their entrance so perfectly.'

A heavy silence descended on the room as they thought through what I'd said.

After a few beats I asked Serova why he'd invited Helen to his party.

'I met her through a fellow Russian entrepreneur named Alexander Orlov,' he said. 'We used to be in business together. You may have heard of him.'

I told him I had. Alexander Orlov was another big-spending Russian who had settled in London in recent years. He was in the papers more often than that other famous oligarch, Roman Abramovich.

'She's a terrific lady and I thought she would add an element of glamour,' Serova said. 'Plus, I wanted to wish her luck. She was planning to fly to the South of France tomorrow to make an appearance at the Cannes Film Festival. And next week she's due to embark on a world tour.'

'So how many people knew she was coming here?'

The woman who was on Helen's management team spoke up. She explained that plenty of people would have known because their PR department had issued a press release and Helen herself had tweeted that she was going to attend the event.

It didn't surprise me. Good publicity is the life-blood of every celebrity, and an appearance at a film premier or top London nightclub almost guarantees getting their picture in the papers and causing a ripple on social media.

'We're going to have to check the mobile phones of everyone who was here tonight,' I said. 'And I'm afraid nobody can leave until we've done that.'

'We can appreciate that, Inspector,' Serova said. 'The important thing is to find Helen before those men do something bad to her.'

'I doubt it will be easy, Mr Serova,' I said. 'This abduction was carried out by a team of highly organised professionals. They knew exactly what they were doing.'

'But why would they kidnap Helen, for God's sake?'

'Well the obvious reason is so that they can demand a ransom,' I said. 'And since Helen Troy is wealthy and famous my guess is she'll command a very high price.'

Chapter 6

I couldn't be sure about the motive, of course. But kidnapping usually involves a ransom.

The UK had seen an upsurge in this particular crime in recent years. This was mainly due to the rise in illegal immigration, and the growing number of eastern European gangs in the cities.

I knew for a fact that there'd been almost 200 kidnappings in London alone last year. The vast majority were carried out by criminal gang members targeting rival groups. They think nothing of taking hostages over disputes involving drugs, money or other property.

The ransoms are usually small and quite often the police aren't told until they've been paid and the hostages have been released.

More serious kidnappings involving people with a public persona are comparatively rare. But in truth it has never been easier to snatch a high-profile celebrity.

Too many like to reveal everything about themselves through the internet and social media. A gang intent on kidnapping someone famous can find out where they live, what they're doing and where they'll be at a particular time.

Helen Troy, it seemed, was a case in point. She'd made it easy for the gang to get to her. She'd informed them through Twitter that she'd be at the Tequila Club, and they would have known that at some point she would visit the VIP toilets. All they needed was someone inside the club to alert them as soon as she did.

Nevertheless, what the three men had done had been extremely bold. It was a miracle that no one had been killed or seriously injured. At least one of the men had been armed, and I didn't doubt that he or his accomplices would have shot anyone who got in their way. Bob Adams had been a very lucky man.

*

Helen's bodyguard, Simon Nail, was understandably distraught when Anna and I spoke to him after leaving the hospitality suite. He felt he was to blame for allowing her to go into the VIP toilet area by herself.

'I should have checked it out,' he told us. 'This was my first visit to the club and I had no idea the corridor led to a service entrance. If I had I would have been more cautious.'

He said it was only the second time he had acted as Helen's minder, and he knew it'd be the end of his job with the agency that employed him.

'Had you been with her all evening?' I asked.

'I picked her up from her house at half past seven,' he said. 'She lives out in Chiswick. I then brought her straight here.'

'So you're her driver as well as her bodyguard?'

'That's right. It's a valet service out front so the limo was parked for me.'

I didn't get the impression that he was involved in the abduction, but just the same I asked him to show me his mobile phone. There were no incriminating text messages on it and the last call he'd made had been to Helen herself earlier in the evening.

We left Nail to wallow in his own misery and caught up with DI Taylor, who was ready to provide some updates.

'I've sent two officers to Helen Troy's house in Chiswick,' he said. 'And two more are on their way to speak to her widowed mother who lives in Barnet. I don't want her to hear about it from the TV.'

I made a note of both addresses and then told Taylor that none of the guests or staff was to leave until their mobile phones had been examined.

'And I want a trawl of the traffic and security cameras within a half-mile radius,' I said. 'It shouldn't be difficult to pick up the van after it left the alley.'

'That's already in hand,' Taylor said.

'Good. So what about the interviews? How are they coming along?'

'We're down to the last 20 people, but we've got nothing so far. Most of them saw Helen when she was here and a few even got her autograph. But they all say they didn't realise what had happened until the alarm was raised.'

'Well, the gang must have been tipped off by someone inside the club,' I said.

Taylor moved his shoulders. 'I've already viewed the CCTV footage covering the interior, but it doesn't help us. People keep walking in and out of shot, and at the precise time Helen went to the toilets I didn't spot anyone using a phone or acting suspiciously.'

'Do we know if anyone apart from Bob Adams was in the toilets at the same time?'

'The door that provides access from the VIP area can be seen on the footage throughout. It shows Helen going in shortly after Adams. Everyone who went in before then had already come out.'

Taylor went on to say that a media posse had gathered on the street out front and were demanding to speak to whoever was in charge.

'They know what's happened because those we've allowed to go have been giving interviews,' Taylor said. 'Plus, the BBC is already running it as a breaking news story.'

Before going outside to face the reporters and TV crews I called Lattimer and updated him.

'We need the media on our side from the start,' he said. 'Get them to put out a description of the van and tell them we'll shortly be releasing video footage of it.'

I told him I was convinced they'd had help from someone on the inside.

'Trouble is there were more than a hundred people here,' I said. 'And that includes the Russian millionaire who was holding the party and invited Helen Troy.'

'Who is he?'

'His name is Leon Serova. An oligarch living in London.'

'The name's familiar. I'll have him checked out.'

'And see if we have anything on a bloke named Mike Dennis. He manages this place and he could have been the one who left the service entrance door unlocked.'

After ending the call, I walked outside and was taken aback by the size of the crowd. Thankfully the uniforms were managing to keep them away from the entrance, and the reporters and photographers were corralled behind yellow tape that stretched across the pavement to the right of the club.

Questions came at me like rapid machine gun fire as I approached the cordon. It seemed most of the hacks recognised me because they were shouting my name. I had to raise my arms, and my voice, to calm them down.

I began by confirming what they already knew – that Helen Troy had been abducted. I then went into details about how it was done and gave them a full description of the van.

'I can confirm that at least one of the three men was armed,' I said. 'So they shouldn't be approached under any circumstances by members of the public. If anyone spots the van or thinks they know who might be behind this, then they should call the police immediately.'

There were more questions. More flashing lights. Then came a chorus of expletives when I said that was all they were going to get for now and there'd be a full briefing when we had more information to impart.

I went back into the club intent on speaking to the staff and having another look at the CCTV footage of the gang making off with Helen. But I didn't get to do it because Taylor was waiting for me in the reception area with news of a significant development.

'We've just had a call from the fire brigade,' he said. 'The van's turned up in Bermondsey. They've dumped it on a patch of derelict land and set light to it.'

Chapter 7

I left Anna at the club and made my way across town, using the Beemer's satnav to guide me to the patch of derelict land in Bermondsey.

The spot nestled in the shadows of some high-rise office blocks, a stone's throw from the Thames. I knew the area well from my days with the Murder Investigation Team. It used to have a well-deserved reputation as a rough inner-city district, with more than its fair share of violent crimes.

But in recent years it had undergone something of a transformation with the appearance of upmarket blocks of flats and an invasion of well-heeled residents.

A lot of the old buildings had been demolished, and some of those sites that had not been redeveloped had become dumping grounds for discarded mattresses, broken kitchen appliances, supermarket trolleys … and even abandoned vehicles.

The fire had been put out by the time I got there, so what confronted me was the charred wreckage of the van. It had been driven onto the site through a high, rusty gate that had been forced open. I noted that the road leading to it was poorly lit and quiet, and there were no street cameras. The kidnappers had chosen a good spot to dump the van and had presumably moved their cargo to a vehicle parked close by.

There was a single fire tender in attendance and two patrol cars. The officers had been forewarned that I was on my way and the first this thing they did was point out to me that the van's registration plate hadn't been completely destroyed by the flames. It was indeed the same one I'd seen on the van in the alley behind the Tequila Club.

One of the officers identified himself as PC Stu Kendal and said: 'Looks like they did a good job of getting rid of any evidence.'

I refrained from telling him that he was stating the bloody obvious. I knew it was unlikely we'd be able to retrieve any fingerprints or DNA traces.

'Nevertheless, I want you to get a forensics team out here,' I said. 'It's possible we'll get lucky.'

But I seriously doubted it. The van was a mess. The gang had made sure that the fire would do a lot of damage before the brigade arrived. A woman cleaner in one of the nearby office blocks had called it in after hearing a loud explosion and looking out of the window.

'I don't suppose she saw the men leaving the site,' I said.

PC Kendal shook his head. 'I'm afraid not, sir. She was waiting at the gate when the brigade arrived. I talked to her a minute ago, and she told me she didn't see a thing before or after the explosion.'

That didn't surprise me. The gang would have been in and out within minutes. And by the time the flames reached the fuel tank they'd have been well on their way.

'Let's start checking traffic cameras,' I said. 'We know roughly when the kidnappers swapped vehicles. So that should help us. And get your officers to walk around the site. See if there are any potential witnesses.'

I knew it would probably be a waste of time. There were very few lights on in the offices, which was to be expected late on a Saturday night. In fact one of the buildings looked as though it was unoccupied.

I got up close to the burned-out van. Some smoke was still rising from the soaked bodywork, and the smell made my nostrils flare.

The rear doors had been left open, and one of the fire officers pointed at what remained of a petrol can inside.

'They would have poured petrol over the van and thrown the can in before setting light to it,' he said. 'It would have been engulfed in flames within a minute.'

It struck me again how wickedly efficient the gang had been. They knew the van needed to be abandoned as quickly as possible, and that they had to destroy all traces of evidence.

It was now going to be difficult, if not impossible, to identify the vehicle they made off in. Despite the hour the surrounding streets were still busy with traffic. And they would surely have worked out a route that would enable them to avoid cameras.

I experienced a fierce wave of sympathy for Helen Troy. I couldn't even begin to imagine how scared she must be. Here was a girl who probably thought she was invincible – a celebrity with a capital C who even had her own bodyguard.

Yet now she was at the mercy of a ruthless gang who were in a position to do anything they wanted with her. Even if their aim was to demand a ransom, it didn't mean they wouldn't subject her to any amount of physical and psychological abuse. Her star status made her particularly vulnerable in that respect.

My whole body felt tight with tension as I thought about it. History was littered with kidnap cases that had gone wrong and where the victims had never been seen again. I just hoped to God that this one would have a successful resolution.

I looked at my watch. It was 11pm. I decided to head back to the Tequila Club since there wasn't much I could do here.

But as I was heading towards the BMW my phone rang. It was Anna.

'I thought you should know that I'm on my way to Helen Troy's house,' she said. 'I've just heard back from the officers we sent there and they got a bit of a shock. It's in a real mess apparently.'

'You mean someone turned it over?'

'Not only that, guv. Whoever did it also smeared blood over the walls.'

Chapter 8

Chiswick is situated just west of the city centre. To get to it I had to drive back across the river.

Like everywhere else in London, it's an expensive district in which to live, with the value of many homes running into millions.

Helen Troy's Tudor-style house was in one of the tree-lined streets around Grove Park, a much sought-after area with sky-high property prices. It was a two-storey detached affair with a driveway, a double garage and a neatly trimmed hedge at the front. There was no gate, and my initial impression was that it didn't provide the level of security that someone as famous as Helen required.

I parked up behind one of three patrol cars, got out and showed my ID to the officer standing on the pavement. A small group of neighbours had gathered across the road, but it seemed the press hadn't yet arrived.

Anna's ageing Mazda was parked on the driveway next to an expensive-looking Porsche Carrera which probably belonged to Helen.

Anna herself was standing to the left of the property's arched porch alongside two more uniforms.

'I've had a quick look round, guv,' she said, 'but forensics are on their way so I thought it best not to spend too much time inside compromising the evidence.'

'So what have we got?' I asked.

'The place is empty and the security alarm had been deactivated,' she said. 'We gained access through the back door which had been left ajar. And there's a lot of damage to the living room and kitchen.'

She pointed to a security camera above the garage. 'There's a basic video set-up back and front, but the monitors and recording equipment inside have been smashed to pieces.'

'Burglary?'

She shook her head. 'It doesn't look like anything's been stolen. Just messed up. It's more like the work of a psycho with a grudge.'

'What about the blood you told me about? Do we know who it belongs to?'

'Indeed we do,' she said. 'We found the poor bugger upstairs on Helen Troy's bed. And it's not a pretty sight.'

*

The victim wasn't a man or a woman, thank God. It was, or had been, a pure white Persian cat. Its stomach had been sliced open and its entrails were poking out. Its little head was resting on a pillow and there was blood all over the duvet cover.

Anna had been right. It wasn't a pretty sight. But it came as a huge relief that it was a cat and not a human.

'His name was Biscuit,' Anna said.

Without taking my eyes off the bed I asked her how she knew.

'There's a small room downstairs with a load of cat stuff inside, including a cat bed and playthings. And the name's on the door.'

'Must have been Helen's pampered pet,' I said.

'That's what I figure,' Anna said. 'No self-respecting celebrity would be without one.'

It was clear that the cat had been killed downstairs in the living room – probably gutted with a knife – before being carried up here. There was a trail of blood on the stairs and across the bedroom carpet.

'This is Helen's room,' Anna said. 'The wardrobes and en-suite bathroom are full of her things. There are three other bedrooms and they appear to be untouched.'

I had a quick look around, treading carefully to avoid the blood spatters. There was no damage in any of the other upstairs rooms, and it didn't seem as though the drawers and cupboards had been disturbed.

But downstairs it was a different story. The living room walls had been daubed with the cat's blood and it had been smeared over the white leather sofas and patio doors. The large flat-screen TV had been knocked off its perch and was lying on the floor. Table lamps were broken along with the glass coffee table. A sideboard had been emptied of bottles of wine and spirits. Some of them had been opened and the contents poured over the carpet.

There was more mess in the kitchen, which was huge by any standards. All the cupboards were open and the floor was covered with broken crockery, utensils and food and drink from the fridge. Two wall-mounted monitors which had displayed the feeds from the outside security cameras had been smashed. In an adjoining utility room the video recording equipment had been wrecked, presumably to destroy any footage of the perps entering and leaving the house.

'This must have happened soon after Helen left to go to the club,' Anna said. 'The cat's body's still warm and some of the stuff from the fridge is still cold.'

'Did the neighbours hear anything?'

'Don't think so. The houses either side are empty. The family to the right are on holiday apparently, and the one to the left is unoccupied most of the time because the owner lives abroad and stays here only occasionally.'

'Terrific.'

'Two uniforms are going house to house as we speak to see if anyone saw or heard anything.'

There was a separate dining room on the ground floor as well as a study. Those rooms were neat and tastefully furnished. In the study the walls were adorned with framed photographs of Helen Troy at various showbiz events and with a bunch of other celebrities. On the desk was a picture of her holding her cat and beaming at the camera.

I put on a pair of latex gloves and opened the desk drawers. But there was nothing that stood out as unusual. There were lots of glossy publicity photos and at least a dozen scrapbooks filled with newspaper and magazine cuttings in which she featured.

I switched on the desktop computer but I couldn't get into it because it was password-protected. Instead I took out my phone and went online. I put Helen's name into Google and unsurprisingly the search engine signalled that there were over a million hits.

I scanned some of the news stories and checked out her website. I discovered that she was an only child and that her parents, Sarah and Ronan Troy, had decided before she was born to name her after the Helen of Troy in Greek mythology. It was a name that helped raise her profile when she started on her singing career.

Her father died from throat cancer when she was 12 and her mother, a nursing assistant, had remained single.

I also learned that Helen had moved into her house four months ago after paying £2.5million for it. Previously she'd lived with her mother in Barnet, and before that she'd shared a flat in Wandsworth with her boyfriend. But they had split up soon after she hit the big time.

There was speculation in some of the feature articles about her personal wealth. The consensus seemed to be that after two years as a pop star she had accumulated a £10m fortune. It was more than enough to attract the attention of criminal gangs with an eye on securing a ransom.

The ex-boyfriend was definitely someone we'd need to speak to. His name was Paul Rhodes and according to the web articles he was a 25-year-old city trader who was wealthy in his own right. I came across several photographs of him. He was a good-looking guy with fair hair and an athlete's body. In one photo he was posing with Helen on a beach in Barbados where, according to the attached report, the couple announced that they were in love.

Back outside I told Anna that we should talk to Paul Rhodes and find out if Helen had a current boyfriend.

'We also need to know who has a key for this house apart from Helen herself,' I said.

Anna pursed her lips. 'Her mother will probably be able to tell us that.'

'Let's hope so. I'll go see her next. With any luck she might also be able to shed light on what's happened here.'

'Do you want me to go with you, guv?'

'No. You stay here and liaise with the SOCOs. And make sure we pull in the traffic camera footage from the surrounding streets.'

Anna said she'd stay on top of things and then lit a cigarette. We both knew it was going to be a long night and that there was little chance of either of us getting any sleep.

We were now effectively dealing with two major investigations – Helen Troy's abduction and the criminal damage done to her house.

Chapter 9

I made several calls from the car on the way to Barnet. I told Lattimer about the state of Helen Troy's house, and asked DI Taylor to track down her ex-boyfriend.

I then got central control to send a message to every member of the Celebrity Crime Squad telling them to report for duty.

The questions were piling up in my head. Who had abducted Helen? Where had they taken her? Who inside the club had tipped them off? Why had they chosen to do it in such a public place and under the watchful eye of security cameras?

I also wanted to know if those same men had trashed Helen's house and killed her cat. If so, then perhaps this wasn't a straightforward kidnap-for-ransom case, after all. Maybe the pop princess had got involved with the wrong people and done something to upset them. Now they were exacting a brutal revenge.

It was a plausible theory. I could summon up the names of a dozen or more showbiz stars who had compromised themselves by getting involved with drugs and other nefarious activities. At least three became victims of blackmail, and two were actually beaten to a pulp. They failed to realise that fame and fortune do not act as a buffer against the more ruthless elements of the London underworld. But as far as I was aware no hint of scandal surrounded Helen Troy.

Despite her rapid rise to fame she came across as likeable, grounded and clean-living. She probably hadn't been in the limelight long enough to become tainted by the vagaries of fame.

Her songs were sweet rather than sexy, and her music videos tended to be light-hearted and self-deprecating, not crude and explicit.

But that didn't mean it wasn't a façade created by her PR machine and that in truth she was a very different person.

*

It took me half an hour to get to Sarah Troy's house in the outer London borough of Barnet. I couldn't remember the last time I'd done so much driving around the capital at night, and I'd also forgotten how stressful it could be.

When I arrived I was glad to see that the media hadn't yet laid siege. There was a single patrol car parked outside and no spectators in sight.

Helen's mother's house was a post-war semi that was half the size of her daughter's. The street was quiet and there were only a few lights on in the neighbouring properties.

The door was opened by a uniformed officer who filled me in on what the mother had been told as he led me through to the living room where Mrs Troy was waiting.

She was sitting in an armchair opposite another PC who acknowledged me with a half-smile.

'I'm DCI Quinn from Scotland Yard,' I said by way of introduction. 'I'm leading the investigation into your daughter's abduction.'

Sarah Troy was a small woman in her 50s, with shoulder-length hair that was too dark to be natural. As I crossed the room towards her I saw the unshed tears in her eyes and the cracked capillaries in her cheeks.

'Is there any news?' she said, her voice shrill with shock and fear. 'Please tell me you've heard something.'

The PC stood up and gestured for me to take his place on the sofa. A hard lump formed in my throat as I sat down and explained that we had no idea where Helen was.

'We're doing everything we can to find her, Mrs Troy,' I said. 'There's a good chance that whoever took her will get in touch soon if it's a ransom they're after.'

She bit into her bottom lip and laced her fingers in a tight, tense ball.

'I'd always feared that something like this would happen once she became famous,' she said.

I cleared my throat and said: 'When was the last time you spoke to Helen?'

'This morning. She phoned to remind me that she's flying to the Riviera tomorrow to attend the film festival. She was so excited because she's never been before.' Her voice rose in a desperate cry. 'Oh God, I can't imagine what she must be going through. This is so awful.'

Her hand flew to her mouth and she closed her eyes, squeezing out some of the tears, which trailed down her cheeks.

I waited a few seconds before giving her more disturbing news.

'You need to know that I've just come from Helen's house,' I said. 'And I'm afraid it's been vandalised.'

Her jaw dropped and she listened in stunned silence as I told her about the extent of the damage and what had happened to the cat.

Her breath caught, and she shook her head.

'I can't believe anyone would do that to Biscuit,' she said. 'He was so small and harmless. I bought him for Helen when he was a kitten and she treated him like her baby. I look after him when she goes away.'

'Have you any idea who might have done it?'

She pulled a tissue from the sleeve of her cardigan and wiped her eyes with it.

'Everyone loves Helen,' she said. 'She doesn't have any enemies.'

'So you don't know if there's someone out there who bears a serious grudge against her?'

She took a couple of deep, ragged breaths. 'I know a lot of people resent her success, Inspector. I've seen some of the nasty, anonymous tweets that have been posted about her. But I can't imagine that anyone would have reason to abduct her or kill her cat.'

I asked her if she knew who had a key to Helen's house.

'I've got one,' she said. 'And so has Clara Pike. She's Helen's cleaner and goes round twice a week.'

'So she'll also know how to deactivate the burglar alarm.'

'She would have to. There's a code you've got to tap into the wall machine once you're through the front door. I can never remember what it is.'

Mrs Troy did not have any contact details for Clara Pike but said her number was probably on Helen's phone.

'Does your daughter have a boyfriend at present, Mrs Troy?' I asked.

She shook her head. 'If she does she's kept it to herself. I don't think she's had the time to get involved with anyone since she broke up with Paul.'

'Is he still on the scene?'

'No, although I'm sure he'd like to be. He was very upset when Helen ended it. But he only had himself to blame.'

'How do you mean?'

'Well he became jealous and possessive when her career took off. He struggled to handle it. She put up with his moods and tantrums as long as she could.'

'Was he very angry with her?'

'He was distraught. He pestered her with calls for weeks and turned up here several times. But eventually he got the message and left her alone.'

'Do you have an address or phone number for him?'

'I'm afraid not. But why do you want to talk to him? Surely you don't think …'

'We'll be talking to everyone who knows Helen, Mrs Troy. That doesn't mean we suspect them of wrongdoing.'

I then broached the subject of her daughter's financial situation. She confirmed that Helen was indeed very wealthy.

'So who apart from her would have access to her bank accounts?' I said. 'I have to know because the kidnappers might approach whoever it is to pay a ransom.'

She thought about it and said: 'Well her manager and her lawyer could be in a position to withdraw her money, I suppose. But I can't think of anyone else. But that might not be necessary anyway. I spoke to Mr Orlov by phone just before you arrived and he said he would help to get her back no matter what it cost.'

'Do you mean Alexander Orlov?'

'That's right. He called from Cannes after he heard what had happened. He's flying back first thing in the morning.'

She went on to explain that Helen had been due to fly to France tomorrow afternoon on Orlov's private plane. She was going to be a guest on his yacht for a few days.

'So are they close friends?' I asked.

'Not really,' she said. 'Mr Orlov's business empire includes an entertainment magazine and a publishing company. He pays Helen a great deal of money to write a regular column for the magazine, and he bought the rights to her life story. The book's due out later this year.'

I could see why he had decided to head back to London. The man had obviously made a significant investment in Helen Troy – an investment that the kidnappers had put at risk.

I spent another 20 minutes with Mrs Troy. But the more we talked about her daughter, the more upset she became.

She was in a dreadful state when I left her, and I couldn't help thinking that her suffering was not going to end any time soon.

Chapter 10

Sometimes I get a bad feeling about a case. I just know it's going to be a hard one to crack.

That was how I felt as I arrived back at the Tequila Club. Despite the hour the street outside was hosting a full-blown media circus. There were satellite trucks, flashing lights, reporters talking into cameras.

The news hounds far outnumbered those members of the public who were still hanging around, presumably because they reckoned it was the most interesting show in town.

I decided to front an impromptu press briefing and announced that the van used by the kidnappers had been abandoned in Bermondsey. I said it had been set on fire and that Helen must have been transferred to another vehicle.

I then told them that we were also investigating criminal damage to Helen's home, and that we couldn't be sure if the two events were linked.

I'm not always so forthcoming when dealing with the press, but on this occasion I agreed with Lattimer; we needed whatever help they could give us.

I confirmed that we hadn't heard from Helen's kidnappers and that we didn't know if or when they would demand a ransom.

'We're very concerned about Miss Troy,' I said. 'We fear she's in grave danger and I would appeal to anyone who thinks they may have information on her whereabouts to contact us without delay.'

I spent a further ten minutes answering and dodging questions and promised to give one-to-one interviews later in the morning.

Inside the club it was much quieter than it had been earlier. Most of the guests and staff had been allowed to go home, and those who remained looked shell-shocked.

Among them was Simon Nail, the bodyguard, who was being quizzed again by DI Taylor when I entered the hospitality suite.

'Mr Nail was about to leave when he remembered that Helen had left her overnight bag in the limo,' Taylor said, pointing to a Gucci holdall on the floor. 'She'd apparently been planning to spend the night at Mr Serova's house in Mayfair.'

'So why weren't we made aware of this earlier?' I asked, directing my question at Nail.

He gave a tired shrug. 'It didn't occur to me to mention it. I'm sorry. When I saw the bag on the back seat it struck me that you ought to know.'

'So were you going to drop her off there after leaving here?'

He nodded. 'Either that or she would have gone with Mr Serova in his car. It hadn't been decided.'

'So are we to assume from this that they were involved with each other in some way?'

'I really don't know, Inspector. And that's the truth. It was only the second time I'd been assigned to Miss Troy.'

'One final question, Mr Nail,' I said. 'When you picked Miss Troy up at the house did you go inside?'

He nodded. 'She wasn't ready so she invited me in and I waited for her in the living room.'

'And was the house in a mess at that time?'

He arched his brow. 'I'm not sure what you mean. It looked really tidy to me.'

'That's all I needed to know. Thank you.'

The fact that Leon Serova hadn't mentioned his relationship with Helen gave me cause for concern. After Nail left I raised it with Taylor.

'Serova didn't give me the impression that he was in any kind of relationship with Helen Troy,' I said.

'That might be because the guy's married,' Taylor said. 'I know that much about him from what I've read in the papers. The wife apparently spends most of her time at their other home in Monte Carlo.'

'Is that where she is now?'

'I don't know. I'll have to check.'

'Is Serova still around?'

'No. He left a short time ago.'

'Then we need to talk to him later.'

'Do you really think he could be involved in this?' Taylor said.

I shrugged. 'We can't rule it out. After all, he is the person who invited her here.'

We were interrupted then by Mike Dennis, the manager, who wanted to know when he could have his club back.

'Not until we're finished here, Mr Dennis,' I told him. 'But it won't be for a few more hours.'

He creased his brow. 'But what's left to do? Your people have checked over the corridor and the alley. Surely if there was any forensic evidence they would have found it by now. And you've already taken the security camera footage.'

'You'll just have to be patient,' I said. 'The club is a crime scene and we have to carry out a thorough examination.'

He blew out his cheeks in exasperation, and it made me want to slap him.

'In that case I'll be in my office if you need me,' he said.

Before he left the room I asked him if he was aware that Helen had been planning to spend the night at Serova's house.

'It's news to me,' he said. 'But it wouldn't be a total surprise. I've heard rumours that there's something going on there.'

'You mean an affair?'

'Either that or they're just fond of each other's company. According to gossip they've been on a couple of discreet dinner dates.'

There's nothing at all shocking about a young pop star and a multi-millionaire businessman getting together, even if one or both of them is married. But in the circumstances I felt it warranted further investigation. It was always possible it had a bearing on what had happened.

So Leon Serova was on the list of people I intended to talk to in the coming hours, along with Helen's ex-boyfriend Paul Rhodes and her cleaner Clara Pike.

Chapter 11

It didn't take us long to come up with addresses for Paul Rhodes and Clara Pike. The ex-boyfriend lived in Highgate, and the cleaner lived only five minutes away from Helen's house in Chiswick. So I went there first and arrived at 2am.

Her home was a first-floor flat on an insalubrious council estate. A dog started barking as soon as I rang the bell. And it carried on barking after the door was opened by a brutish-looking man who was wearing only a pair of baggy pyjama bottoms.

'Shut the fuck up, Tiger,' the man yelled at the animal which he was thankfully holding back by the collar.

Tiger was a large German Shepherd and it didn't look very friendly. But it promptly stopped barking and settled for just bearing its sharp teeth at me instead.

'Whoever you are you'd better have a bloody good reason for knocking us up at this time of the morning,' the man said.

He was a surly, muscular guy about my age, with a range of ugly tattoos across his arms and chest. His foul breath swept over me and it stank of booze and cigarettes.

I took out my warrant card and showed it to him.

'I'm here to speak to Clara Pike,' I said.

His eyes narrowed. 'What for? Has someone died?'

'It's nothing like that,' I said. 'Is she here?'

'She's in bed asleep.'

'And you are?'

'I'm Russell, her husband. So you can tell me what it's about.'

'I don't think so, Mr Pike. This is very important so I need to come in and ask her some questions.'

'And what if I tell you to piss off?'

'Then I'll call for back-up and have you arrested for obstructing an investigation.'

He clenched his jaw and pulled his lips back, revealing a set of crooked, yellow teeth.

I could see his mind whirring as he tried to decide how far to push it. Sheer arrogance seeped out of his pores like perspiration.

'I haven't got all night, Mr Pike,' I said. 'So I suggest you invite me in and let me do my job.'

He took a moment more to think about it, twisting his lower jaw as he did so. Then he stepped back and motioned for me to enter the flat.

'Put the dog out of harm's way first,' I said. 'I can tell he's not in the mood for company.'

The corners of his lips slipped into a faint smile before he pulled the dog back along the hallway and ushered it into the kitchen. Then he turned and beckoned me over the threshold.

'Wait in the living room,' he said, pointing to an open door on my right. 'I'll go upstairs and get the missus.'

I turned the light on as I entered. The room was small and drab and I could see dust motes floating in the air. Everything was old and worn, except a huge flat-screen TV that dominated one corner and looked brand new.

I crossed the room and stood with my back to an electric fire. After only a few seconds I heard voices, and then footfalls on the stairs.

Mrs Pike shuffled into the room behind her husband. She was much shorter than him and painfully thin. She wore a bright blue towelling robe belted at the waist, and her brown hair was cut in a boyish style around the ears.

She looked about ten years younger than her husband, early 30s maybe. Her face was slack and listless, and I got the impression that she was a down-trodden wife who lived in the shadow of her domineering partner.

'I'm detective chief inspector Quinn,' I said. 'I apologise for disturbing you at this unholy hour.'

They both stood in the middle of the room, and it was the husband who spoke first.

'Just get on with it so that we can go back to bed,' he said. 'Clara has to be up at the crack of dawn to go to work.'

I knew nothing about Clara Pike and yet I already felt sorry for her. Living with a Neanderthal could not have been easy.

'I understand you're a cleaner, Mrs Pike,' I said.

She threw a nervous glance at her husband before responding. When she spoke her voice was soft and scratchy.

'I clean houses for a dozen people around here,' she said. 'Am I supposed to have done something wrong?'

'I very much doubt that. My visit relates to one of your clients. Helen Troy.'

Her features stiffened and she stared at me, her mouth agape.

'What about Helen Troy?' her husband said. 'Has the bitch made a complaint or something?'

I told them about Helen's abduction. It came as a shock because they hadn't heard the news.

'My God that's terrible,' Mrs Pike said, and her concern seemed genuine. 'But what has it got to do with me?'

'It's not the abduction that I want to talk to you about,' I said. 'Something else happened last evening. Miss Troy's house was wrecked by intruders and her cat was killed with a knife. Whoever did it was able to let themselves in and switch off the alarm system.'

Clara Pike grabbed her husband's arm and pulled him closer to her. Her eyes grew wide and her lips trembled.

'Are you here because you think my wife had something to do with it?' Mr Pike said accusingly.

I ignored him and spoke to her. 'You're one of the few people who has a key to the house and knows the alarm code, Mrs Pike. I need you to account for your whereabouts last evening.'

'She was here with me,' her husband said. 'We watched the telly and went to bed about nine.'

'Can anyone else confirm that?'

'Nobody dropped by if that's what you mean. We were by ourselves just like we usually are.'

His wife suddenly found her voice again and said: 'I would never do anything to hurt Miss Troy. She's always been good to me.'

'So how many keys do you have to her house?' I said.

'Just the one. It's on my key ring. You can see it if you want.'

'And have you lent it to anyone or allowed it to be copied?'

'Of course not. And I've never passed on the alarm code either.'

Tears gleamed in her eyes now and panic distorted her voice. It was impossible for me to know if she was telling the truth.

'How long have you cleaned for Miss Troy?' I asked her.

She licked her lips and swallowed. 'Since she moved in. I cleaned for the previous owners of the house. They recommended me and she kept me on.'

'So when were you last at the house?'

'Two days ago. She asked me to go back on Monday. It's not an everyday arrangement.'

Her husband put his arm around her shoulders and squeezed until she flinched.

I sensed that there was something not quite right about the way they were acting, but I couldn't put my finger on what it was. I could have sworn, though, that the look on Clara Pike's face was a mixture of shock and guilt. It was based on nothing more than instinct – and years of experience dealing with liars and cheats.

Her husband, on the other hand, was giving nothing away. His face was calm and calculating, and his eyes never left mine.

After a few awkward moments, I said: 'Do you happen to know if Miss Troy was due to have any visitors to the house either today or yesterday?'

'I've no idea,' she said. 'We never talk much when I'm there. It's a big house and there's always a lot for me to do.'

'Did she seem all right when you last saw her?'

'She was fine. More cheerful than usual in fact. I think she was planning a trip.'

I realised I wasn't going to get much more out of her, at least not at this time. But that didn't mean I wouldn't be talking to her again, preferably when the husband wasn't around. I needed to satisfy myself that she wasn't holding something back.

'I might ask you to pop along to the house later to see if anything has been stolen,' I said. 'Would that be all right?'

She inhaled sharply and nodded. Then, as I walked towards the door, she started to say something. But her husband got in first and spoke over her.

'For what it's worth I hope you get her back safely,' he said. 'That woman pays bloody well, and the money's a godsend with me being out of work.'

Chapter 12

After leaving Clara Pike's flat I called at Paul Rhodes's upmarket mews house in Highgate, but there was no one at home. The mobile number I'd been given for him kept going to voicemail.

I then paid a last visit to Helen Troy's house in Chiswick, and discovered that the forensic sweep hadn't so far turned up anything we could work with. In other words there were no clues as to who had gone on a wrecking spree there and why.

Finally, Anna, Taylor and I regrouped at the Celebrity Crime Squad's headquarters in Caxton Street, just around the corner from New Scotland Yard. By then most of my team were in, bleary-eyed but raring to go.

Our second floor HQ was plenty big enough to accommodate the lads from the kidnap unit, and the office manager set about allocating work stations and explaining where everything was.

The layout was open plan with three offices, a kitchen area and four side rooms for small meetings and for viewing CCTV footage.

For the next couple of hours we opened up various lines of inquiry and monitored the rolling news channels in the hope that the blanket coverage would offer up a lead.

But as dawn broke over London, Helen Troy was still missing and there had been no word from her kidnappers. I was growing increasingly concerned for her.

I could feel my insides knotting up like a ball of twine. And the questions spooled inside my head. What if there wasn't going to be a ransom demand? What if money wasn't the reason behind the abduction? But then why else would the three men have snatched her and taken such a huge risk in the process?

We pressed ahead with preparations for the morning meeting. We set up two white boards in the operations room and to one of them we pinned a collection of photographs. These included shots of the alley behind the Tequila Club, the inside of Helen Troy's house, the burned-out wreckage of the van and frames from the CCTV footage showing the kidnapping.

On the other board I wrote a list of names and questions. The names were Paul Rhodes, Clara Pike, Leon Serova and Mike Dennis.

The questions: Was this a kidnap-for-ransom? Who in the club tipped off the men in the van? Were the two crimes connected?

I also listed the things that needed to be done and which officers were going to be assigned to which tasks.

There was going to be no shortage of manpower. We had six full-time detectives on the squad and four admin staff. Plus we were joining forces with Taylor's crew so that would boost the numbers.

I was also pretty confident that if we needed more bodies then I would only have to ask. The Commissioner wouldn't shy away from busting the budgets on a case as big as this.

One thing I'd learned since taking charge of the Celebrity Crime Squad was that money and resources were always forthcoming. It was a PR thing as much as anything. The brass wanted everyone to know that crimes against the rich and the famous in London were always treated as a top priority.

So far, thanks in part to this strategy, we'd been strikingly successful. We had solved every case that had been assigned to us – from the Premier League soccer star shot while leaving his lover's flat in Islington, to the TV presenter who was warned that every time she appeared on screen someone would be murdered.

It was a record the powers that be were proud of and were desperate to maintain – whatever the cost.

By 6.30am I was ready to give a full briefing. But before it kicked off there was a sudden development. Much to my annoyance we learned about it from the BBC, which flagged up a breaking news story.

It announced that someone had offered a £1million reward for Helen Troy's safe return.

Chapter 13

I was still processing the news about the reward when another development was brought to my attention.

It concerned Helen Troy's mobile phone. It had been in her clutch bag which she'd dropped in the club's corridor when she was seized. Luckily for us the kidnapers hadn't picked it up, either because they'd been in too much of a hurry or because they hadn't thought they needed to.

DCI Taylor had sent it to the tech guys because it had been password-protected. But now we had access to the call log and text messages, and they were more than a little revealing. I tasked Anna with going through them while I got the meeting started.

The room was buzzing. Officers with legal pads and Styrofoam cups were sitting on chairs and the edges of tables. Some were standing. As well as my own team there were detectives from the kidnap unit and civilians from the media department. Detective Chief Superintendent Lattimer also turned up.

He stood next to me at the front of the room, his expression grim. He was a big bear of a man with a thick neck and greying hair. He was actually in charge of the Met's Homicide and Serious Crime command, which was made up of various specialist sub-divisions including the Celebrity Crime Squad.

He had already been updated, so none of what I was about to say would come as a surprise to him.

I began by explaining that this was to be a joint operation between the CCS and the kidnap unit and made some brief introductions. Then I ran through what had happened while making constant references to the white boards.

'We can't be sure that the events at the club and at Helen Troy's house are linked,' I said. 'But for now we assume that they are and treat this as a single investigation.'

Then I played the CCTV footage showing Helen being manhandled across the alley and into the van. I froze an image at one point to show how one man had his hand over her mouth while another held a knife to her throat. You could just make out the wide-eyed look of terror on her face.

'I don't need to tell any of you how famous Helen Troy is,' I said. 'She's an A-list star, and that means the eyes of the world will be on us. An hysterical media will be following our every move and on occasion they're likely to be one step ahead of us.'

This was my cue to mention the reward.

'It's being offered by a Russian billionaire named Alexander Orlov,' I said. 'The BBC interviewed him by phone last night and he made a direct appeal to the kidnappers, saying that in order to secure Helen's quick and safe release he would pay them £1million.'

I explained that Orlov owned a magazine that Helen wrote a column for, and a publishing company that had acquired the rights to her life story.

'He's apparently flying back from the South of France this morning so I intend to talk to him,' I said. 'He's clearly jumped the gun on this, but if the kidnappers do respond then we need to be across it. I don't want him doing deals without our knowledge.'

It was one of the aspects of a kidnapping that made them tricky investigations. Relatives and friends of the victims were always eager to pay a ransom in the hope that it would result in a quick resolution to their nightmare. But quite often it backfired and there were tragic consequences.

At this point I invited DCI Taylor to update us on the interviews conducted with the staff and guests at the Tequila Club. He started by reading from the statement given by Bob Adams, the man who was confronted by the kidnappers in the toilet.

'Nobody else saw or heard anything,' Taylor said. 'We checked their mobile phones but found no text messages informing the kidnappers that Helen had gone to the VIP toilets. And not a single person used their phone at that precise time. We're now checking all the phone records to see if messages were deleted. But it'll take time.'

'Could someone have used an unregistered phone and dumped it?' Lattimer asked.

Taylor nodded. 'That is a possibility. Everyone in the club was searched along with the premises. But before we arrived on the scene quite a few people went outside and I'm told that some of them drifted off. We're going through the invitation list, but we can't know for sure if any of them had an unregistered phone with them.'

I then relayed my conversation with Clara Pike and her husband.

'I could be wrong, but I had the distinct impression there was something she wasn't telling me,' I said. 'So I want background checks carried out on both of them. It really wouldn't surprise me if the husband has form.'

Lattimer then confirmed that checks had already been carried out on Leon Serova and Mike Dennis. He took a pad from his pocket and read from his notes.

'There's not much to say about Mike Dennis,' he told us. 'He's managed the Tequila Club for a year and before that he ran a club in Manchester. He's single and lives in Maida Vale.

'Serova is far more interesting. He's a Russian oligarch with a French wife and a shady past. The National Crime Agency suspect him of laundering money by buying up outrageously expensive properties in the capital. He already owns four homes ranging in price from £10million–£30million. He also happens to be part-owner of the Tequila Club and therefore Mike Dennis's boss.'

I took the opportunity to reveal that Serova had also been having an affair with Helen Troy.

'Until a few minutes ago we couldn't be sure it was true,' I said. 'We knew only that she had been planning to stay at his house last night and that rumours were flying around that they were dating. But we've now gained access to Helen's mobile phone and what we found pretty much confirms it. The pair have been sending lovey-dovey messages to each other.

'But I'm going to leave it to Anna to provide the details. And she can also tell us about some other text messages on the phone that are not so friendly. In fact they're altogether more sinister.'

Chapter 14

Anna had only had time to look at some of Helen Troy's calls and messages. But it was enough to provide confirmation that the singer was romantically involved with Leon Serova – and that her ex-boyfriend Paul Rhodes was far from happy about it.

'It's clear she's conducting an illicit affair with the Russian,' Anna said. 'But for obvious reasons they're both trying to keep it low key. He because he's married and she because it would be bad for her image if it was widely known.'

The texts between Helen and Serova were actually fairly innocuous. They made arrangements to meet up, exchanged compliments, and agreed that their relationship should not become public knowledge.

'Let's take it slowly,' he wrote. *'We've both got a lot to lose if it gets out xx.'*

'You're right,' she replied. *'But in a way that makes it far more exciting xx.'*

A couple of the messages alluded to the fact that she had stayed at Serova's mansion in Kent. In one dated three weeks ago he wrote: *'Wife in Monte Carlo this weekend. Can u come to my place in the country again? Will make sure we r alone.'*

'But as we know they didn't manage to keep the fling a secret,' Anna said. 'That's no great surprise, of course, considering who they are. And it seems that the ex-boyfriend is among the people who got wind of what was going on.'

Over the past six or seven weeks Rhodes had sent Helen a string of angry and offensive text messages. Anna read some of them out:

'I hear you are seeing some Russian prick who is almost old enough to be your father.'

'How can you do this? You know I still love you and want you back.'

'You fucking bitch. Just because you're famous you think you're better than everyone else.

'I've checked up on your lover. Rumour has it he's linked to the Russian mafia. Think it's time I told the papers who you're shagging.'

'That last message was sent to Helen's phone just two days ago,' Anna said. 'And she actually replied to it. She told him to grow up and that if he didn't stop harassing her she'd go to the police. And perhaps she would have if she hadn't been kidnapped.'

The text messages from Rhodes made it imperative that we questioned him as soon as possible. They were evidence of a serious grudge – and therefore a clear motive for wanting to hurt her.

Was it conceivable then that he had done the damage to her house and killed her cat? Or had he paid someone to do it for him?

And was he also behind the abduction?

His veiled threats certainly made him a prime suspect, and I could sense the ripple of excitement in the room. But as yet we had no idea where Rhodes was. He hadn't been answering his mobile or home phones. What we did know was that he worked as a trader for an investment bank in the City and he did not have a criminal record. We'd be speaking to his company as soon as there was someone available. Meanwhile, a patrol car had been sent to watch his house in Highgate.

'Right now the ex is our only lead,' I said. 'And based on what we've just heard he's got serious potential. But we shouldn't get carried away. He might be entirely innocent, which means we have to consider all other possibilities and pursue every line of inquiry, however tenuous.'

I then asked to be updated on what information we'd so far gathered. DI Doug Ellroy was the first to speak. Doug was the closest person I had to a real friend on the force. We had worked together on the Murder Investigation Team, and he was the first person I recruited when the CCS was set up.

He was inclined to be a little cocky and sure of himself, but he was also dependable, predictable and unflappable, which was why I'd asked him to oversee the gathering and viewing of all the CCTV and traffic camera footage.

'We're obviously focusing on all three locations,' he said, 'the Tequila Club, Helen's house, and the site where the van was dumped. We've got about ten hours of footage so far. We're noting the plates of all vehicles so we can see if any turn up at more than one of the locations.'

With traffic camera footage it's usually a question of luck, especially if those you're hoping to spot are doing their best to avoid detection. Even with so many cameras throughout the city, it's not that hard to avoid many of them with enough forward planning.

A detective named Brady, who was with the kidnap unit, then let it be known that he had spoken to Helen's manager and agent, but neither had offered up much useful information. However, they'd both said that Helen disliked having a bodyguard as a constant companion and had often gone out by herself without telling anyone.

'To their knowledge she's never been targeted by stalkers and internet trolls,' Brady said. 'But she did confide in her agent that the ex-boyfriend had become a bit of a nuisance.'

The meeting went on for another half an hour, during which I handed out a whole bunch of assignments. DCS Lattimer wrapped it up by announcing that a full press conference would be held at 10am and that no one was to talk to the media without authorisation.

But even before he had finished speaking everyone's attention was drawn to the three television monitors that were mounted on stands around the room.

The BBC was trumpeting another newsflash, and this one sent a cold dread through my lungs. The studio anchor spoke slowly, his voice deep and grave.

'In the last few minutes a photograph of Helen Troy has been posted anonymously on the internet,' he said. 'It was purportedly taken last night after she was kidnapped, and it has already been widely circulated.

'In the photograph she's lying on the floor and appears to be unconscious. But a short caption beneath it claims that she's no longer alive. We have chosen not to show the photograph and we've alerted the police to its existence.'

Chapter 15

The online news sites and blogs were not as cautious and sensitive as the Beeb. The photograph in question was popping up all over the internet.

It took me and the rest of the team mere seconds to find it. My initial reaction was that it looked authentic, and this caused my heart to leap in my chest.

Helen Troy was lying spread-eagled on her back on a beige carpet. There was a large red stain beneath the back of her head that I took to be blood. The photo had been taken from directly above her, and a flashlight threw her features into sharp relief.

She was wearing a tight silver party dress – the same one she'd had on at the Tequila Club. The hem was pushed up around her thighs and both her feet were bare.

Below the photo was a caption which read: *'Helen Troy is now a dead celeb. It's what she deserved.'*

The impact the image had on me and the rest of the team was immediate. There were audible gasps and some loud swearing. Then everyone fell silent as they tried to process what they were looking at.

There were no clues in the photo as to where it had been taken. All it showed was Helen and the carpet she was lying on.

'I don't think there's any doubt that it's her,' I said. 'That's exactly how she looked last night. Same dress, same hairstyle.'

'We need to find out who posted the picture,' Lattimer said. He was standing behind me, peering over my shoulder at the computer screen on my desk.

I shook my head. 'We haven't got a hope in hell. I'm assuming that whoever did it knows how not to leave a trail. They would have used a fake IP address for starters, and there are all kinds of ways to disguise the source of online content. They probably sent the image to an unregulated news blog and it went viral from there.'

I turned in my seat to look at Lattimer. The muscles around his eyes had tightened, and his face had lost some of its colour.

'So how do we play this, guv?' I said. 'Has our kidnapping become a murder investigation?'

He gnawed on his lower lip and spoke without taking his eyes off the screen.

'We can't be sure that she's dead, Sam. They might just want us to think she is.'

'But why would they do that? It doesn't make sense. They went to a lot of trouble to snatch her.'

Neither of us knew the answer, of course, just as we couldn't be certain that Helen Troy wasn't still alive. She was most definitely unconscious in the picture, and it appeared as though she had suffered a head injury. But the wound itself wasn't visible, and for all we knew that could have been ketchup on the carpet.

'The media will want our reaction to this,' Lattimer said. 'So we tell them we're taking the photo seriously and it's now a part of our investigation into Helen Troy's abduction. There's really not much else we can say. But you and I both know that the chances of finding her – dead or alive – are now greatly diminished.'

*

The appearance of the photo made it necessary for me to address the team again. I told them we had to do what we could to verify its authenticity.

To that end I asked a young DC named Charlotte Manning to liaise with the computer wizards at the Yard. She was by far the most savvy on matters relating to the internet and social media.

'It's a long shot I know, but let's see if we can find out who uploaded it and where,' I said.

I then instructed another detective to get forensics to examine the picture.

'Ask them to compare it to the CCTV footage and paparazzi pictures from last night,' I said. 'It seems pretty obvious to me that the woman in the photo is Helen Troy, but I want us to be a hundred per cent sure.'

What I'd put in motion were routine procedures. But there was nothing routine about the way the investigation was panning out. It was now much more than a straightforward kidnapping. The photo added a new and terrifying dimension.

'It's been just over 11 hours since Helen was abducted,' I said. 'If she is dead then we have to assume that she was murdered. The blood on the carpet suggests that she suffered a blow to the back of the head, but we can't be sure without a body. It could be that she was simply rendered unconscious so that they could take the picture and make us think they'd killed her, though why they would do that is beyond me.'

A few unsettling theories were then discussed, including the idea that the men might be planning to sell her to some rich pervert.

'They probably think that if they can convince the world she's dead we'll be minded to scale back the search for her sooner rather than later,' Doug said.

It was a valid point and it made my blood run cold.

Another theory that quickly gained traction among the team was equally disturbing. This was that the men had abducted her just so that they could kill her, probably because they had been paid to do so.

Was that it? I wondered. Had Helen Troy been the victim of an elaborate hit, engineered by someone who had a serious beef with her?

It sounded improbable, but I knew there were plenty of people in London who were prepared to carry out contract killings for the right price.

'We know of at least one person who was seriously pissed off with Helen,' Anna said. 'And that's her ex-boyfriend. We also know he has enough money to pay someone to do his dirty work.'

'We have to find him before we can talk to him,' I said. 'So let's redouble our efforts.'

I then made the point that we needed to find out more about Helen.

'Check her bank accounts and her computer,' I said. 'And talk to everyone who knows her. Does she have secrets? Does she have enemies that we're not aware of? Who else might harbour a grudge against her?'

Ten minutes later I wound up the meeting and headed for my little office in order to draw up a list of the things I needed to do.

But as soon as I sat down behind my desk, Lattimer appeared in the open doorway. He was clutching his mobile phone and looking anxious.

'They've brought the press conference forward,' he said. 'It kicks off in 15 minutes and I think we should both be there.'

Chapter 16

The press conference was taking place at the Yard. Before leaving our building in Caxton Street, I drew up a list of the things I needed to do during the rest of the day.

It included having another conversation with Leon Serova about his affair with Helen, and talking to Alexander Orlov, the man who had offered the £1million reward for her safe return. I also hoped to question Paul Rhodes as soon as he surfaced. I gave the list to Anna and asked her to set things up.

'We'll work through it together,' I said. 'I want to get started as soon as the presser is over. I'd also like you to arrange for a family liaison officer to go check on Helen's mother. If she hasn't seen or heard about the picture already then she will soon and it's going to be hard for her.'

I keep a suit and clean shirt in the office, and I just had time to change into them. But there was no time to shave or freshen up, so when I walked into the crowded conference room I knew I looked rough.

I felt it too. There was a buzz at the base of my skull and my eyes felt dry and gritty.

The media pack was there in force. In fact the room was full, and a number of reporters and photographers were having to stand.

I sat behind the desk alongside the head press officer and Lattimer, who started the ball rolling after loudly clearing his throat. He explained that the Celebrity Crime Squad and the kidnap unit were working together on the case and that I was the senior investigating officer.

'We will shortly be releasing actual video footage of Miss Helen Troy being abducted,' he said. 'You'll know by now that the van she was taken away in was later abandoned and set on fire. You'll also be aware that a photograph of Miss Troy, allegedly taken after she was abducted, has been posted on the internet.'

That was when the room exploded, with everyone raising their arms and shouting questions at the same time.

At first Lattimer struggled to make himself heard and it fell on the press officer to calm things down. He spoke as if addressing a classroom full of children. But at least he restored order after insisting we would only take one question at a time.

It was easy for me to understand the high level of excitement. In the eyes of the media this was one of those stories that would be talked about for years to come. It would boost ratings and sell newspapers. And because the victim was someone famous, it would appeal to readers and viewers of all ages and demographics.

When an Associated Press reporter asked if we believed that Helen Troy was dead, Lattimer said: 'We're keeping an open mind. I won't deny that this case has taken a shocking turn. But we can only hope that the photograph isn't what it seems.'

More questions came thick and fast, and it quickly became evident that we didn't have answers for most of them.

'Should we assume that Helen Troy's world tour will now have to be cancelled?' This from a French journalist.

'That's really an issue for her management team,' I said. 'We're only concerned with finding out what has happened to her. And so should you be at this stage.'

The Q and A session lasted another 20 minutes, by which time the same questions were coming around. I felt a jolt of relief when Lattimer finally called a halt and promised to stage another press conference later in the day.

Several reporters requested one-to-one interviews with me, but I said I was too busy. Lattimer agreed to do them instead and told me to get back on the case.

'We need fucking answers, Sam,' he whispered as we both got to our feet. 'You can have whatever's required in terms of people and resources. Just find out what the bloody hell is going on.'

Chapter 17

'Did you know that there are over 70 billionaires living in London?' Anna said. 'And most of them are Russian.'

'I didn't know,' I said. 'But it doesn't surprise me since the most expensive parts of town have been dubbed Londongrad and Moscow-on-Thames.'

We were in my car heading towards Belgravia, one of those areas which had been colonised by Russian oligarchs in recent years. Anna had managed to set up a meeting with Alexander Orlov, who had flown in from the South of France a few hours earlier. He was one of the many Russians who had been buying up property in the capital like it was going out of fashion.

Some of them did it using dirty money funnelled through offshore companies. It was seen as an efficient way to launder the mountains of cash they had plundered in their home country, and at the same time escape the economic downturn there.

To them Britain was a soft touch and a safe haven. And their extravagant lives had become a source of fascination to the British public since they started buying up football clubs and the most luxurious homes in London.

'Alexander Orlov paid £40million for his humble abode,' Anna said. 'That was three years ago. But it's nothing compared with the £90million that Roman Abramovich reportedly paid for his pad.'

'So what else have you found out about Orlov?' I asked.

Anna took out a notebook and slipped on a pair of reading glasses that I hadn't seen before. They triggered a memory – her telling me a while ago that she was having problems with her eyes. I couldn't resist a peek and decided they suited her; gave her an air of sophistication that evaporated as soon as she started speaking.

'Well for one thing I can tell you he's filthy fucking rich,' she said in that familiar South London vernacular. 'In fact he's apparently one of the richest men in the country. He's got a yacht on the Riviera, his own jet, and homes all over the place.

'He's aged 54, twice divorced and currently single. He started out as a humble civil servant in Moscow before he got involved in private banking. In the Nineties he became one of the beneficiaries of the sweetheart deals that saw state assets sold off for a fraction of their value. He now runs a string of companies across Europe, including a publisher's and a showbiz magazine.'

'And that's how he got involved with Helen Troy?' I said.

She nodded. 'That relationship actually began 11 months ago when he paid her £100,000 to sing at the party marking the launch of the magazine. He then signed her up to write a column and did a book deal with her.'

'Any suggestions of impropriety on his part, or is he one of the straight ones?' I said.

'I only came up with one piece of negative publicity. He was involved in a public spat with Leon Serova of all people. This was ten months ago. The reports were confined to the financial press so I doubt you came across them.'

'What was it over?'

'Well Serova was a significant shareholder in the showbiz magazine, but he and Orlov fell out just before the launch. They said at the time that it was over creative differences, but some commentators suspected there was more to it. Anyway, Serova suddenly agreed to step down from the board after they'd been bad-mouthing each other for a few days. He sold all his shares to Orlov.'

'Do you know what finally made him throw in the towel?'

'The details were never made public, hence the speculation that it wasn't just to do with creative differences.'

'Interesting,' I said. 'It might be worth asking Mr Orlov if there was another story behind those headlines.'

Chapter 18

The stucco-fronted house was at the end of a terrace so it was semi-detached. It faced a communal garden that was packed with so many trees it looked like a mini rain forest.

The street was smart and exclusive, and all the properties had four upper floors. There was parking for residents only so I stuck a 'Police on duty' notice on the dashboard.

A tall, thin woman in her 30s opened the door to us. She introduced herself as Lena Belov, the housekeeper, and had a broad, toothy smile.

'Mr Orlov is expecting you,' she said. 'He's waiting in the sitting room.'

The entrance hall was bland and luxurious in equal measure. The colours were muted, but the walls and surfaces were adorned with fabulous paintings and sculptures.

We followed the housekeeper past a sweeping staircase and into a huge L-shaped sitting room. It was filled with designer furniture and modern art, and was more like a movie set than someone's home.

Alexander Orlov was sitting behind a small desk when we entered. He immediately stood up and stepped forward with his arm outstretched.

He was wearing neatly pressed black trousers and a white open-neck shirt. He was short in stature and thinning on top, with a distinct paunch and double chin.

When we shook hands I couldn't help wondering how much the heavy gold watch strapped to his wrist had cost him.

'You're detective Quinn,' he said. 'I saw you on the television at the press conference.'

I nodded and introduced him to Anna. He gave a slight smile and dimples appeared either side of his mouth.

'Thank you for seeing us, Mr Orlov,' I said.

He waved a hand. 'Please sit down. Would you like tea or coffee?' There was barely a trace of an accent and his English was careful and correct.

'We're both coffee drinkers,' I said.

'Then Lena will get some for us.'

As the housekeeper left the room Anna and I sat down on the sofa, but Orlov remained standing with his arms crossed, his expression weighty and intense.

'The photograph that was posted online is truly disturbing, Inspector,' he said. 'Please be honest with me. Is there any chance that Helen could still be alive?'

I drew in a breath. 'I'm afraid I can't really add to what was said at the press conference, Mr Orlov. At this stage we're just not certain. The photo is undergoing a thorough examination by experts.'

He cast his eyes downwards as he considered my answer. Then he raised them after a few seconds.

'I just don't understand,' he said, shaking his head ruefully. 'Why would those men kill her? I've made it clear that I'm willing to pay them £1million to get her back safely.'

It had been my intention to tell him that we weren't happy about the gesture he'd made on the grounds that it would hinder the investigation. But given the latest development I didn't see the point.

Instead I said: 'It's possible they didn't kidnap her in order to demand a ransom.'

'Then what motive could they have?'

'That's anybody's guess, Mr Orlov. Are you aware that her house was wrecked and her pet cat was killed last night? It must have happened shortly before she was abducted.'

He looked shocked. 'On the news they said there had been a break-in. There was no mention of a cat or damage being done.'

'Well we're still trying to determine whether or not it's linked to her abduction. And that's why we're having to talk to all her friends and acquaintances. We're hoping that someone can tell us if Helen had upset anyone recently. Or had she got involved with any dubious characters?'

His eyebrows drew together. 'I haven't known her for long, Inspector. As you're no doubt aware we became acquainted through the magazine and through my publishing company. But I can say that she's a charming, down-to-earth young woman who hasn't let her celebrity status go to her head.'

'Does she take drugs?'

'Not to my knowledge. And if I'd suspected it then I would not have done business with her.'

'So you can't think who might want to harm her?'

Before answering, he sat down in the armchair facing us and clenched his jaw.

'I wouldn't put it past that ex-boyfriend of hers,' he said. 'I've only seen her get upset once, and that was when she received a phone call from him. He said something that made her cry. She told me he'd been pestering her to get back with him, but she didn't want to. And he'd recently become abusive and threatening because he'd found out that she was seeing someone else.'

'What do you know about that, Mr Orlov?' Anna asked him.

He looked at her and pushed out his bottom lip. 'I knew she was seeing Leon Serova, Inspector. And I told her it was a big mistake. But she told me it was none of my business.'

'So why do you disapprove? Is it because he's married?'

'That's partly it,' he said. 'But it's mostly because being with him could do irreparable damage to her career. You must know yourself that he's under investigation for money laundering. He's also a serial adulterer. And I know from bitter experience that he can't be trusted.'

'We heard that you fell out with him,' I said.

'That's true. At one time we were good friends.'

'So what caused the rift? And why did he quit the magazine business?'

At that moment the housekeeper arrived with the coffees. She placed a tray on the marble table between us and handed out our drinks in delicate china cups.

After she left the room again, Orlov said: 'The official explanation for Leon's departure from the business was 'creative differences'. And that was true up to a point.'

'What does that mean?' I asked.

It took a couple of moments for him to respond. Before he did he let out a heavy sigh.

'Leon wanted the magazine to be gossipy and salacious,' he said. 'But I was keen for it to be fun and frivolous. I was convinced it was the way to go if it was going to be a success. He dug his heels in and managed to get the support of other board members. He became quite aggressive, and it got to the point where he started trying to force me out.'

'So what happened?'

'Well I'm not a man who can easily be intimidated, Inspector. I therefore decided to fight back. He didn't see it coming and he had no choice but to agree to my demands, which were to leave the company and sell his shares to me.'

'How did you manage it?'

He shrugged. 'I had evidence that one of the women he'd been having an affair with was none other than the wife of a prominent figure in the Russian mafia. I simply suggested that it wouldn't be good for Leon if the man in question found out about it.'

'So you blackmailed him.'

'Not at all. I merely pointed out that his actions would have consequences. I was actually doing him a favour.'

Yeah, right, I thought.

'He can't have been happy about that?' I said.

'Oh, he wasn't. He swore that one day he would get his own back. And I'm sure he intends to.'

Chapter 19

'So what do you think, guv?' Anna said.

'I think that Mr Orlov raised some interesting points about his business rival,' I answered. 'If what he claims is true then we have to consider that Leon Serova may have decided to use Helen as a way of getting his own back on the man who effectively blackmailed him.'

It was wild conjecture, of course, but the thought of it had my pulse racing as I drove us towards Serova's house in Mayfair.

'Are you suggesting that he could have arranged to have Helen kidnapped?' Anna said.

'I'm saying it's possible. I've known stranger things to happen.'

'But they're in a relationship.'

'So what? It doesn't mean he has true feelings for her. If he's a serial adulterer then perhaps it's purely sexual. Or maybe he entered into it just to wind Orlov up.'

Anna took off her glasses and pondered the idea. Then she said: 'It seems a bit extreme to me, guv.'

'Well, what's extreme to you might not be to him,' I said. 'The hunger for revenge can distort a person's perception of things and make him or her behave irrationally.'

Anna still wasn't convinced. 'Then let's imagine that did happen,' she said. 'Serova wanted to stuff Orlov so he got some men to abduct one of the man's prize assets after inviting her to his party. But then why kill her?'

'Good question,' I said. 'Except that we can't be sure she's dead. And if she is then maybe he just couldn't resist going all the way.'

*

We parked in another upmarket street, this time close to Berkeley Square Gardens in Mayfair.

Leon Serova's house was, if anything, even more impressive than the one we had just left. Late Victorian, with five floors and a red brick façade.

Anna had arranged an appointment for us, but before getting out of the car we listened to the mid-day news on BBC Radio Two.

Helen Troy was still the headline story, and it included a short interview with Lattimer given straight after the press conference. There were also soundbites from Helen's agent and a representative of her recording company. Both of them referred to her in the past tense, presumably because the photograph that had been posted had convinced them she was dead.

As we listened, Anna used her smartphone to check the reaction on social media.

'It's all anyone is talking about,' she said. 'Helen's own website has crashed because so many people are trying to post messages. And Twitter and Facebook are on fire.'

On the radio the newsreader said that Helen's world tour had been cancelled, and her showbiz friends were lining up to voice their concern. One prominent actress said that all celebrities lived in fear of being targeted by stalkers, kidnappers and demented fans.

It made me think about my wife, and how she'd been cut down in her prime by a psycho with a grudge against the rich and famous.

I shook my head to dislodge the memory. Now was not the time to allow myself to be distracted by the numbing pain of the past. I owed it to Helen Troy to be totally focused on the case.

It was a case that I already suspected was going to end in tears.

Chapter 20

Our meeting with Leon Serova got off to a bad start. He was yelling into his mobile phone when a man I assumed was his bodyguard showed us into his sumptuous office on the ground floor and invited us to be seated in front of the desk.

Serova didn't even acknowledge us as he paced the room with the phone to his ear.

'I've already told you,' he was saying, 'the rumours are not true. Helen Troy and I are just good friends. If you publish anything to the contrary you'll be hearing from my lawyers.'

He switched off the phone and swore under his breath. He didn't move for several moments, just stood in the centre of the room breathing heavily through his nose. Blue veins stood out on his neck, and he had grim, tight lines at the corners of his mouth.

'That was the Daily Mail,' he fumed. 'The second paper to call me this morning asking me if I'm having an affair with Helen.'

'So why are you denying it?' I said.

'Because it's nonsense.'

'That's not what we've been told, Mr Serova. In fact that's why I wanted to see you again. I want to know why you didn't volunteer that information when I spoke to you last night at the club.'

He was clearly surprised. He stood there slack-jawed, his eyes like slivers of ice.

I gave him a few seconds to respond, and when he didn't, said: 'Don't bother lying to us, Mr Serova. We're aware that Helen was going to spend the night here with you. Her bodyguard told us. We also know that you two have been dating for some time. We've seen the text messages you sent to each other.'

He fixed me with a hard stare and blew out a lungful of air.

'I don't see why my relationship with Helen is an issue,' he said. 'It's got nothing to do with you or the media. And it has absolutely no relevance to what has happened to her.'

'So why didn't you tell me about it?' I said.

He stepped behind his desk and sat down in a high-backed leather chair before answering the question.

'I wasn't being deliberately evasive,' he said. 'It just didn't occur to me. I'm sure if you had asked me outright I would have told you.'

'But surely it must have occurred to you that we'd want to know that you were her current boyfriend.'

'I'm not her boyfriend,' he snapped. 'We've been out and slept together a few times. But that's all. Just a bit of fun. Nothing serious.'

I gave a thoughtful nod. 'I suppose that's why you didn't appear to be that upset.'

His eyes flared. 'What's that supposed to mean?'

I shrugged. 'Well looking back you came across as remarkably calm considering what had happened. You weren't acting like someone who is in a relationship with Helen.'

'I'm not a man who is inclined to show his emotions, Inspector. And the last I heard that's not a crime in this country.'

I held his stare and saw anger vibrating beneath his composure. I could tell he wasn't used to being on the back foot, or being asked to account for his actions.

Anna entered the conversation at this point with a question that made him blush.

'Is it true that you're a serial adulterer, Mr Serova?' she said. 'And that Helen is just one of many?'

For a moment I thought he was going to explode. Instead he jabbed his tongue against the inside of his cheek and sat back in the chair.

'I get it now,' he said. 'You've obviously been listening to the vitriol that's often spouted by my one-time friend and business partner, Alexander Orlov. He's too fond of spreading malicious gossip. You shouldn't listen to it.'

'Did you know that he wasn't happy that you started seeing Helen?' I said.

'Of course, but that's only because he regards her as one of his assets. The truth is he gives her the creeps. She told me so. He tries to be a father-figure to her and she doesn't like it.'

'But is what he told us true?'

'Again, my personal life is really none of your business, Inspector.'

'It is if it has a bearing on Helen Troy's abduction,' I said.

He frowned. 'But I don't see how it could.'

'Well, according to Mr Orlov you threatened revenge after he forced you out of the magazine business. One way to get back at him would be to arrange for Helen to disappear.'

His eyes grew wide and he spoke in a low, barely controlled voice. 'Are you actually telling me that I'm a suspect?' he said.

'At this stage everyone we speak to is a suspect, Mr Serova.'

'Then it's no wonder you're getting nowhere with the investigation. You have no idea if she's dead or alive and yet you see fit to come here and make outrageous allegations. You're wasting your time and mine.'

'That's not how we see it,' I said. 'You were, after all, the person who invited Helen to the Tequila Club. And it's alleged that you have links with the Russian mafia, which I assume is one of the reasons you're the subject of a money-laundering investigation by the National Crime Agency.'

He suddenly pushed himself forward and banged a fist on top of the desk.

'That's enough, Inspector. I'm not listening to anymore of this rubbish. I'd like you to leave my house right now and if you want to speak to me again you'll have to go through my lawyers.'

The door to the study flew open and his bodyguard appeared without being summoned. I saw two other men in dark suits standing in the hallway.

I thought about trying to talk Serova around by assuring him that I wasn't actually making an accusation, but I decided not to bother. He was well within his rights not to say any more, and I would have done the same in his position.

We were clutching at straws and he must have known it. He would also have known that we had not a shred of evidence linking him to the kidnappers.

Nevertheless I planned to talk to him again after I'd spoken to my contact in the NCA and got the team to see what they could dig up on him.

As we were being escorted out of the house my mobile phone rang. The call was from a withheld number.

'Hello,' I said.

'DCI Quinn?'

'That's right.'

'It's Paul Rhodes here. I'm Helen Troy's former boyfriend. I gather you want to talk to me.'

Chapter 21

'Where are you, Mr Rhodes?' I said.

He sounded breathless. 'I'm at my place in Redhill, but I'm just about to set off for London. Should be back home in just over an hour, traffic permitting.'

'Are you aware that we've been trying to contact you since last night?'

'I am, but my phone's been switched off. I spent the whole of yesterday doing up the cottage. I went to bed early and didn't want to be disturbed.'

'How long have you been in Redhill?'

'Why do you want to know that?'

'Just answer the question, Mr Rhodes.

He tutted. 'I've been here since Friday. I've only just bought the place as a weekend retreat and it needs a lot of work. So I took a day's leave. I still don't have a television so the first I heard about Helen was when I just turned my phone back on. That's when I saw the messages from the police. I was told to call you on this number.'

I asked him for his address in Redhill. He was on speaker so Anna made a note of it.

'I'm going to arrange for the local police to come straight there,' I told him. 'So I want you to stay put. Would you have any objection if they carried out a search of your cottage or do I have to get a warrant?'

'Are you serious? Do you really think Helen is here?'

'We need to be sure that she isn't, Mr Rhodes, and I strongly suggest that you cooperate.'

'But why would she be here? I didn't kidnap her for heaven's sake.'

'But we know that you've been harassing her, so it's necessary for us to eliminate you from our enquiries. I hope you can understand.'

'Not really. I've got nothing to do with what's happened.'

'Then there's no reason why you should object to us searching your premises. It'll happen anyway, Mr Rhodes. All I have to do is get a warrant.'

He hesitated briefly before telling me that he had no objection.

'I'm also going to arrange for a car to bring you to London,' I said. 'I'd like to meet up with you at your house in Highgate.'

'You're making me nervous now,' he said. 'Do you really think I had something to do with Helen's kidnap?'

'I honestly don't know,' I said. 'So the sooner we can satisfy ourselves that you didn't the better for all concerned.'

As soon as the call ended, Anna was on the phone to Surrey police. She filled them in and asked them to send detectives and a forensics team to the cottage.

'Check his car as well,' she said. 'And then have him brought straight to London.'

She gave them the address in Highgate and then made another call to our own ops room in Caxton Street. She told them to put a team of SOCOs on standby so they could meet us at Highgate as soon as we gained access to the house.

But it wasn't going to be for a couple of hours, which gave Anna and I time to grab some lunch. We were both famished as well as tired.

I drove to Highgate and found a trendy pub with tables outside. The sun had disappeared behind low, menacing clouds, and the air was heavy with the promise of rain. But it was still warm, so I treated her to an al fresco meal of pie and chips. We washed it down with coke to give us both a caffeine jolt.

We talked about the case, and I told her we now had to assume that Helen Troy was dead until we could prove otherwise.

'This will put the fear of God into other celebrities,' Anna said. 'Personal protection companies will be doing a roaring trade for a while.'

She was probably right on that score, I thought. But then maybe that wasn't such a bad thing. Celebrities needed to be far more aware of the threats they faced.

In my view they had never been so at risk, particularly in London, a city teeming with the rich and famous.

Hordes of celebs live, work and play here. They flaunt their wealth and success and bask in the adulation. At the same time they tell the world what they're doing and what they're thinking through blogs, online postings and newspaper interviews.

So it's no wonder they attract the attention of obsessive fans and hate-filled individuals.

I remembered what Lattimer told me when he asked me to head up the Celebrity Crime Squad. This was after a series of newspaper headlines attacking the Met because of the poor detection and conviction rates in celebrity-related cases.

'The criticisms are justified, Sam,' he'd said. 'Barely a week goes by when a celebrity isn't robbed, threatened, blackmailed or even murdered. And too often the crimes against them are unsolved because of fuck-ups on our part. We can no longer expect ordinary, mainstream detectives to handle these cases.'

And he'd been right, of course, which was why the CCS had been created.

Cases involving people like Helen Troy used to be rare. But now they were far more common, partly because of the growing tide of resentment against celebrities.

And with the gap between the rich and poor becoming ever wider, there was every reason to believe that the problem was set to get much worse.

Chapter 22

When Paul Rhodes arrived at his house in Highgate we were waiting for him outside – along with a forensics team.

I didn't recognise him from the pictures I'd seen online. In the flesh he was sallow-faced and unshaven, with sweat sparkling like fine dew across his forehead.

He also looked tired. His shoulders were hunched and his eyes were heavy and red from where he'd been sobbing in the patrol car.

We'd already heard back from the team in Redhill who had searched his cottage. They'd found no evidence to suggest that Helen Troy had been there.

They said the property was detached, and it appeared that Rhodes had been painting the inside walls and fitting new units in the kitchen. None of the neighbours had been able to confirm that he'd been there all day, but the local pub landlord did remember that Rhodes popped in for a sandwich lunch between about 2pm-3pm.

'We appreciate your cooperation,' I said as he opened the door to his smart mews house.

He shrugged. 'I didn't see that I had any choice. And what about my car? It's still in Redhill and I'll need it tomorrow.'

'We've arranged to have it brought to London later today,' I said.

He asked me if there had been any more news about Helen. As we stepped into the hallway I told him there'd been no further developments since the posting of the photograph.

'I saw it on my phone,' he said. 'I can't believe somebody would do that to her.'

I asked him again if it was all right for the SOCOs to check the house.

'If you object then I'll obtain a warrant,' I said. 'It's up to you.'

Another shrug. 'They can come in as long as they don't make too much mess.'

Anna signalled for the forensic team to come in and I said to Rhodes: 'Why don't we have our chat in the kitchen while they get on with it? Perhaps we can blag a cup of tea at the same time.'

His house was immaculate, and it was clear that no expense had been spared on furniture and decorations. On the ground floor there was a huge designer kitchen, a study and a spare bedroom.

Rhodes explained that the living and dining rooms were on the first floor and there were two more bedrooms on the top floor.

He gestured for us to sit at the kitchen table. I thought he was going to make the tea then, but instead he stood in the downdraught from the ceiling fan and turned back to me.

'I feel like I've walked into a bloody nightmare,' he said. 'It's bad enough knowing that Helen might have been murdered. But the fact that I'm under arrest as a suspect makes it a thousand times worse.'

'You haven't been arrested, Mr Rhodes,' I assured him. 'And there's no need for you to worry if you haven't done anything wrong.'

'Well that's what it feels like. I'm beginning to think I should have consulted my lawyer before letting you in here.'

'I've already told you, Mr Rhodes. We have to go through the motions because you sent offensive text messages to your ex-girlfriend during the past few weeks and in at least one of them you made a threat.'

'I don't remember that.'

'Then let me remind you. In a text sent just a couple of days ago you said you were going to expose her relationship with Leon Serova. Not that it appears to have been a well-kept secret.'

'That was because I was upset,' Rhodes said. 'And jealous. I've wanted desperately to get back with her.'

'Well it seems you went the wrong way about it.'

'But that was because she kept ignoring me. It drove me fucking crazy.'

'So why didn't you just leave her alone?'

'I tried, but I was wound up. I wanted to talk to her face to face, but she wouldn't have it. She was treating me with contempt and it wasn't fair.'

I got him to sit down and asked Anna to make the tea. I didn't want his nerves to get the better of him. I needed him to stay focused and compliant.

'Look, just relax,' I said. 'Answer the questions and we'll be out of here before you know it.'

I started with his alibi. He insisted he drove to Redhill on Friday afternoon and spent all day Saturday painting walls and ceilings. But the only person he spoke to was the pub landlord, and there was no one to confirm that he was there throughout the evening.

'I went to bed about seven,' he said. 'I was totally knackered. And I slept right through until this morning.'

'So you're saying you did not return to London in the evening?'

'That's right. I had no reason to. And before you ask, I didn't pay anyone to abduct Helen. Why on earth would I? I'm a city broker, not a gangster.'

'Are you aware that her house was broken into just before she was kidnapped?'

He said there had only been a brief mention of it in the online reports he'd read. So I told him about the damage and the fate of the cat and he appeared visibly shaken.

'Blimey,' he said. 'That's bad. But no way would I have done it. I'm not some psycho. Sure I was pissed off with her and I told her so. But you would have to be sick in the fucking head to do something like that.'

'Have you seen Helen recently, Mr Rhodes?'

He shook his head. 'I told you. She wouldn't meet me. That's why I had to resort to phone calls and text messages.'

'Have you been stalking her as well?'

'No I fucking haven't. I did go to her house once – about a month ago – but she wouldn't let me in so I didn't go back again.'

Rhodes was clearly an angry young man. There was a dark rage burning beneath the surface and I could see why Helen had been alarmed and had threatened to call the police.

As Anna poured us each a mug of tea I got him to tell me more about himself and his relationship with Helen. He said it became strained when she became successful and spent increasing amounts of time away from home. It fostered resentment on his part and he acknowledged that he became possessive and argumentative.

'The shock of living with a celebrity hit me hard,' he said. 'Just as I was finally coming to terms with it she decided to end it. And yes, I was angry and heartbroken at the same time. I admit I couldn't leave it alone. She accused me of being a pathetic pest, and it just made things worse. But despite everything that happened I've always loved her and I can't bear the thought that she might be dead.'

There was no doubt that he still had strong feelings for his ex-girlfriend, but that didn't mean he wouldn't want to hurt her. She had dumped him, after all, and he had reacted badly.

But if he had been involved in what had happened then it was going to be hard to prove it without any physical evidence and with an alibi that stood up to scrutiny.

Nevertheless he'd remain firmly in the frame until I was convinced that what he had told me was the absolute truth.

I wrapped up the interview at the same time as the SOCOs finished what we'd agreed would be a fairly superficial sweep of the house. If there'd been a shred of evidence to indicate Rhodes had been complicit in Helen's abduction then they would have carried out a more thorough examination. But they'd found nothing at all suspicious.

Just to be on the safe side they'd collected various samples in plastic bags to be checked over in the lab, and Rhodes gave us details of his email accounts so that we could go through them.

As we left him sitting forlornly at the kitchen table I felt a wave of disappointment wash over me. It seemed that our most promising line of inquiry had taken us no further forward.

Helen was still missing. We still didn't know for certain if she was alive or dead.

And my head was aching from the flood of unsettling thoughts rushing through it.

Chapter 23

Thankfully there was something to offer up when Lattimer convened another press conference in the late afternoon.

It was a short video clip from a street camera near Helen Troy's home. It showed a man in a hooded cardigan walking towards her house about the time she left to go to the Tequila Club.

He was then picked up again on the same camera 40 minutes later walking in the opposite direction. Several other pedestrians were captured on that particular camera, but none of them walked back and forth or moved as quickly as he did.

The man was too far away to make identification possible, though. His face wasn't visible and his hands were thrust into his pockets. Even when a freeze frame was enhanced it was still too blurry. We couldn't even be a hundred percent certain the figure was male, but that was our conclusion based on his shape and how he walked.

Unfortunately we hadn't so far spotted him on any other CCTV cameras in the area, which raised the possibility that he had gone out of his way to avoid them.

But at least we had something to give to a frenzied media pack that was hungry for news.

There were no other fresh developments. The trawl of dozens more traffic cameras hadn't produced a result and neither had any of the forensic evidence.

The prints, hairs and fibres from Paul Rhodes's house all belonged to him, and whoever had messed up Helen's place hadn't left a single clue.

The jury remained out on the photograph of Helen posted online. The techies said it was impossible to know if she was dead or merely unconscious in the picture. We also drew a blank in respect of her ex-boyfriend's email and phone accounts. The only text messages to and from Helen were those we'd already seen on her phone, and there was nothing that could be deemed incriminating.

I did decide to pursue further the line of inquiry relating to Clara Pike. This was because a criminal records check showed that her husband had served two years in prison for aggravated burglary and 18 months for an attack on a man in a pub. Clara herself also had form – a fine and suspended sentence for benefit fraud. It begged the question as to why Helen – a top notch celebrity – had seen fit to employ her as a cleaner. But then it was already evident that the singer was far too complacent about her own security.

'Let's dig a little deeper,' I said. 'Check their phones, emails and bank accounts. And we should arrange for Mrs Pike to go to Helen's house to tell us if anything is missing.'

By 6pm the lack of sleep was catching up on me. My senses were dulled by fatigue and I was finding it hard to concentrate.

I sent Anna home because she dropped off at her desk while going through social media sites looking for anything that might prove relevant to the investigation.

Before I took off myself I decided to make one final call – to a contact inside the National Crime Agency.

*

Joe Deakin was a senior investigator with the NCA, which has been dubbed Britain's FBI. Its remit is to investigate organised crime, including money laundering, human trafficking and the illegal sex trade.

Joe had been one of the few people I'd confided in during those dark days when my gambling addiction ruled my life. That was because he had also been an addict, and it had led to the break-up of his marriage.

We weren't close friends, but we did stay in touch and meet up for the occasional drink, during which we tried to reassure each other that we finally had the demons under control.

'I'm surprised you found the time to call me, Sam,' he said. 'The Helen Troy case is a biggie.'

'That's actually why I wanted to talk to you,' I said. 'I've got a few questions about a couple of Helen's acquaintances.'

'I take it you mean Leon Serova and Alexander Orlov?'

'How did you know?'

'Well there's Orlov's offer of a reward, and the fact that Serova is part-owner of the Tequila Club. And I gather that Helen was having a fling with him, which is why she went there to help celebrate his birthday.'

I briefed Joe on my conversations with the two Russian oligarchs and he confirmed that the NCA was investigating Serova.

'But it's not just because he's building up his London property portfolio with laundered money,' he said. 'We're just as interested in his links to a major drugs and prostitution racket that provides a high-end service to rich Russians living in London. There's an insatiable demand for classy girls and cocaine, and of course to those guys money is no object.'

'So what's Serova's connection to that?'

'We've been carrying out surveillance on the man we believe is behind the operation. His name is Anton Drach. He's a leading figure in the Russian mafia and we know he's supplied girls for sex parties held by Serova and others. Sometimes dozens of girls at a time are flown by private jet to exotic locations around the world. The oligarchs use Drach because he's part of the same Russian clique here. He's the London end of a huge international operation.'

'So why hasn't he been arrested?'

'Because he's a canny operator, and we haven't been able to get enough evidence together to put before the DPP.'

'Is Alexander Orlov also among Drach's clients?'

'We believe so. In all there are 15 or so oligarchs based in London who use Drach's services on a regular basis. You have to remember that the men we're talking about are among the richest in the world. So naturally they have expensive habits.'

'Orlov told me that Serova was having an affair with the wife of a Russian gangster,' I said. 'He used it to blackmail him. Could it be Drach?'

'I suspect it is,' Joe said. 'Drach's wife Natalia resides in Moscow and we know that Serova goes there about once a month. On one occasion he was photographed having dinner in a hotel restaurant with Drach's wife. The photo came into our possession about six months ago. Maybe Orlov got his hands on it too.'

I asked Joe if he thought that Drach might have been involved in Helen's kidnapping.

'Personally I think it's highly unlikely,' he said. 'For one thing he wouldn't do it unless it was to collect a huge ransom. And for another he wouldn't want to get on the wrong side of Alexander Orlov, who is rich and powerful enough to cause him no end of problems.'

'What about Serova?' I said. 'Presumably he wouldn't have the same qualms about upsetting Orlov?'

'That's a fair point,' Joe said. 'And of all the oligarchs residing in London, he appears to be the most ruthless as well as the most crooked.'

Chapter 24

By the time I got home to my sterile flat near Canary Wharf my temples felt like they were going to explode. The place seemed emptier than usual – a hollowed out shell.

A sudden weariness came over me as soon as I closed the front door, and with it memories of better times when my life wasn't blighted by loneliness; when I had Karen for company, and the evenings were cosy and warm and complete.

I undressed and stepped into the shower. The water came down like a tropical storm and it made me feel a little better.

I put on my dressing gown and fixed myself a JD with coke and ice. I carried it out onto the balcony. The rain hadn't materialised, and a full moon now shone in a clear, starry sky.

The flat was five floors up with a view across the Thames to South East London. Looking west I could see the spectacular city skyline, including the London Eye and the 87-storey skyscraper known as The Shard.

The beauty of it never ceased to amaze me. I couldn't imagine living anywhere else, despite the darkness that lurked beneath the gloss.

From up here it all looked so pretty and serene. But in truth London was a melting pot of rival cultures, criminal gangs and a festering animosity between the rich and poor.

Every day bad things happened and there were victims galore. Helen Troy was among the very few the public ever got to hear about. And that was only because she was famous.

Worrying thoughts chased through my mind and I wondered if she was out there somewhere, waiting to be rescued – or waiting to be buried.

I couldn't get the photo of her out of my head. It was stressing me out and making my stomach churn like a pit of acid.

I fired down the JD, but it didn't help. It felt like someone had removed my battery and replaced it with hot coals.

What I needed was to go to sleep and escape into blessed oblivion. But I knew I would probably lie awake for a couple of hours fretting over the case and wondering why life had to be so bloody cruel.

After downing two more JDs I decided I needed a distraction, and against my better judgement I fired up my laptop.

As I logged in to a familiar online poker site I felt a rush of guilt as well as adrenaline. But a voice in my head told me not to overreact, that I was suffering a minor relapse. It was no big deal, just a way of dealing with the pressure of arguably the biggest case of my career.

So I decided to go for it and play a few hands – just until I felt I was ready for bed.

Of course, it was a big mistake, but I didn't realise that until it was far too late.

PART 2

Chapter 1

'Where are you taking me?' she said.

'Somewhere nice,' the driver told her. 'It's quiet. You'll like it.'

The sedative they had given her was starting to wear off. She knew because her senses had begun thumping, and a raw terror was rushing through her body.

She had lost track of time, but she was aware of exactly what was happening to her. And what was going to happen.

She was in a car with two of the men who had abducted her. She had served her purpose and now they were going to kill her. She didn't want to die, but at least it would bring an end to the pain and humiliation that had become increasingly difficult to endure.

She sniffed back a shuddering sob and looked out the window. They were driving through dark countryside. The car's vents drew in the smells of the woods and fields.

She felt nauseous and dizzy, and at the same time every muscle in her body was taut, her shoulders rigid.

She knew that the driver had just told her a lie because before setting out she'd overheard their muted conversation.

The other one, who was sitting next to her on the back seat, had said they'd been instructed to take her to the wood because 'it was time to bury her with the others.'

That had been just after the sedative was administered so she'd been too spaced out to react. Now there was no point. She knew only too well that they didn't respond to her screams and pleas for mercy, and she felt too weak to put up a fight. Her ordeal had turned her into a physical and mental wreck. She was no longer the beautiful, talented celebrity with a glittering future to look forward to. Now she was damaged goods, a burned-out shell of her former self.

She clenched her eyes shut and forced back the tears. Every nerve in her body was jumping at the prospect of what they were going to do to her. Would it be quick or slow? Would they take turns to rape her first? Would they use a knife or throttle her with rope?

'It was time to bury her with the others.'

Those words leapt unbidden into her mind again. They could only mean that she wasn't the first victim, that other women had suffered the same terrible fate.

Before they seized her she would never have believed that such things could happen. Now she knew better, having been exposed to unimaginable cruelty.

She thought again about her friends and family. They'd be frantic with worry. And so too would her fans. And they would probably never find out what had happened to her.

'Not far now,' said the man beside her. 'A few miles at the most.'

He was tall and sinewy, with a narrow face and slits for eyes. It was the first time he had spoken to her. Usually it was the driver, much older and rougher looking, who told her what to do.

She opened her eyes and looked out of the window again, just as they crossed a bridge that took them over a motorway. Through the railings she saw the lights of fast-moving traffic down below.

She took a deep breath, expelled it, said, 'Please let me go.'

They both chose to ignore her. Then the man beside her started to whistle and tap his shoe on the floor.

'I beg you,' she said. 'I won't tell anyone where I've been. I promise.'

This time it was the driver who spoke.

'You know that can't happen,' he said. 'So do as you've been told and keep quiet.'

Her mantra had always been 'never give up'. It had helped her to do well at school and then to become a star. But she couldn't see how it could help her now.

She was no match for the two thugs, especially with the sedative sloshing around her system. And they knew it. That was why they hadn't bothered to tie her up or cuff her wrists. They weren't expecting her to try to escape or make things difficult for them.

But it struck her now that it had been a mistake on their part because she wasn't as shaky and disoriented as they thought she was. And this made her realise that she didn't have to give up. At least not yet. Not until the moment she was about to take her dying breath.

And that moment hadn't yet arrived … which was why she suddenly felt compelled to do something.

Propelled by anger and desperation, she threw herself forward and thrust her right arm around the driver's face so that his eyes were covered.

He cried out and tried to shake himself free, at the same time slamming on the brakes. The car veered to the left, mounted the kerb, then lurched back onto the road and went into a dramatic spin.

She was then forced to release her grip as she was thrown back against the seat.

A split second later the car collided with a solid object, and the side windows caved in.

In the brief silence that followed she saw that the collision had caused the rear door on her side to be flung open.

She prayed she had the strength to hurl herself through it.

The tall thug tried to stop her but he wasn't quick enough. She managed to clamber out of the door before he could reach her. Then she pushed it shut behind her and stumbled away from the car.

It took a moment for her scrambled brain to register the scene around her. The car had smashed side-on into a lamppost on the edge of a village. The driver was struggling to contend with an inflated air bag while shouting at her through the side window.

She gave an involuntary gasp, turned away from him, and started running for her life.

She chose not to head towards the village because it was too far away and too exposed. Instead she ran into the woods bordering this side of the road.

Her lungs started burning almost immediately, and her legs felt weak and rubbery.

But she willed herself forward into the brooding embrace of the trees, with her heart pounding like a drum, and her arms flailing wildly in front of her.

Ahead of her through the trees she could hear the hum of traffic. She guessed it was the motorway they had crossed over just minutes before.

She wasn't sure she would get to it before they caught up with her, but she was determined to try. If she could flag down a car or lorry then she could save herself.

But she was struggling just to stay upright. It was too dark to see the ground, which was covered with low bushes and rocks. She was wearing jeans and a T-shirt, and sharp branches were tearing at her arms and legs.

She heard one of the men call her name. He sounded close. And angry. She didn't stop. Terror and panic carried her forward, and she quickly discovered that the motorway was closer than she thought.

It was suddenly there in front of her, an unlit section with vehicles thundering in both directions.

She had to climb over a fence to get to it, but it was low and not really an obstacle.

As she launched herself down the steep embankment she lost her balance and fell. She rolled some of the way through tall grass before she was able to pull herself up again.

She heard a panicked voice behind her as she ran onto the hard shoulder. She started waving and yelling to attract attention. But her screams were drowned out by the roar of the traffic, and she didn't think the drivers could see her.

Out of desperation she stepped onto the carriageway and held her arms in the air in the hope that she could force someone to stop.

But she chose the wrong moment to do so.

A lorry was bearing down the inside lane. The driver must have seen her because he sounded his horn. But there was no way he could stop in time even though he applied the brakes. They wailed like a banshee as the lorry slammed into her.

Chapter 2

The alarm woke me at 6am. I keep the clock on the chest of drawers rather than the bedside table so I have to get out of bed to turn it off. If I don't it's just too easy to go back to sleep.

I knew that waking up this morning was not going to be a pleasant experience. I felt like total crap and I only had myself to blame.

I'd stayed up playing online poker until 3am. And if that wasn't bad enough I'd also lost just over £1000. A bloody disaster, and more than a minor relapse.

I'd let the pressure get to me. Other coppers release it through the bottle or slapping people around. With me it's through gambling – the crack cocaine of the new Millennium.

I was angry and disappointed. I'd been telling myself that I'd finally found the strength to resist the rush of adrenaline, the pull of what was for me the ultimate high.

I thought about the Gamblers Anonymous session. It was hard to believe I was there just the night before last. It seemed like ages ago. I would definitely be going back, especially now that I'd fallen so spectacularly off the wagon.

Shit.

I hauled myself into the kitchen, filled the kettle and put it on to boil while I had a shave and then jumped in the shower.

I didn't switch on the television until I was sitting at the breakfast bar, fully dressed and drinking my first cup of coffee of the day.

Helen Troy's kidnapping continued to dominate the news agenda. The BBC was now showing the photograph of her, along with the caption claiming she was dead. All the stations were also running the video clip of the hooded man seen near her home.

There had been no new developments overnight, but Sky News had managed to get a short interview with Helen's mother, who broke down on camera after saying that she wanted to believe her daughter was still alive.

I felt a tightening in my gut, a fierce apprehension, at the thought that Helen was probably dead. But if she was alive then we needed to find her – and quickly.

But there was still nothing in the way of solid evidence linking any of those people in her life with her abduction.

Leon Serova was certainly a shady character, but would he really have snatched her just to get back at his business rival?

And would Paul Rhodes have gone to the extreme of paying someone to do it because he was jealous of her involvement with another man?

And then there was the trashing of her home. Should we be treating that as an entirely separate incident? And was it conceivable that the cleaner Clara Pike knew more about it than she was letting on?

I was still not convinced that she and her husband had been totally upfront with me. Was it possible that Clara had fallen out with Helen and had ripped up the house and killed the cat in a violent rage? Or was it more likely that her husband had done it on her behalf?

There were too many questions and too few answers. I'd been up for less than an hour and already I could feel the pressure building.

On the TV the anchor had moved on to other news. A car bomb had gone off in Tripoli, killing 12 people. Forest fires were raging across Southern California. And a young woman, who had yet to be identified, had been killed by a lorry on the M4 motorway just west of London.

The start of a typical day, I thought. Death and destruction everywhere.

But at least outside the sun was shining.

Chapter 3

The caffeine had started to kick in by the time I got to headquarters. But I still felt pretty rough and I probably looked it too.

Anna, on the other hand, was looking fresh and alert. She greeted me with a bright, easy smile and a cup of steaming black coffee.

'Morning, guv,' she said. 'How did you sleep?'

'Like a baby. Is everyone in?'

'Just about. The DCS called to say he'll be late so you should start the briefing without him.'

'Anything happened overnight that I should know about?'

She shook her head. 'Nothing apart from a raft of calls from cranks and time-wasters. The appeal hotline was swamped apparently. At least a dozen people rang in to say they'd spotted Helen Troy in the street. Four said they were part of the gang that took her. And one nutter claimed he'd killed her because he didn't like to hear her singing.'

'So what's being done about them?'

'Well most calls were anonymous, but those where names were given are being followed up.'

Whenever there was a high-profile case the mischief-makers came out of the woodwork. They took a perverse pleasure in wasting police time and raising the hopes of friends and relatives of the victims.

But all calls had to be checked out if possible because there was always the slim chance that a member of the public really did have information that was relevant to the case.

I convened the morning meeting as soon as I'd checked my emails and messages.

It began with a handover from the officers who had worked through the night. They'd been allocated various tasks and I wanted updates.

'Give me some good news people,' I said. 'We need to move forward on this. And that means working our socks off. Helen Troy is still missing and every hour that passes makes it more likely that even if she is still alive then we'll never find her. So try to imagine what her mother's going through. We have to do everything we can to end her suffering.'

The first progress report came from Doug Ellroy, who looked bleary-eyed having trawled through hours of CCTV footage.

'We've drawn up a list of about 200 vehicle registration numbers,' he said. 'Most belong to cars and vans that were close to the derelict site in Bermondsey when the kidnappers dumped the van there. The rest are from vehicles in the vicinity of Helen's house around the time it was trashed.

'The numbers have been fed into the system and we're in the process of collating owner IDs. We've also circulated the list to all forces. I'm hoping that the more units who have access to it the more chance of something coming back.'

Before leaving the previous evening I'd told the team about my conversation with Joe Deakin at the NCA. I'd asked them to pull together what information they could on Anton Drach, the gangster who was providing Russian oligarchs with whores and drugs.

One of the detectives with the kidnap unit had assumed responsibility for pulling it together. He was a sharp young officer named Derek Fallon and he made use of a laptop linked to a TV screen to show us what Drach looked like.

The man was tall and heavy-set, with short dark hair and a pockmarked face.

The NCA had provided several surveillance photographs of him. He'd never been charged with an offence so we didn't have a proper mugshot.

'He lives alone in a flat in Chelsea and has an office in Vauxhall,' Fallon said. 'He runs an escort agency that on the face of it is legit, and a security company that provides muscle for clubs and pubs across the capital. The NCA believe they're covers for the drugs and illicit prostitution.

'He's been questioned and put under surveillance a number of times, but so far he's managed to keep a clean sheet.'

Fallon went on to say that Drach was the son of a notorious Russian mobster who lived and worked in Moscow. He'd moved to London four years ago and it was believed he'd been sent by his father to set up mob operations here.

Fallon pointed to one of the photographs and said: 'That was taken outside the Tequila Club a month ago. He's been a regular visitor apparently and is on first name terms with the part-owner Leon Serova and the manager Mike Dennis. However, there's no suggestion that he was there on the night Helen Troy was kidnapped – unless, of course, he was one of the men wearing a balaclava.'

The information on Drach gave me an excuse to talk to him and to have another chat with Serova and Dennis.

'We need to work up this line of inquiry,' I said. 'I'd like to know if Drach has ever met Helen Troy. Maybe Serova introduced them. And let's find out more about the blokes who work for him. I should imagine he's got guys on the payroll who would be more than capable of kidnapping someone.'

This led to another discussion about the motive for the abduction and whether or not we believed Helen was dead. It was dispiriting to know that we were still in the dark about that.

I was dishing out assignments when DCS Lattimer entered the room and signalled for me to follow him into my tiny office. He looked anxious, so I asked Anna to finish what I'd started and joined him.

After closing the door behind us, he said: 'Have you heard about the fatal accident that happened on the M4 motorway last night west of Slough?'

I frowned because it seemed an odd question to ask.

'I saw something on the news about a woman being hit by a lorry,' I said. 'Why?'

'Well the victim has just been identified.'

I felt a twist of alarm. 'Don't tell me it's Helen—'

He interrupted before I finished saying her name. 'No, not Helen. But if it had been it would have been less of a shock.'

'What do you mean?'

He shook his head. 'Believe it or not the woman killed was none other than Jennifer Booth, the actress.'

It took a moment for this to sink in, and when it did I felt my voice drop low in my chest.

'But she's supposed to be dead,' I said.

Lattimer nodded. 'Exactly. However, I just took a call from a DCI Copeland of Thames Valley Police based at Maidenhead. He's investigating the death and he rang to say he's on his way here with information he wants to share with us as a matter of urgency.'

'What information?'

'Well he reckons there might be a link between Jennifer Booth's death and Helen Troy's kidnapping.'

Chapter 4

While I waited for DCI Copeland to arrive I went to my computer and typed Jennifer Booth's name into Google.

I was already familiar with the actress and what was supposed to have happened to her two months before. Her sudden 'death' had made front page news around the world because she had shot to fame following her performance in two successful movies.

There were countless stories online about how it was believed she had drowned after going for a night-time swim while holidaying at her villa in Southern Spain. Her belongings were found on the beach in front of the property, but her body hadn't turned up despite an extensive search. The Spanish police had concluded that winds and currents had carried it out to sea.

The 28-year-old actress, who was single, was by herself at the detached villa learning lines for her next film role. Neighbours said they'd seen her earlier that day sunbathing on the beach and beside her pool. And they confirmed that she'd often swum in the sea, sometimes at night.

Even so, her disappearance had been regarded as a mystery. But of course that was nothing compared with the fact that she had mysteriously reappeared on a motorway in Southern England.

It begged a number of questions. Where the hell had she been all this time? Had she faked her own death? Why did she step out in front of a lorry on the M4 two months after she vanished in Spain?

And then there was the question that really made my scalp prickle. What possible link could there be between Jennifer Booth and Helen Troy?

*

All credit to DCI John Copeland. The man wasted no time winging his way across London to deliver his news in person.

I'd never met him before, but as soon as he walked into Lattimer's office I could tell he was a no-nonsense, old-school copper.

He was in his early 50s, of average height and build, with grey hair and a neatly trimmed beard to match.

After Lattimer and I introduced ourselves, he got straight down to business.

'I know this might seem a tad melodramatic,' he said, 'but I felt you needed to know what I'd got as quickly as possible.'

'We appreciate it,' Lattimer said, waving the detective into the chair next to me. 'I have to admit you've aroused our curiosity, and it was quite a shock to learn about Jennifer Booth.'

'It was for me too,' he said. 'It was actually an assistant at the mortuary who recognised her. Luckily her face wasn't too badly damaged in the accident, unlike the rest of her.'

'Was it an accident?' I asked. 'They're saying on the news that she stepped out in front of a lorry.'

'According to the driver she was trying to flag him down, but he couldn't stop in time. He applied his brakes, but he was doing about 60mph when he struck her. She suffered multiple injuries and died instantly.'

'Was she carrying ID?' I said.

'No. She was wearing a T-shirt and jeans and there was nothing at all in her pockets. I got involved as soon as we got the call from the mortuary.'

'Are you sure it's Jennifer?'

'No question. Her parents, who live in Manchester, are on their way down to make a formal identification. But she has two distinctive tattoos which confirmed it for us. One is her name which is written on her left ankle. The other is a small bird on her right shoulder. They're an exact match with photographs of tattoos that she posted on her Facebook page a year ago. Her father also told us that Jennifer has a three-inch scar on her left shin from a childhood accident. And so does the dead girl.'

'How did her father react when you spoke to him?' Lattimer asked.

'As you would expect, it came as a massive shock. He assumed, as did everyone else, that she died while swimming in Spain a couple of months ago. But as you must know yourselves, her body hasn't been found.'

'So why did she suddenly turn up on the M4?' I said.

Copeland reached into his pocket and took out a computer memory stick. He held it up and said: 'On here is footage from a CCTV camera showing that minutes before she died she was in a car that crashed into a lamppost on a road close to the motorway. And it also shows her running away from the scene with two men chasing her.'

I felt my pulse quicken. 'So it's possible she was being held against her will?'

'Absolutely.'

'Jesus.'

Lattimer leaned forward across his desk and sucked on his bottom lip in concentration.

'So is that why you think there's a link with the Helen Troy case?' he said.

Copeland shook his head. 'That's just part of it. I'm saving the best bit until last. But I suggest you view the footage first and then I'll tell you why I came rushing over here.'

Chapter 5

DCI Copeland handed the memory stick to Lattimer, who inserted it into his desktop computer and turned the screen so that we could all see it.

'There's a camera on the road that runs parallel to the motorway,' Copeland said, taking control of the mouse to open up the file. 'Last night a motorist rang the emergency services to say that a car had collided with a lamppost outside his village. A patrol responded but by the time they got there the car was gone. The camera was then checked this morning as a matter of routine and that's when we realised the incident was related to what had happened on the nearby motorway minutes later.'

As soon as the video sequence was running it was obvious why Copeland had been called in. It was grainy footage, but I watched, mesmerised, as a silver Mercedes appeared in the distance and drove towards the camera.

Suddenly it started to veer from one side of the road to the other, before its nearside wing rammed into the post.

The impact forced open the rear passenger door and as soon as the vehicle was stationary a woman in a T-shirt leapt out. She slammed the door shut behind her, then looked around as though confused, before darting off into the woods.

Two men then got out of the car, one from the front and the other from the back. They were both big guys in dark clothes, and when Copeland froze the image we saw their faces. But their features were blurred even when Lattimer zoomed in on them.

'The picture's not too good I'm afraid,' Copeland said. 'I've asked our tech guys to work on it, but we might struggle to ID them from this.'

'They look to be in their 30s or 40s,' I said.

Copeland nodded. 'I think you're right.'

He then pressed play again, and we watched the two men run out of shot as they chased the girl into the woods. Shortly after that another car – an SUV – came from the other direction, slowed, then stopped next to the Merc. The male driver got out, looked around, then climbed back in and drove off.

'He's the guy who rang 999,' Copeland said. 'He said there'd been an accident, and he wasn't sure if anyone had been hurt. But he didn't have time to hang around.'

The detective then pressed fast-forward until the two men reappeared. They quickly assessed the damage to the side of the Merc before getting back in and driving away. I noticed that they didn't look towards the traffic camera, which suggested to me that they'd been too busy to notice it.

'We have to assume they chased her through the woods to the motorway,' Copeland said. 'It's a distance of about 100 yards from the road.'

Copeland then opened up another video clip on the memory stick.

'This sequence is from a motorway gantry camera,' he said. 'You can just see Jennifer in the distance before the lorry hits her.'

The quality was much better but the distance far greater. The section of motorway was unlit, and Jennifer appeared only briefly as a tiny figure caught in the lorry's headlamps before she was struck down.

Copeland rewound the tape and paused it, then enhanced the picture so we could see that she'd taken several steps onto the inside lane and was waving her arms in the air.

'The lorry would have found it hard to miss her,' he said. 'As you can see if the driver had swerved into the middle lane he would have hit another vehicle.'

Lattimer leaned back in his chair and shook his head, his eyebrows knitting together in an anxious bundle.

'The poor girl,' he said.

What had been caught on camera was a real tragedy. The scene sucked the breath out of my lungs, and I had to blink my eyes a few times to rehydrate them.

'Now for the reason I'm here,' Copeland said. 'It has to do with the Merc. When we put the registration number into the system it was red-flagged. Turns out the same vehicle is on the list you guys circulated overnight.'

'What list?' Lattimer said, and I realised he didn't know because he hadn't been at the briefing earlier.

I explained that we'd pulled together a list of vehicle registrations spotted on traffic cameras near Helen Troy's house when it was wrecked, and those seen close to where the white van was dumped.

'Well, you've got a match,' Copeland said. 'The Merc was one of those caught on video near the derelict site in Bermondsey. It could be an amazing coincidence, but somehow I doubt it.'

Chapter 6

DVLA records showed that the Mercedes belonged to a Russian national named Ivan Kulik, with an address in Notting Hill.

The revelation caused my stomach to clench, and I felt the adrenaline fizz through my veins.

This was our first real lead, and I dismissed the notion that it might be a coincidence, partly because the owner was yet another Russian.

As far as I was concerned the Mercedes provided us with a bizarre link between Helen Troy and Jennifer Booth.

That was how I presented it when I went back into the ops room and called the team together. There were looks of disbelief on their faces when I gave them the news about Jennifer.

'I know it's hard to take in,' I said. 'She'll be formally identified by her family later today, but we've no doubt they'll confirm what we already know.'

I showed them the two video clips that DCI Copeland had brought over, and as I watched them again I found them just as unsettling.

'The man who was driving the Merc was probably Ivan Kulik,' I said. 'All we know about him is that he's not on the criminal records database, but that doesn't mean he hasn't got form back in Russia.'

While I was talking, Doug Ellroy was sifting through the CCTV footage from around the site in Bermondsey where the kidnappers' van was abandoned. When he found it he switched it through to the TV from his computer.

The Mercedes was seen for several seconds as it passed under a traffic camera two streets away from the derelict site. Doug paused the video and magnified the image. We could only just discern the vague outlines of two people sitting in the front seats.

But it was the same car all right, and Doug explained that it was captured on camera just minutes after the gang's van was set on fire.

'So there's a good chance that's the car they switched to,' I said. 'Helen would probably have been in the back with the third bloke or in the boot.'

My brain pulsed as I tried to grasp the significance of this latest development. The investigation had suddenly taken an unexpected turn. It now involved two female celebrity victims. One had been kidnapped and might have been murdered. The other had in effect come back from the dead, only to die again for real while running away from two men who might have been holding her against her will for two months.

It added more questions to the pile of those that still hadn't been answered. Had Jennifer also been abducted? If so, then did it happen in Spain and did the kidnappers make it look as though she'd drowned in the sea? Was she brought back to the UK soon after she disappeared? Was she taken by the same three men who kidnapped Helen? What would have happened to Jennifer if she hadn't managed to run away from the car after it hit the lamppost?

'Hopefully Ivan Kulik will provide some or all of the answers,' I said. 'I intend to pay him a visit asap with a tactical support team. At the same time I want us to find out everything about the guy. Where does he work? Who are his friends? Has he ever been linked to either Jennifer or Helen? And is he connected in any way to the Russians we've already spoken to?'

Lattimer pointed out that the media would soon be all over the Jennifer Booth story, and there was no knowing when they'd become aware that there was a link with our case.

'There's a press conference scheduled for this afternoon,' he said. 'It would be great to announce then that we've made an arrest.'

Chapter 7

We had a legitimate reason to mount a full-blown raid on Ivan Kulik's house in Notting Hill, so Lattimer was able to fast-track a warrant.

And since at least one of Helen's kidnappers had a gun, most of the team were armed.

We couldn't afford to waste time putting the place under surveillance or making sure there was someone at home. A sudden, surprise assault was called for rather than the softly, softly approach.

Before setting out we recced the street and the house via Google Earth. It was a terraced, two-storey property with parking along both sides of the road. Its rear garden backed onto an alleyway which ran the length of the street.

The tactical support team arrived mob-handed, their vans screeching to a halt in front of the house, blocking the street. I was behind in a pool car with Anna.

Officers in helmets and body armour piled out and went straight up to Kulik's front door. A battering ram was used to force it open and in they went, shouting at the tops of their voices.

Anna and I held back, and while we waited for the all-clear I looked up and down the street at the parked cars. There were no silver-coloured Mercedes, which was why I wasn't surprised to learn that the house was empty.

But it hadn't been cleared out. It was full of Ivan Kulik's belongings, and the woman next door told us that he lived alone and she'd seen him leave the house earlier in the morning.

'I was coming in as he was going out,' she said. 'His car was involved in an accident last night, and he was going to get it repaired.'

The middle-aged woman, whose name was Rita, described Kulik as a quiet foreigner who kept to himself and had the occasional male visitor.

'He told me he's from Russia,' she said. 'And that he works for a security firm. He usually doesn't come home until well after midnight.'

Kulik was renting the house apparently, and during the search we came across the tenancy agreement.

The interior was sparsely furnished, with empty walls and wooden floors. There was little in the way of personal possessions. We found his passport, which gave his age as 38. In the photo his face was blunt and square, and he had a neck like a tree trunk.

On the kitchen worktop was a laptop, which was password-protected, so I told the officers to seize it.

'You need to see this, guv,' Anna called from upstairs.

In the main bedroom the officers had pulled a suitcase from under the bed. Inside were two revolvers, a steel knuckle-duster, and a large army knife.

'I think it's safe to say that Mr Kulik is not an upstanding member of the community,' I said to Anna. She was already on the phone calling forensics and excitedly briefing the team back at base on what we'd found.

I felt she sounded too up-beat. After all, our timing had been off and we'd missed Kulik. I thought about delaying a forensic sweep of the house and clearing the street of vehicles so that we could lie in wait for him to return. But I decided that was too risky. Most of the neighbours were aware of what was happening and for all I knew one of them had already alerted him, which meant he wouldn't be coming back.

It was possible that he and his accomplices weren't aware that they had been captured on a street camera. On the footage from the previous night they certainly hadn't looked directly at it or pointed to it. So Kulik wouldn't necessarily know why the raid had taken place. But he would know we'd find the weapons and that being in possession of them would mean a lengthy prison sentence.

One of the uniforms drew my attention to a notepad that was lying open on the coffee table in the living room. Scrawled in black ink was an address:

'JJ Cosson

Auto Body Repairs

Canford Road, Notting Hill'

There was also a phone number and web address, and I guessed it was where Kulik had taken his car to be repaired. Anna looked up the company on her phone.

'It's just five minutes from here, guv,' she said.

I felt a frisson of excitement. 'Then let's get moving. Maybe he's is still there.'

Anna and I set off in the unmarked pool car, followed by armed officers in an incident response vehicle.

Chapter 8

The garage was only three streets away and it was easy to find. It was sandwiched between a small tyre outlet and an electrical wholesalers. The 'JJ Cosson' name was writ large above the entrance.

I drove straight onto the premises and the response vehicle followed.

Anna spotted Kulik's Mercedes before I did and pointed to it. It was parked outside the workshop next to a battered Mondeo. The offside wing and front door were badly dented and the side windows were missing.

Two men in dark overalls suddenly appeared, one from out of the workshop, the other from a small office next to it. They were both clearly startled by the sight of armed officers.

'No need to be alarmed,' I said to them as I whipped out my warrant card and held it up. 'Just stay calm.'

One of the men was in his 50s, the other half that age. It was the older guy who spoke.

'I'm John Cosson, the proprietor. What's going on?'

I stepped up to the Mercedes and tapped on the roof with my fist.

'We're looking for the owner of this vehicle. I understand it was brought here a while ago to be repaired.'

He nodded. 'That's right. A Mr Kulik. He's agreed to pay over the odds to get it fixed in a hurry.'

'Is he still here?'

He shook his head. 'He left about an hour ago. He waited around while we arranged for a loan car to be delivered. He's coming back tomorrow to pick the Merc up.'

'I'll need details of the car you loaned him, and I don't want you to touch the Merc.'

'What's this about?'

I ignored the question. 'Did he leave a phone number?'

'Of course. It's in the office with the paperwork.'

'Then I need you to give it to me.'

I followed him into the windowless office and he ruffled some papers on his desk until he found what he was looking for. He handed me a sheet of paper containing Kulik's mobile number, credit card details and information on the car he'd been loaned, a red Peugeot 307.'

'Did Kulik by chance tell you where he was going?'

'No, but he did ask me where he could get a cooked breakfast around here. I told him the best place is Joe's café. It's at the end of this street.'

'And you think that's where he went?'

He shrugged. 'Who knows? But he did say he was starving so I wouldn't be surprised.'

*

We left two officers at the garage and set off for Joe's café. It was only about 300 yards away, and as we were approaching it a car pulled away from the kerb out front.

'That's it,' Anna shrieked. 'A red Peugeot. And it's the same number plate as the one we've been given.'

Instinctively, I put my foot down with the aim of overtaking it, but a car was coming in the opposite direction, and I had to hit the brakes and swerve to avoid it.

The blast of a horn gave the game away. I saw Kulik's head snap towards the rear-view mirror. He must have spotted the response vehicle and realised we were onto him. Suddenly the Peugeot shot forward.

It was the last thing I wanted – a high-speed pursuit of a suspect through a built-up area. There was nothing more dangerous.

I felt an electric charge run over my skin as I pressed down on the accelerator.

'Call for back-up,' I yelled at Anna, and behind us the response vehicle's siren started wailing.

The Peugeot bolted down the street at breakneck speed and I tried to keep up. But it wasn't easy. I'm not a great driver at the best of times and going too fast, even on a motorway, makes me nervous.

The Peugeot reached a T-junction and screeched to the right without stopping. The gap between us widened because I slowed to take the corner. And I was glad I did because we came within inches of colliding with a bus.

Horns blared and vehicles swerved as the chase continued along a busy shopping street. Pedestrians scattered when the Peugeot mounted the pavement in order to pass a motorcyclist who'd stopped in the road before turning left.

By the time I reached the spot the motorcyclist had moved, so I hurtled forward.

Beside me Anna was shouting our latest position into the radio. In the distance I could hear other units already closing in, sirens screaming.

Ahead, the Peugeot sped through a red light, causing some vehicles to shunt together, while others veered wildly to avoid the chaos.

My stomach convulsed as I narrowly missed crashing into a van that blazed across the junction.

Beyond the junction the road was less busy, and this encouraged Kulik to drive faster. The Peugeot overtook two cars and struck the kerb of a traffic island. Then its nearside wing hit a pedal cycle, sending its helmeted rider flying onto the pavement.

I managed to keep pace, but in doing so I realised I was putting lives in danger. The pavements were full of pedestrians and if I lost control God only knew how much damage I'd wreak.

I could feel the sweat beading on my forehead and the breath was stuck in my lungs.

'Why not let the response vehicle take the lead, guv?' Anna shouted above the roar of the engine.

'I will the first chance I get,' I said, knowing it made sense.

But in the event there was no need because seconds later the Peugeot blistered through another red light and came unstuck when a Lexus clipped its rear end.

The Peugeot went into a wild spin and jumped the pavement before smashing head-on into a low wall.

I slammed on the brakes and we skidded to a halt about 15 yards back from the Peugeot. The response vehicle came to a stop behind us.

Anna and I got straight out of the car. I was relieved to see that no pedestrians had been hit. That was thanks to the wall which had stopped the Peugeot from ploughing into a busy precinct.

But the damage to the Peugeot was not extensive. The bonnet and front bumper had been crushed and the windscreen had shattered. But most of the bodywork remained intact.

There was a good chance that Kulik was not seriously injured. I could see the back of his head through the rear window, and he wasn't moving. Did that mean he was unconscious or maybe trapped behind the wheel?

I was anxious to find out so I threw caution to the wind and started walking towards the Peugeot. I was aware of Anna to my left and an armed officer to my right.

Other officers were shouting for people to stand back as a small crowd started to gather on the precinct.

We got to within about ten yards of the Peugeot when the driver's door was suddenly thrown open and Kulik stumbled out. I recognised him straight away – the hard face and thick neck.

He was wearing a brown leather jacket and jeans, and I didn't realise he was clutching a revolver until he raised his arm and aimed it in our direction.

I froze on the spot as a shot rang out. I expected to be blown off my feet, but the bullet went wide.

In the same instant a volley of shots came from the officer next to me and Kulik was cut down before he could fire a second time.

Relief surged through me as I rushed forward and squatted beside the Russian. He'd been hit three times, twice in the chest and once in the throat, and he was unquestionably dead.

I took a deep breath and swallowed my disappointment. I'd lost my only lead. I was gutted, but then at least I was alive.

I shook my head and stood up. Then I looked back and saw something that caused my heart to explode.

Anna was lying on the road in a pool of her own blood.

Chapter 9

Kulik's indiscriminate shot hadn't gone wide, after all. The bullet had struck Anna's right shoulder. She was unconscious and bleeding profusely.

One of the uniformed officers was kneeling beside her, trying to stem the flow.

'She's alive and I think she'll be all right,' he said to me. 'The bullet's gone straight through. We just need to get her to hospital.'

The driver of the response vehicle had already summoned an ambulance. I just hoped it would get here quickly enough.

I crouched down and held Anna's hand, and as I did so I felt the panic rush through my veins. This wasn't supposed to have happened. I should have stayed in the car and left it to the armed officers to approach the Peugeot. Anna had followed my lead and had paid a terrible price.

I felt the throb of tears behind my eyes and prayed that we wouldn't lose her.

I wasn't as confident as the officer appeared to be. I had seen people die from gunshot wounds even though the bullets had missed vital organs and arteries. Blood loss, shock, any number of other factors could reduce the chances of survival.

A moment of anger flared up in me and I wanted to go and kick the shit out of the Russian's lifeless body. I was glad he was dead even though I'd been hoping he would lead us to Helen Troy. Now we were back to square one and a valuable member of the team was seriously wounded.

I wasn't shocked or even surprised at what Kulik had done. I'd seen it happen more times than I cared to remember – desperate men resorting to extreme measures to avoid being taken.

Given the circumstances I doubted that Kulik had thought it through. He'd have reacted instinctively and probably hadn't realised that the officers pursuing him were armed.

Anna's eyelids fluttered open suddenly, and her eyes seemed to be floating around in their sockets. It was a good sign, and I couldn't help but smile.

'Hang in there, Anna,' I said. 'The ambulance is on its way. You're going to be okay.'

I squeezed her hand and she tried to speak, but nothing came out and phlegm bubbled at the edges of her mouth.

Then she grimaced as the pain registered. Her jaw went tight, and the tendons in her neck stood out. I reached forward and brushed a tendril of hair from her wet forehead.

She managed to turn her head towards me and tried again to speak.

'Wha ...happ ...?'

'You were shot, Anna,' I said. 'But it's a shoulder wound. You'll be fine. Honest.'

She blinked away the tears of shock and mumbled, 'Did ... we ... ge ... him?'

I experienced a blast of emotion and an overwhelming sense of admiration for the young detective.

'We got him, sweetheart,' I said, ignoring protocol by using a term of endearment I usually reserved for wives and girlfriends. 'The bastard's dead. But you're going to live and will be back on your feet in no time.'

*

Anna remained conscious until the ambulance arrived. I went with her to the University College Hospital on the Euston Road where she was delivered straight into the capable hands of a trauma team.

I got a coffee from the machine and sloped off to the small waiting room. I felt physically weak, drained of energy. My stomach was churning with dread and my brain had slipped into numb. I knew I was going to feel this way until I was certain that Anna would be all right. Despite reassurances from the paramedics I still feared the worst.

I stood at the window to make some calls. Outside, dark swollen clouds had built in the sky, and the streets looked grey and miserable.

As I held the phone to my ear, I realised that my hand was shaking. What had happened back in Notting Hill had jolted me to the core. It was something I would need to take account of during the rest of the day. It would likely impair my judgement and dull my senses.

The first call I made was to Lattimer, who had been trying to reach me and had left several messages. He had already been put in the picture and I gave him an update on Anna's condition.

'I've already contacted her boyfriend,' he said. 'Her parents live in Margate so I've arranged for the locals to go and see them.'

I felt bad because I didn't know much about Anna's private life. I was sure she had filled me in at some point, but I'd forgotten.

Lattimer went on to say that the team were dealing with the aftermath of what had happened and the media were all over it. The shooting of a police officer was big news.

'SOCOs are at Kulik's house as we speak and Doug Ellroy is overseeing the scene in Notting Hill,' he said. 'I'm sure we'll get a result from this even though Kulik's dead. My gut tells me he'll have left a trail of evidence. Hopefully there'll be something to link him to Helen Troy. That's why he panicked. He must have known his only option was to shoot his way out or face the prospect of years in jail.'

I told Lattimer I would call him back as soon as Anna was out of surgery. I then rang Doug so I could brief him and find out how things were going in Notting Hill.

'We're waiting for the meat wagon to take Kulik's body away,' he said. 'And I've got a team of officers getting eyewitness statements.'

'Have you checked his pockets yet?'

'Just about to. If I find anything I'll ring you straight back.'

I finished the coffee and sat on an overstuffed sofa. It felt like my heart was trying to punch through my ribs. I let my head hang forward and closed my eyes.

I was still sitting like that half an hour later when a doctor came to see me. He was young and black, with skin so dark it shone.

He told me Anna was doing fine. The surgery was successful and the wound had been patched up.

'Luckily she didn't lose as much blood as we feared,' he said. 'And the damage caused by the bullet was to tissue and bone. No vital organs.'

It was good news, and there was more to come a few minutes later when Doug called me back.

Before I could tell him about Anna, he said: 'I just checked Kulik's mobile phone, guv. You won't believe what I've found.'

'Well, don't keep me in bloody suspense.'

'There's a text message that proves he was one of the men who carried out the kidnapping. And what's more we now know the name of the person who tipped them off from inside the club.'

Chapter 10

I saw Anna briefly before I left the hospital. Her face was pale and blotchy, and there were great dark crescents under her eyes.

She was still sleeping off the anaesthetic, and I would have waited for her to wake up if her boyfriend hadn't arrived. His name was Josh, and he had a round, kindly face that was grey with shock.

I told him what had happened and then arranged for family liaison support to come to the hospital. As I was exiting the building two uniformed officers, sent by the Met, arrived to stand guard outside Anna's room.

It was a necessary precaution even though I didn't believe that Anna would be a target for anyone Kulik had been working with. But I did believe his death would cause them to panic, given what Doug had told me on the phone.

I was still trying to settle the revelation in my mind. The contents of the Russian's mobile had propelled the investigation forward. We now knew for sure that Kulik was not only one of the three men who abducted Helen Troy – he had also chased Jennifer Booth to her tragic death on the M4 motorway.

I strongly suspected that he and others had snatched her in Spain and made it look like she'd drowned in a swimming accident.

But I still had no idea why the two celebs were taken, or why there hadn't followed huge ransom demands. I would know by the end of the day, however – if I could persuade Mike Dennis, the manager of the Tequila Club, to spill his guts.

*

Mike Dennis was implicated by virtue of an exchange of text messages between Ivan Kulik's mobile phone and one that wasn't registered.

Doug showed them to me as soon as he arrived back at Caxton Street shortly after I did.

The exchange took place a few minutes before Helen was abducted at the club by the three men in balaclavas.

Kulik: '*You there Mike?*'
Mike: '*Yes.*'

Kulik: '*We r in the alley. Has she arrived?*'
Mike: '*Yes. I've unlocked back door and taken key.*'
Kulik: '*Let us know when she goes to toilet.*'
Mike: '*Dnt worry. I knw wot am supposed to do.*'
A few minutes later Mike sent a text to Kulik.
Mike: '*She's gone through door. Check mens room. Guy in there.*'
Kulik then sent a final message a few minutes later.
Kulik: '*We have her. Well done.*'

'It's Mike Dennis for sure,' Doug said. 'I checked the list of all the other guests and staff members. No one else named Mike was in the club on Saturday night.'

'Are we bringing him in?'

'Units are on their way to his home and to the club. We should hear back any minute.'

So now we knew how the men in the van had been made aware that Helen Troy had gone to use the VIP toilets. They were tipped off by Mike Dennis.

'He must have used an anonymous phone,' Doug said.

I nodded. 'I wonder if anyone else knew what was going on. Dennis is the manager but he didn't invite Helen Troy to the club. Leon Serova did. And Serova is part-owner, which effectively makes him Dennis's boss.'

'That doesn't mean Serova was involved,' Doug said.

'I realise that. But there's definitely something dodgy about the bloke. The NCA believes he launders money and has links to the Russian mafia. Plus, he chose not to tell us he was seeing Helen.'

'Shall we bring him in as well?'

'Later. Let's wait and see what Dennis has got to say for himself first.'

I went to Lattimer's office to brief him on what we had. He'd been about to call me with information he'd received.

'I just got confirmation that Ivan Kulik was employed as a security officer – meaning a bouncer or minder – by a company called Capital Protection. It's run by none other than Anton Drach.'

Drach. The Russian villain Joe Deakin had told me about. The man who was allegedly running a drugs and prostitution racket whose clients were oligarchs living in London.

'We need to talk to him,' Lattimer said.

'I'll get right onto it.'

There was something else he had to tell me that caused my gut to twist in a knot.

'A preliminary post-mortem report on Jennifer Booth has come through,' he said. 'The conclusion is that she died from massive injuries suffered when she was hit by the lorry. But the pathologist says her body was covered in a range of older wounds. Cuts and bruises that must have been inflicted during the past couple of months. He believes she was subjected to systematic abuse and torture after she went missing in Spain.'

Chapter 11

'Systematic abuse and torture.'

The words were hard to take in and made my mouth go dry. The disgust I felt was compounded when I opened up the PM photos on my computer.

The pathologist had circulated shots of the wounds inflicted on Jennifer Booth before she was killed by the lorry. They had also been sent to DCI Copeland who was still officially in charge of the investigation into her death.

There were close-up images of severe bruises and swollen areas on her thighs, buttocks and lower back. And there were scabs on her neck and shoulders.

The pathologist noted that there may have been other wounds that were obscured by the more severe injuries she'd suffered. These included a crushed chest and arms, and lacerations across her stomach and face.

'The earlier wounds, some of which have almost healed, were inflicted by various means,' the pathologist wrote. 'The bruises and swellings on her buttocks and back appear to be marks left by a whip.'

A sour taste leaked into my mouth as I tried to imagine the terrible ordeal that Jennifer Booth had been subjected to. The poor girl had been whipped and beaten, and as I read more of the report I learned that as well as being malnourished she'd been drugged. Toxicology tests had revealed the presence of a variety of sedatives, including one that was administered shortly before she died.

Anger balled like a fist inside me. This was surely the stuff of nightmares, and I promised myself that I would find out who was responsible.

It was obvious now why Jennifer had fled from her captors as soon as she got the chance. I wondered where they were taking her in the Mercedes when it crashed into the lamppost. And what else they were planning to do to her.

I also wanted to know why she'd been targeted. And why the same men had seized Helen Troy.

Was it because they were both celebrities? Or were they kidnapped for an altogether different reason?

Chapter 12

Mike Dennis was brought into the interview room at 4 pm having been picked up at his club after returning from lunch at a West End restaurant.

He was wearing a smart, charcoal grey suit. His red tie was crisp and neat and symmetrical, and he reeked of aftershave.

I was struck again by the resemblance to Rod Stewart, a look I was pretty sure he cultivated.

'Thank you for coming in, Mr Dennis,' I said.

His eyes shifted between Doug and me. We were sitting facing him across a table.

'It's not as though I was given a choice,' he said. 'What's this all about, Inspector Quinn?'

'Please sit down and I'll tell you.'

He remained standing and fixed me with a brimstone stare.

'Do I need a lawyer?'

'That's up to you, Mr Dennis. I just need to ask you some questions relating to Saturday night. If you decide you want a brief at any point then by all means call one.'

He looked at his watch and sucked in his cheeks. Then he pulled out the chair and sat opposite us.

I didn't get the impression he was overly worried. He appeared calm and quite relaxed, but I knew that wouldn't last once I got started.

'My first question is this, Mr Dennis. Are you aware that there was a shooting in Notting Hill earlier today? A man was killed and a police officer was wounded.'

'I heard a report on the radio. But what's it got to do with me for fuck's sake? I've not been to Notting Hill and I've got witnesses to prove it.'

'Oh, I'm not suggesting you were there, but I'm afraid a friend of yours was. He was the man who was shot dead – after he shot and wounded a police officer.'

His face fisted into a frown.

'Who was he and what makes you think he was a friend of mine?'

There was an envelope on the table in front of me. I picked it up and took out Kulik's passport. Slid it across the table towards him.

'His name was Ivan Kulik,' I said. 'He was Russian and he drove a Mercedes.'

He tried not to react but it was a poor effort. A vein pulsed in his temple, and he couldn't stop himself from swallowing.

'I'm sorry to be the bearer of bad news, Mr Dennis. Were you close?'

He pursed his lips and raised his eyebrows until they almost met in the middle.

'The name doesn't ring a bell, Inspector. He certainly wasn't a friend and I'm sure I've never met him.'

As lies go it was a pretty convincing one. He'd recovered well from the initial shock and was going all out to regain his composure.

'Why don't you pick up the passport and take a look at his picture?' I said. 'It might jog your memory.'

He spread his lips into a thin line and shrugged. Then he reached for the passport, opened it and stared at Kulik's mug for several seconds.

'No, I've never met this man before. I'd know if I had. Now perhaps you can tell me why you're so convinced that I have.'

I reached into the envelope again, took out a sheet of A4 paper and placed it on the table.

'The words on this piece of paper prove that you're lying to me, Mr Dennis. And they also prove that you were involved in the abduction of Helen Troy.'

His body tensed, and his eyes grew wide as saucers.

'That's fucking preposterous,' he said, his voice trembling over the words. 'Are you really serious?'

I shoved the sheet towards him. 'Read it yourself. Then we can get down to the serious business of finding out what's going on.'

He picked up the sheet and read through the transcript of the text messages that passed between him and Kulik.

'You've got this wrong,' he said, dropping the sheet back on the table. 'That's not me. It's another Mike. You can check my phone.'

He reached into his pocket, took out his mobile and handed it to me. I took it from him and put it on the table.

'You used another phone,' I said. 'And for your information there was no one else in your club on Saturday night named Mike.'

'That doesn't prove a thing. Anyone could have sent those texts.'

'Well, maybe the messages in themselves won't be enough to bring charges against you,' I said. 'But they give us grounds to search your house and delve into every aspect of your life. I'm sure that once we start stirring things up some dirt will rise to the surface.'

'This is bollocks,' he seethed through clenched teeth. 'No way would I have got involved with kidnapping someone, especially from my own club. I'm a respectable businessman, not a fucking criminal.'

'Then why do you associate with gangsters?' I said. 'I hear you're also on first name terms with Anton Drach, the Russian racketeer who was Ivan Kulik's boss up until a few hours ago.'

His face drained of colour. 'Drach comes to the club. I don't associate with him. He's just a paying guest.'

'Oh, he's more than that. I've heard it on good authority that he also supplies drugs and whores to a bunch of wealthy Russians, including your employer Leon Serova.'

He wiped his mouth with the sleeve of his expensive suit, and when he next spoke his voice was pitched high.

'I don't know what the bloody hell you're talking about. This is outrageous. I played no part in Helen Troy's abduction, and I did not know that man Kulik.'

'That's not true is it? You tipped him off about Helen after you unlocked the back door to the club. Then you pretended that someone had taken the key.'

He shook his head. 'That's nonsense.'

'Was Leon Serova also involved?' I said. 'Is that why he invited Helen along to the party? So that you and your accomplices could grab her?'

He poked a finger into his shirt collar, which suddenly appeared too tight for him.

'It's time I consulted my lawyer,' he said. 'I don't have to sit here and take this.'

I nodded. 'I think that's probably a good idea since I've got a lot more questions to ask you. For instance, I'd like you to tell me what you know about the actress Jennifer Booth. It seems she also fell into the clutches of your mate Kulik.'

His eyes popped out on stalks and he seemed genuinely perplexed.

'I don't understand,' he said. 'She died months ago. It was all over the news.'

'Well, we should all know by now not to believe everything we read in the papers and watch on the television,' I said. 'You see last night she suddenly turned up again. And she managed to run away from Kulik who had obviously been holding her against her will. It's what led us to him. And it's how we discovered that you helped him to kidnap Helen Troy.'

That was when Mike Dennis refused to answer any more questions and insisted on calling his lawyer. I was happy to oblige. I told him that while we waited for the brief to turn up I'd be obtaining warrants to search his home and his club.

'By the time we get together again in this room I've no doubt we'll have enough incriminating evidence to charge you.' I said, leaning towards him across the table. 'And once that happens your accomplices will start to worry that you're going to drop them in it. So my advice is to come clean and tell me everything, including what's happened to Helen, and I promise to keep you out of harm's way. I might even be persuaded to put in a good word at your trial.'

Chapter 13

Mike Dennis was allowed to make one phone call, before his phone was taken away from him. I waited until he'd finished so that he could give me the name of his brief and tell me when he'd be turning up.

'It'll be at least an hour,' he said. 'They're sending one of their top guys. He'll sort this out.'

It suited me. The longer the better in fact. I wanted him to sweat a little. I also wanted to give the teams time to find some more evidence against him. He'd been right about the text messages. Unless we found the unregistered phone with his prints on it then we couldn't prove they were sent by him.

I told him he could wait in the interview room and arranged for tea and biscuits to be sent in. I then called reception downstairs and gave them the lawyer's name.

Back in the ops room the team were waiting anxiously for me to update them. Before I began I called the hospital to check on Anna. She was progressing well, they said, and a cheer went up when I passed the news on.

I then explained why Mike Dennis was in the frame and gave them the gist of the interview.

'The bloke's as guilty as sin but we need more than just the text messages,' I said. 'So let's dig up what we can. We have to throw something else at him.'

Lattimer said he was chasing up a warrant to search Dennis's house and club. He also confirmed that forensics were wading through everything collected at Kulik's flat.

'I've just heard back from DCI Copeland,' he said. 'He told me the parents of Jennifer Booth have formerly identified the woman killed on the M4 as their daughter. And it won't come as a surprise to anyone that the story is already out there. The Beeb have started running it, and the press office is being inundated with calls from the papers.'

'Are they tying it in with our case yet?' someone said.

Lattimer nodded. 'Questions are being asked apparently. That's why I'm planning to confirm there's a link at the delayed press conference. I also intend to make a statement about what happened in Notting Hill.'

I could feel the growing sense of anticipation and determination among the troops. This was due in part to the fact that we were now making headway. But mostly it was a reaction to what had happened to Anna. She was one of our own, and it was a miracle we hadn't lost her.

Ivan Kulik had shot her, but he was just one of the people responsible. There were others, including Mike Dennis, and nobody was going to rest until they were all behind bars.

'I want Anton Drach and Leon Serova brought in for questioning,' I said.

I pointed to Serova's photo on the whiteboard to my left.

'Let's consider the facts. Serova is part-owner of the Tequila Club. He decided to hold a private function to celebrate his birthday. He invited Helen Troy along because he's been having an affair with her. Then on the night his manager, Mike Dennis, made it possible for three men, including Kulik, to enter the club and kidnap her. I find it hard to believe that Serova didn't know what was going on.

'Let's also see if we can establish a link between him and Jennifer Booth. Maybe he dated her as well. And how close is he to Drach and the Russian mafia? Is he more than just a customer? Is he actually part of Drach's prostitution and drugs racket?'

The detectives took it in turns then to say what leads they were following and what progress they were making.

Known associates of Kulik and Dennis were being traced, and the NCA had sent over a file on Anton Drach, plus a detailed report on how the Russian mafia had become one of the biggest criminal organisations operating in the UK. It cited an MI5 analysis which stated that in recent years London had turned into a playground for Russian mobsters.

It came as no surprise to be reminded of the power they wielded and the extent of their activities. In addition to drugs and prostitution, they were into human trafficking, illegal firearms, internet porn, extortion, gambling and cyber-crime.

I'd come across more than a few in my time. They were usually beefier, rougher, coarser than your average villain, and were notorious for covering their bodies with elaborate tattoos.

Anton Drach was one of three Russian faces who controlled things in the capital. But he was the only one who had apparently built up a relationship with the capital's oligarchs – which was why he was firmly in the frame.

One aspect of our case that still baffled me was the damage done to Helen Troy's house the night she was snatched. And the latest development made it even more intriguing.

'I did as you asked, guv, and ran some checks on Helen's cleaner Clara Pike and her husband,' said a young detective named Boyd. 'And something unexpected showed up in their joint bank account. Three days ago the husband made a cash deposit of £8000, which is a lot for a guy who's on benefits and a woman who doesn't earn much more than that over the course of a year.'

'Did you ask them about it?'

'I did. The husband said they'd been saving it in a tin under the bed for years and had decided it was time to put it into the bank. But I'm not sure I believed him. And the wife seemed desperately nervous. He made sure she didn't contribute to the conversation.'

I recalled how domineering he'd been when I spoke to them at their flat. And how he had answered most of the questions on her behalf.

'I'll talk to her myself away from the husband,' I said. 'I assume we haven't taken her to Helen's house to see if anything is missing.'

'Not yet, guv. I was planning to do that tomorrow.'

'Well, arrange it so that I can be there. And make sure she goes alone.'

When I ended the briefing, Lattimer said he wanted me at the press conference. It was due to take place in half an hour. I grabbed a coffee from the machine and went to my office to write up some notes and check my emails.

A call came through on my mobile from Alexander Orlov. He wanted me to know that dozens of people had responded to his £1million reward offer for Helen's safe return.

'Some of them are claiming they know where she is,' he said. 'They insist she isn't dead. I've got their names and contact details. What do you want me to do with them, Inspector?'

I told him that most were probably time-wasters, but that we would nevertheless have to check them out. I said I'd arrange for an officer to go to his house to pick them up.'

'I've been following the news,' he said. 'They're saying the man shot in Notting Hill may have been one of the kidnappers and that another suspect is under arrest. Is it true?'

'There'll be a press conference shortly,' I said. 'We'll be making a statement then.'

'But surely you can tell me if you're any closer to finding out what's happened to Helen.'

'I believe we are, Mr Orlov. In fact while you're on perhaps I can ask you a couple of questions.'

'Of course. I'll be happy to answer them if I can.'

'Then tell me – have you heard of a man named Ivan Kulik?'

A pause, then: 'I can't say I have. But he's obviously Russian.'

'He is. He worked for Anton Drach, who I assume you do know.'

'Ah yes. Mr Drach. The man of dubious character who has his finger in many pies.'

'So have you ever done business with him?'

'Occasionally, yes. He runs an escort agency here in London and he's provided women for parties and events I've held. It's always been strictly above board, of course. The women were employed as hostesses. They talked and interacted with guests. What they did beyond that and in their own time was their business.'

It was his way of saying that he did not engage them as prostitutes who'd be willing to have sex with his friends and business acquaintances. But of course that was nonsense.

'Has Drach also supplied you with drugs, Mr Orlov?'

He sounded offended. 'Of course not, Inspector. I'm really not into that and I will never knowingly break the law. But I have heard rumours that he supplies certain types of drugs to a number of other wealthy and influential people in London – including members of parliament and high-ranking officers within the Metropolitan Police.'

'I don't suppose you're prepared to give me names,' I said, knowing what the answer would be.

'You suppose correctly, Inspector. I don't want to blacken the reputations of individuals given that I can't guarantee that my sources are totally reliable.'

I would have spent more time picking Orlov's brain, but one of the detectives poked his head around the door to tell me that Dennis's lawyer had turned up. I didn't want the brief talking to his client until I'd had a word with him.

So I thanked Orlov for calling and hung up, then hurried along to the interview room.

The suited lawyer, briefcase in hand, was waiting outside in the corridor with a uniformed officer. He was tall, well over 6ft, and somewhere in his 40s, with blond hair slicked into a quiff and dark-tinted spectacles. He plucked a card from his top pocket, holding the tip of one corner between his finger and thumb, and handed it to me.

'My name is Leonid Esmond,' he said in a thick Russian accent. 'I'm here to represent my client, Mr Dennis.'

The card identified him as a lawyer with LJP Solicitors and Advocates of Knightsbridge.

'Would you care to tell me why he has been apprehended and if you intend to charge him with a criminal offence?' he said.

I handed him a copy of the text exchange between Dennis and Kulik.

'We have evidence linking your client with the kidnapping of Helen Troy,' I said. 'And we believe he may also have been involved in the disappearance of the actress Jennifer Booth.'

Edmond listened as I explained that we were searching Dennis's home and office. When I was finished he gave a thin smile, briefly exposing a gold canine tooth that seemed at odds with the rest of him.

'I would like to speak to my client now and I insist we have total privacy,' he said.

'That goes without saying, Mr Edmond. I'll be back in under an hour. That should give you more than enough time to hear what he's got to say for himself.'

Chapter 14

The press conference turned out to be another raucous affair. This time there was a lot more for the media to get its teeth into.

Lattimer read out a pre-prepared statement in which he confirmed we were linking Helen Troy's kidnapping with Jennifer Booth's disappearance. He also confirmed that it was indeed Jennifer who had been killed on the M4 when she stepped in front of a lorry.

This prompted an avalanche of questions about what had happened to her in Spain and where she'd been for the past two months. The boss didn't reveal the injuries that had shown up during the post-mortem. But he did describe how she had fled from Ivan Kulik and his accomplice after their Mercedes had crashed into the lamppost.

I then gave a detailed account of what had happened in Notting Hill, and lavished praise on detective Anna Crick for the part she had played in trying to arrest him.

'She was wounded when the suspect fired at officers as he tried to run away,' I said. 'I'm pleased to say that she's in a stable condition in hospital. The suspect was killed when armed officers returned fire.'

Lattimer then made it known that as far as we were aware there was no obvious connection between Helen and Jennifer apart from the fact that they were both A-list celebrities.

'We don't believe they ever met,' he said, 'either in a professional or a personal capacity. Helen was – or rather is – a singer. Jennifer was an actress. They've been represented by separate management teams and agents.'

What Lattimer neglected to mention was that they had both visited the Tequila Club and this was pointed out by a reporter from The Guardian.

'That's true,' Lattimer responded after an awkward pause. 'However, we've not been able to determine from our inquiries if they were ever there at the same time.'

'But surely it's significant anyway,' the reporter added. 'As is the fact that Helen Troy was in a relationship with the club's owner, Leon Serova.'

I was obliged to say that we couldn't comment on claims of an affair between Helen and Serova.

But for this lot that was as good as confirming it. It gave them a fresh, juicy angle on what was already a multi-faceted story, a story that was like manna from heaven for rolling news stations around the world.

And even as the press conference was playing out there came another dramatic development.

I was informed about it via a text message on my mobile phone which I'd placed in front of me on the table.

As a read it I felt my stomach clench into a hard ball.

'Mike Dennis is dead, guv. He's been murdered.'

Chapter 15

I showed Lattimer the text and hurried out of the press conference just as the entire building was locked down.

Alarms screeched and corridors suddenly filled up with uniforms as I made my way back upstairs.

By the time I reached the third floor I'd convinced myself that it must be a mistake. It couldn't possibly be true. Surely to God.

But it was, and when the evidence was right there in front of me I thought I might be sick.

I couldn't believe it. Mike Dennis had been murdered in one of our own interview rooms.

It was obvious he had been killed by his lawyer – or rather someone masquerading as a lawyer.

Dennis was slumped in the same chair he'd been sitting in when I'd interviewed him earlier. His head was thrown back and there was a bright red ligature mark a few centimetres wide around his neck. I'd seen marks like it before on people who had been strangled to death.

A police doctor arrived at the same time as I did, and after a brief examination he confirmed what was already pretty obvious.

'From the look of the ligature mark I'd say the murder weapon was a length of nylon cord or rope,' he said. 'There's a deep groove so whoever did it is strong. I'd say this man lost consciousness very quickly and was dead in perhaps 15-20 seconds.'

I thought about the guy I'd met and didn't doubt that he was strong enough to squeeze the life out of another man. He would have caught Dennis by surprise, perhaps lulled him into a false sense of security before walking around the table to grab him from behind. He would have had to stifle his screams and somehow stop him from kicking the table over. But for a professional hitman it wouldn't have been that hard to crush the victim's windpipe and carotid arteries in the front of the neck.

And the man who had carried out this cold, calculating assassination was most definitely a pro, who had presumably been sent to stop Dennis from revealing what he knew.

It was a shocking thing to have happened inside a police building, and it was going to cause a shit storm. Procedures would have to be re-examined and there'd be an urgent internal inquiry, which would be extremely embarrassing for the Met.

But before that there was the profound impact it was going to have on the investigation. We'd lost another suspect, and it was the second major set-back in a matter of hours.

The scene outside the interview room was chaotic. People were shouting and dashing around in a state of confusion. But despite that it quickly became evident that the killer had left the building long before the alarm was raised.

The white-faced officer who had been standing outside the interview room had been the one who discovered Dennis dead when he opened the door to check on him.

'The lawyer was only in there for about ten minutes,' he told me. 'Then he came out and said he had to go and make an urgent call. He insisted his client should not be disturbed. But when he hadn't returned after about 20 minutes I decided to go in.'

'Was the man searched before he went in there?'

'Of course,' he said. 'His briefcase was checked downstairs and it also went through the scanner. But a length of rope or nylon could have been concealed easily on his person and we wouldn't have detected it.'

It was a fair point, I supposed, but that wasn't going to stop the wave of criticism that would be coming our way. What had happened was a disaster and it made us look foolish. Made me look foolish.

I took out the card the lawyer had given me. I remembered how he had held it so delicately between his forefinger and thumb, and I wondered now if that was to avoid leaving a print.

I re-read the words on it. Leonid Edmond – LJP Solicitors and Advocates of Knightsbridge.

I whipped out my mobile and tapped in the office number. I wasn't at all surprised when it failed to connect. I then went online and did a search for the company. It didn't exist.

The man calling himself Leonid Edmond was a killer and not a lawyer. We had allowed him to enter the inner sanctum of a police building so that he could commit a brutal murder.

Should we have carried out a thorough check of his lawyer's credentials? With hindsight, of course we should have. But the man had been expected. Dennis himself had told us he was coming. And he'd passed through a security check, albeit one that was designed to detect guns, knives and explosives.

There had therefore been no reason to believe he wasn't who he said he was when he turned up to speak to his client.

Chapter 16

Lattimer was fuming, even after I explained to him what had happened. But he held back from attributing blame because he knew it wasn't really the fault of any individual. This was a failure of the system and it was bound to trigger a tightening-up of vetting and security procedures at police stations across the country.

'The media rabble are still downstairs,' he said. 'They know something serious has happened and I've now got to go and tell them that our prime suspect has been murdered while in police custody.'

The DCS's face looked grey and waxy and I was glad he didn't want me to go with him into the bear pit. It was not going to be a pleasant experience.

Instead I was told to help find out who had murdered Mike Dennis and who had ordered the hit. There was no question in our minds that the killer was a paid assassin who was probably heading out of the country.

And there were only a handful of criminal organisations with the clout to arrange such a ruthlessly efficient assassination in such a short space of time. The Russian mafia was one of them. And since the man who killed Mike Dennis was a Russian that was who my money was on.

I immediately thought about Anton Drach, who we were apparently still trying to track down. I wondered if he was the one who Dennis had contacted when he pretended to call his lawyer.

I retrieved his phone from the officer who had been holding it and checked the last call on it. It was to a mobile number that was switched off when I rang it. A quick check told us it was an unregistered number and there was no way we could trace who had it unless it was switched on and we managed to triangulate the signal.

Shit.

While this was going on my team had been pulling together the security footage from cameras inside the building and CCTV cameras out on the street.

I sat down with a bunch of anxious detectives and watched the man who called himself Leonid Edmond enter the building and present himself at reception.

I suspected that the tinted glasses he was wearing were to help disguise his face. It was also obvious that he was deliberately avoiding looking at the cameras.

When he left the building he was caught on a CCTV camera walking to the end of Caxton Street and flagging down a black cab. We got the registration number but I knew it wasn't going to help much. The Russian would almost certainly have got the driver to drop him in the busiest part of town so he could disappear into the crowds.

I turned away from the screen and rubbed my face, trying to erase the stress. But it was no use. It felt like my mind and body were in meltdown.

I'd never known a day like it. Our valued colleague Anna Crick was in hospital, and our two leading suspects had been killed – one shot, the other strangled.

The investigation had been derailed and we still didn't have a clue as to what had happened to Helen Troy.

I couldn't imagine that things could get much worse. In fact right there and then I was willing to put money on it.

But in view of what we would soon discover I was glad I didn't.

Chapter 17

Leon Serova appeared to have no qualms about coming in to be questioned again. He didn't even bother to bring a solicitor with him.

He was no doubt curious to find out what was going on. Three hours had passed since Mike Dennis had been murdered and the story was already dominating the airwaves.

The news channels were understandably making a big thing of it and were even airing his name. They were repeatedly showing the clip of Lattimer explaining to the media that Dennis had been strangled while the earlier press conference was taking place several floors below.

It made for uncomfortable viewing, and the reaction from outside was one of astonishment. One MP was demanding an inquiry, and Mike Dennis's girlfriend was quoted as saying she was heartbroken.

Serova, however, didn't act like a friend who was grieving. He was clearly more angry than upset.

I'd decided to interview him in one of the empty offices because of all the commotion around the interview rooms.

When he sat down opposite Doug and me, he said: 'I find it incredible that not only was Mike killed in your custody, but that you actually believe he had something to do with Helen's abduction.'

'He did, Mr Serova,' I said. 'There's no doubt about it. We believe it's why he was murdered. Someone was desperate to make sure he didn't break under questioning and disclose what he knew.'

'Then perhaps you can tell me what evidence you have. After all, Mike was my employee at the club. And I'm assuming you've got me here because you think I might also have been involved.'

'I need to ask you some more questions, Mr Serova,' I said. 'And I would have been happy to talk to you with a solicitor present.'

He shrugged. 'I didn't see the point. I've got nothing to hide. So why don't you just get on with it?'

I began by asking him if he had known Ivan Kulik. His answer was an emphatic no. I then told him about the exchange of text messages between Kulik and the man we were convinced was Mike Dennis.

Unfortunately we hadn't come up with any further evidence. No unregistered mobile phones had been found at his home and club, and there was nothing else to link him to Kulik.

But Serova appeared to accept that the text messages were incriminating enough, given that there were no other people named Mike in the club on Saturday night.

He affected a surprised look which might or might not have been genuine.

'I had absolutely no idea, Inspector. I'm shocked and disappointed. I had always thought of Mike as an honest and trustworthy person. This is totally unbelievable.'

'Did you not notice him behaving suspiciously at the party?'

He shook his head. 'There was a lot going on. I didn't pay him much attention after the guests started to arrive.'

I asked him then how well he knew Anton Drach. He surprised me by smiling.

'I wondered when my connection to Drach would crop up,' he said. 'I've known the man for some time, as have most other leading figures within London's Russian community. He's been a frequent visitor to the club. On occasion I've acquired the services of one of his female escorts when I've needed a companion. I know he has other business interests but I don't get involved in those.'

'Would you describe him as a friend?'

'Hardly. He's just another face on the scene. Because of his reputation I've made a point of not getting too cosy with him.'

'But that didn't stop you getting cosy with his wife did it?'

He exhaled loudly. 'Is that another nugget of gossip from Mr Orlov, Inspector?'

'No. It came from the NCA. There's a photograph in their possession of you and Mrs Drach together at a restaurant in Moscow.'

He cleared his throat, gave another shrug. 'Well, as I said to you before, what I get up to in my personal life is my business. It has no bearing on what's been happening here in London.'

'But from what I hear about Drach you're taking an almighty risk. The man is after all a leading light in the Russian mafia.'

'He doesn't scare me, Inspector. And whatever might have happened in the past it's over now and has been for a long time.'

'So she was just another notch on your stick.' This from Doug.

Serova blew air out between pursed lips. 'I really have no answer to that,' he said.

'Then instead, why don't you tell us what you know about Jennifer Booth, the actress. Did you have a fling with her too?'

Serova gave Doug a cold stare. 'Of course not. I never met the Booth girl and I was never in the club when she visited. If, indeed, she ever did visit.'

'So you've no idea where she's been since she went missing in Spain two months ago?'

'That's right. Just like I've no idea who kidnapped Helen and why. Or whether or not the poor girl is dead or alive.'

Chapter 18

I'd learned nothing new or significant from the interview with Leon Serova and that left me feeling utterly deflated.

He'd had an answer for everything and had come across as calm and self-assured. I wasn't even sure what I had expected him to say, but whatever it was he hadn't said it.

I discussed it briefly with Doug and neither of us was convinced that Serova had told us the truth. But how we would ever be able to prove it was another matter. The man was rich and powerful and supremely confident. It would be hard, if not impossible, to find out his secrets.

We had a final briefing in the ops room and by the end of it I felt shattered. The events of the day had taken their toll and I realised it was time I went home.

On the way I took a detour to the University College Hospital to see Anna. It was a relief that she was sitting up in bed and able to talk to me. Her boyfriend took the opportunity to go and get something to eat.

Anna's face was lined with emotion and fatigue. She was still on a drip and her shoulder was heavily bandaged. But she looked a hundred times better than she had done earlier.

She insisted on being updated on the events of the day so I filled her in. But she dropped off to sleep before I'd finished, so I left quietly and told the boyfriend I'd be back tomorrow.

When I got home I threw a ready meal in the microwave and poured myself a glass of red wine.

I was dog tired, but I knew I would have trouble sleeping and I didn't want to fall into the same trap I'd fallen into the night before. As tempting as it was to try to win back my money, I was determined to resist.

So instead, I ate my supper in front of the television and flipping through the news channels proved to be enough of a distraction. It was like re-living my entire day.

There were video clips of the Tequila Club and Helen Troy's house. Footage of the spot on the M4 where Jennifer Booth had met her untimely death, and exterior shots of our building in Caxton Street.

There was even a dramatic sequence from someone's mobile phone of the immediate aftermath of the shooting in Notting Hill.

A host of familiar faces appeared on every channel. Helen Troy, Jennifer Booth, Mike Dennis, Anna Crick, Leon Serova.

And of course there were the sound bites from me and Lattimer, and from a range of people who wanted to comment on the investigation and to offer their condolences to the families of Helen and Jennifer.

I stopped watching only briefly, and that was when I went to refill my glass. Soon after that I must have fallen asleep on the sofa because when I woke up the next morning the TV was still on and my glass was still full.

Chapter 19

It was a call from the office that woke me just after six. One of the detectives who had worked the graveyard shift had arranged for me to meet up with Clara Pike, Helen's cleaner.

'A car is picking her up at eight,' he said. 'You wanted us to make sure that she was alone so we're bringing the husband in to question him again about the money paid into their account. This time under caution.'

I thanked him and he told me there had been no overnight developments. Then I hauled myself to my feet. I felt stiff all over and there was a dull pain in my lower back from where I'd been positioned awkwardly on the sofa. But at least I'd slept for a good five hours, which I hadn't expected to.

On the TV a Sky News reporter was doing a piece-to-camera outside our Caxton HQ while telling viewers what had happened inside the day before to Mike Dennis.

He linked to security footage of the killer and said that police were appealing for information on him.

I left it on as I shuffled into the bedroom and shed my clothes before stepping in the shower.

Over coffee and toast – always my breakfast of choice – I made a list of the issues to discuss at the briefing later in the morning.

I wanted to know why we still hadn't managed to run down Anton Drach. Had he done a runner? Was he back in Russia? Or was there an innocent explanation for why we hadn't been able to talk to him.

I also wanted a detailed evaluation of what had been found at the homes of Ivan Kulik and Mike Dennis. Surely there had to be something more linking them to Helen and Jennifer.

I was anxious to keep the momentum going despite the horrendous setbacks.

Helen's face kept pushing itself into my thoughts, reminding me that it was conceivable she was still alive. If so, then she might not be for long if we didn't find her.

I was fearful that the people behind this murderous business were now desperate to cover their tracks. That was why they had given the order to eliminate Mike Dennis. He was a liability because we had evidence connecting him to Kulik and the kidnapping.

I wouldn't have been surprised if those pulling all the strings had begun to panic after Jennifer Booth managed to escape from her captors.

They would not have been expecting that, or the fact that the incident would establish a link between her and Helen.

Not that we were any the wiser about what was really going on. The questions were continuing to stack up – along with the bodies.

I was dead certain of one thing, though. We were trying to get to the bottom of something that had the backing of people who were rich, powerful and incredibly cruel.

Chapter 20

The streets of London were soaked from a storm that had raged during the night. Dark clouds still hung in a sullen mass above the city, but the rain had tapered to a fine drizzle.

As I drove out to Chiswick I called the hospital again to check on Anna's condition. She'd had a comfortable night and was still sleeping. I asked the nurse to tell her I'd phoned.

I got to Helen Troy's house just a few minutes past eight. The squad car with Clara Pike in the back was already outside.

I parked the BMW at the kerb behind it and climbed out. A uniformed officer opened the door for Clara and she stepped onto the pavement as I approached the squad car. I conjured up a smile and thanked her for coming.

'It shouldn't take long, Mrs Pike,' I said. 'I just need you to look around and tell me if anything is missing.'

'I'll do my best,' she said.

She was wearing a dark anorak over her thin frame and her sallow skin was flushed. She also looked very nervous and seemed reluctant to make eye contact with me.

I waved her towards the front door which was standing open. When she reached it she stopped and looked up at me.

'Can you tell me what's happening to Russell?' she said. 'Why is he being questioned again?'

'I assumed it had been explained to you,' I said. 'We need to find out more about the large sum of money that was paid into your joint account last week.'

'But he's already told one of the other detectives who came to see us. It was money we'd saved.'

'Well, we just need to clarify a few points. It is after all a significant amount.'

'What's that got to do with anything? Do you think we stole it?'

I grinned. 'Of course not.'

'Then what—'

'Look, why don't we step inside out of the rain,' I interrupted. 'We can talk as we look around.'

The house was still a crime scene and a few SOCOs were milling around in their overalls. Just inside the door we were asked to put on paper shoe covers.

'We have to be careful not to contaminate potential evidence,' I said.

The house was in less of a mess than when I'd last seen it. But the cat's blood was still on the walls, and Clara gasped aloud when she saw it.

I steered her through the living room into the kitchen, then into the downstairs study.

'I'm pretty sure that nothing is missing,' she said, her voice tight and strained.

She then asked me if there was any news on Helen.

'I'm afraid she's still missing,' I told her. 'But hopefully she is alive somewhere.'

'Do you think she was taken by whoever did this?'

'That's what we're trying to find out. It's why we need to know if anything has been stolen.'

After checking all the rooms upstairs, including the blood-stained bedroom, she said she was certain that nothing had been.

'Can I please go now, Inspector. I really don't like being here.'

When we were back downstairs in the hall I asked her how long it had taken her and her husband to save the £8000 they had supposedly been keeping under their bed.

For a moment I thought she was going to ignore the question as she continued walking towards the front door. But when she realised I'd stopped she turned to look at me.

'About three or four years,' she said.

'So why decide to put it in the bank now?'

'I'm not sure. It was Russell's decision. He takes care of the money.'

She moved her eyes away from me and chewed on her bottom lip.

'Have you ever met a man named Ivan Kulik, Mrs Pike?' I asked.

She frowned. 'I don't think so. The name is not familiar.'

'What about Mike Dennis?'

'I've never met him but I know he was the man who was killed yesterday in the police station. I saw it on the news last night.'

'Do you know if your husband has had any dealings with either of them?'

She shook her head. 'I'm sure he hasn't. He doesn't get out much. But you can ask him yourself.'

'We will. We'll also be asking him if what you've both told us about the money is true. You see, it seems too much of a coincidence that £8000 in cash should suddenly appear a few days before Helen Troy was abducted and her house trashed.'

She looked at me again and held my gaze. I could see what could only have been fear in her eyes.

'I don't know what you mean,' she said. 'We haven't got anything to do with what's happened to Helen. She's always been good to me. I'm as shocked by all of this as much as anyone else.'

'But you can see why we're a bit suspicious can't you?' I said. 'I mean, £8000 is a lot of cash. And you can't be earning much more than that as a cleaner and your husband is on the dole.'

She was confused and flustered now and I could see she was missing the domineering presence of her husband.

'I know what you're doing,' she snapped. 'You're trying to make me admit to something that I haven't done. Well, you're wasting your time. So if you don't mind, I would like to go home now.'

'Please, Mrs Pike,' I said. 'If what you've told us about the money isn't strictly true then now is the time to put it right, before you get into serious trouble.'

'But we've done nothing wrong.'

I held up my hands, palms out. 'Look, you have to understand that you and your husband are suspects in our investigation. You yourself are one of only very few people who had a key to this house. You also knew how to disable the alarm system.'

'That doesn't mean I came here and did this.'

'Then who did?'

'I don't know. I swear.'

Tears welled up in her eyes then and she let out a strangled sob.

I felt a flash of sympathy for her and wondered for a second if perhaps my instincts were wrong. Was she telling the truth about the money? Was she and her husband completely innocent of any wrongdoing?

Just then my mobile rang. I took it out of my pocket and saw it was Doug Ellroy calling me. I answered it because I suddenly had an idea.

'Just bear with me for a moment,' I said to Clara. 'Then I'll arrange for you to be taken back home.'

I turned away from her as Doug said he was calling to find out what time I intended to hold the morning briefing for the team. He also wanted to let me know that Lattimer had assigned a dozen more detectives to the case.

I told him I'd be in within the hour and asked him to start pulling together the reports for the meeting.

After hanging up I turned back to Clara and said: 'That was a member of my team. He told me that your husband has made a statement in which he admitted to us where the money really came from and said that you both took the decision to withhold the information from the police.'

I knew that I was taking a huge gamble and that most people would have seen through the lie. But this woman was in a state of high anxiety, and in the absence of her husband she was clearly weak and vulnerable.

I also sensed that she was consumed by guilt and had been since the early hours of yesterday when I broke the news to her about Helen.

I watched as her face crumbled and the tears spilled from her eyes.

'Oh my God, I'm so sorry,' she sobbed. 'I told Russell we shouldn't do it. That it was wrong. But he wouldn't listen. He said we needed the money.'

Her voice was laced with misery, and as she spoke I stepped forward and put a hand on her shoulder.

'Let's go and sit in my car so that we can talk,' I said, pleased that my gamble had paid off. 'I think it's time you got this off your chest.'

Chapter 21

An hour later I arrived back at Caxton Street with Clara Pike in tow. She wanted to see her husband but I told her it wasn't possible.

Instead I arranged for one of the detectives to get a formal statement from her. I told him what she had confessed to and then went to the ops room to brief Lattimer and the troops.

'At least we've solved the mystery of why Helen Troy's house was trashed,' I said. 'And we know for certain now that it had nothing to do with her kidnapping. It was just a coincidence after all.'

Clara had told me in floods of tears that she and her husband were approached about a week ago by Paul Rhodes, Helen's ex-boyfriend. He told them he had a grudge to settle with Helen and he was willing to pay them handsomely if they would help him gain access to her home so that he could teach her a lesson by causing some damage.

He wanted Clara's spare key in order to make a copy, and he wanted her to give him the code for the alarm.

'My instinct was to tell him to piss off,' she said. 'I was even going to inform Miss Troy of what he was planning. But my husband was all for going along with it, which didn't really surprise me. I suspect Mr Rhodes did some checking and discovered what kind of man Russell is.'

Rhodes had initially offered £4000, but Russell Pike had said they would do it if he doubled the money, which he did. They then gave him the key, which he had copied, along with the alarm code.

'We didn't know he would kill Miss Troy's cat,' Clara said. 'Or that he would do so much damage. After you came to the flat my husband told me we had to keep quiet or we'd be in trouble.'

Russell Pike was still being questioned downstairs so I said I would go and give him an account of what his wife had told us.

'Meanwhile, I want Paul Rhodes arrested and brought here for questioning.'

*

Russell Pike flew into a rage when I confronted him with what his wife had said.

He swore at me and accused me of lying. Then he demanded he speak to Clara and said he would get her to retract her statement.

But after 45 minutes of questioning he finally accepted that we had him bang to rights. He told me they'd made a stupid mistake and asked to see the duty solicitor.

I formally charged him with aiding and abetting a burglary and withholding information from the police. And I warned him that further charges were likely to follow.

*

The first question I put to Paul Rhodes when he was brought into the interview room was whether he had ever met Clara and Russell Pike.

I think he knew straight away that the game was up, but he still insisted that he had never heard of the couple.

'That's funny,' I said. 'Because they've told me you gave them £8000 so they would help you break in to Helen Troy's house.'

'They're lying,' he said. 'I told you before that I don't even know where she lives.'

'But you made it your business to find out,' I said. 'Then you carried out some checks and discovered that Helen's cleaner and her husband were the sort of people who might be open to a bribe.'

He shook his head. 'Come on, Inspector. Why would I risk doing something like that? I've got too much to lose.'

'You wanted to vent your anger because she was seeing someone else and refused to get back with you. It's clear from the tone of the text messages you sent to her that you were in a right old state over it. You told me yourself that you were furious. It made you blind to the risk you were taking.'

'That's ridiculous. You can't possibly prove it.'

'We can and we will, Mr Rhodes,' I said. 'We've got signed confessions from the Pikes, and I'm willing to bet that your bank account will show a recent cash withdrawal of £8000.'

He broke down then and started to cry like a baby. I had no sympathy for him. In fact the anger inside me suddenly felt like an inflated balloon.

Paul Rhodes had caused us to waste a considerable amount of time with his lies. Time that would have been better spent trying to find out who had abducted his ex-girlfriend.

I spent the next half hour listening to his story. How he became consumed by a desire to get revenge on Helen when he learned that she was seeing Leon Serova. He found that out because he'd been stalking her.

So he then made it his business to find out where she lived and while watching the house several weeks ago had seen Clara Pike arrive to do the cleaning. He struck up a conversation with her as she left, asked for one of her contact details, and then set about finding out what he could about her.

'I Googled the name and discovered she'd been done for benefit fraud and that her husband was an ex-con,' he said. 'So I reckoned they would jump at the chance to earn some extra cash. And I was right. The husband especially didn't take much persuading.'

He said he chose to break in on Saturday night after learning that Helen was going to the Tequila Club to help celebrate Leon Serova's birthday.

'I drove up late afternoon from Redhill and parked a few streets away from the house,' he said. 'I wore a hood because I knew there were CCTV cameras around. Then I hung about round the corner from the house until her driver picked her up. That's when I went in. I didn't intend to do that much damage, but I got completely carried away.'

Chapter 22

I left it to Doug to charge Rhodes because I couldn't bear to look at him any longer. He was a pathetic scumbag who deserved everything he was going to get. And that would hopefully include a custodial sentence.

When I shared the news of his confession with the rest of the team their reaction was muted. There was no sense of jubilation since the vandalism of Helen Troy's house had turned out to be just a sidebar to the main investigation.

It was something we had suspected but hadn't been sure of. Now it was confirmed. Rhodes might well have got away with it if the Pikes hadn't put the money they'd been given into their account.

I now intended to wash my hands of the case. It would be passed over to another detective so that I could concentrate on the primary investigation.

It irked me that I'd wasted an entire morning on an incident of criminal damage committed by an ex-boyfriend in a jealous rage.

'But at least now we can cease looking for a connection that isn't there,' Lattimer said.

Unfortunately there was nothing new to report. Anton Drach, the man I now regarded as our prime suspect, still hadn't surfaced. We'd raided his home and office, having obtained warrants, but there'd been no sign of him. Forensic teams had this morning descended on both premises. We were also in the process of visiting all his known associates.

A couple of them had said they'd heard he was out of the country and had been for some time. The man who ran his escort agency – a fellow Russian who was well known to the police – said he hadn't heard from him for a couple of weeks. The guy managing Drach's security company had said the same thing.

It seemed obvious to me that they were all lying through their teeth and that Drach was keeping a low profile in the hope that things would blow over. It suggested to me that he was somehow involved in what had been going on. In fact, based on what we knew it was hard to imagine that he wasn't.

Kulik was on his books and he had links with Leon Serova, Mike Dennis and the Tequila Club. Plus, he had at his disposal the considerable resources of the Russian mafia.

I went to my office after the briefing in order to write up the interviews with the Pikes and Leon Serova. But as soon as I started DC Fallon appeared holding up a computer memory stick.

'This just came up from the lab,' he said. 'It's a copy of a file from Anton Kulik's laptop. You really need to take a look, sir.'

I plugged it into my desktop PC and opened it up. Fallon took control of the mouse and clicked on the first icon which read: 'Targets'.

Coloured photographs of six women appeared. Only two of them I recognised – Helen Troy and Jennifer Booth.

'What the bloody hell is this?' I said.

'They're all celebrities, sir. You know about Helen and Jennifer. Well of the other four two are Russian actresses, one is a French model, and the other is a reality TV star from Italy. And apart from their celebrity status they have one other thing in common. All four have disappeared. And at least one of them is believed to have been kidnapped.'

Chapter 23

Clicking on the photos opened up information on each of the women, including their names.

There were various documents containing their personal details, plus more photographs taken from their own websites and from newspapers and magazines.

'I checked the properties of each file,' Fallon said. 'They show that in all cases the files were created before the women disappeared.'

In Helen Troy's file there were dozens of facts about her spread over several pages: her home address; her phone numbers; the names of her agent and manager; a description of her car; a list of her friends and relatives. There was also a brief summary of her career.

Jennifer Booth's file featured much of the same information. In her case it included details of her villa in Spain, along with dates when she was planning to spend time there.

Looking at the photos it struck me that they were all young, attractive women.

Daniella Moreau was a French model with bee-stung lips and jet black hair. In the photo she was looking directly into the camera and smiling. I thought it was probably a publicity shot because her skin looked soft and flawless.

The file revealed her to be aged 21 and a resident of Paris. She was described as a rising star of the catwalk, and her ultimate ambition was to be an actress in movies. She was single and lived with her parents.

The Italian reality TV star was blonde and beautiful. Her name was Monica Bruni and she was 23 with an address in Milan. She had shot to fame after appearing in a Big Brother-type show.

The two Russian women were also in their 20s. Maria Markov lived in Moscow and had made a name for herself as an actress in a long-running soap. She had red hair and sharp features, and was married to a soldier.

Natalia Skova was an expat Russian who had set up home in Germany and had appeared in several movies made in that country. She had won a couple of awards and apparently spoke fluent English.

She too was a real stunner. A series of photos showed her posing in various locations, including a beach and next to a luxurious swimming pool.

'So how do you know these women have disappeared?' I asked Fallon.

'I ran a search on Google,' he said.

He stood behind me looking over my shoulder while I did the same.

First Daniella Moreau. As I scanned the various reports I remembered reading about her disappearance at the time. It was a year ago and she vanished after leaving a Paris nightclub in the early hours. Friends saw her get into a taxi and she was never seen again. Police had so far failed to trace the taxi driver and nobody had been arrested in connection with the disappearance.

Monica Bruni mysteriously disappeared from her house in Milan 15 months ago. She had gone home at the end of the day after working on her reality show. She lived alone, and when the studio driver arrived to pick her up the following morning, she didn't answer the door.

It was later discovered that she hadn't slept in her bed and had vanished without taking any of her belongings with her. However, she was known to have taken drugs, and there was speculation that she might have fallen foul of criminals, who had abducted her.

The actress Maria Markov told her husband she was going shopping one day six months ago. But she never returned to their Moscow home. A major police investigation had drawn a blank.

However, there was evidence that the Russian expat Natalia Skova was kidnapped near her home in Berlin two years ago. This was another story I vaguely remembered because it was featured in newspapers around the world.

A witness claimed that Natalia's car had been forced to stop in a side street when a van in front of her suddenly applied the brakes. Two men then jumped out of the van and dragged her from her car. She was then bundled into the van which sped away.

No one had heard from her since then, and there had been no ransom demand. In fact there hadn't been ransom demands for any of the women.

After checking out the names through Google I sat back in my chair and felt a cold stab of apprehension in my gut.

'This is bad,' I said.

Fallon stepped around the desk to face me again. 'That's why I brought it straight to you, sir. The title of the file on Kulik's computer says it all. These girls were targets. It's almost certain they were all abducted and in six different countries over a period of two years.'

He didn't need to spell it out for me. It was all there on the memory stick and across the internet. There was only one conclusion to draw from this. The women must surely have been targeted because they were celebrities and because they were attractive.

'We need to contact the police in those other countries,' I said. 'Tell them what we've found here. And we should liaise with Interpol at the same time.'

I told him to run off prints of the photos and the documents in the files.

'And spread the word that they'll be another meeting as soon as you've done that.'

Fallon hurried out of the room to get on with it. After he'd gone I sat for some minutes at my desk staring at the photos of the six women on my computer screen.

Goosebumps broke out along my limbs as I wondered what in God's name had happened to them.

I wondered, too, if Jennifer Booth would be the only one of them who would get to have a proper funeral.

Chapter 24

It was yet another extraordinary development for the team to take in and process.

There were now photographs of six women on the whiteboards. We had to assume that they were all victims of an unscrupulous group of criminals who were targeting young female celebrities. I couldn't see any other explanation for it in view of the file on Kulik's computer.

We knew for a fact that they were created before the women vanished, and not after. We also knew that at least two of them had been kidnapped, and it was a fair bet that the others had too. Only one of them, Jennifer Booth, had so far managed to escape.

She had disappeared in Spain. Did that mean the others who had vanished in Russia, Italy, German and France were also being held somewhere in the UK? Or were they still in those other countries?

Two other questions weighed heavily on my mind. Had the women been murdered? And why hadn't there been any ransom demands?

'Hundreds of women go missing across Europe every day,' I said. 'Many of them are kidnapped by human traffickers. But the difference here is that these ladies are high-profile celebrities. The evidence on Ivan Kulik's laptop suggests they were all deliberately targeted and that a lot of planning went into the abductions.

'Those responsible must be well resourced and well organised. And despite all the attention and publicity they attract, they're clearly confident they'll get away with it every time.'

I assigned four detectives to the task of talking to the authorities in the other countries.

'Share with them everything we have,' I said. 'And get as much information as you can on what they came up with and whether they had any suspects.'

Over the next few hours we got some encouraging news. Various sets of fingerprints had been found in Kulik's house and on his Mercedes. Among those on the Merc were a set belonging to a Ukrainian national named Viktor Franko, who showed up on our database. He had spent two years inside for dealing drugs and had been released 11 months ago. He was married with a five-year-old son.

Like Kulik, Franko was on the staff of Anton Drach's security firm based in Vauxhall, and was among the 30-odd employees and freelancers we were in the process of rounding up.

The fact that his prints were on the Mercedes meant he might well have been one of the two men seen on the traffic camera chasing Jennifer Booth into the woods. The other man, we assumed, was Kulik himself.

Officers were dispatched to Franko's house straight away, but we chose not to disclose the latest development to the media just yet. It wasn't as if they didn't already have enough to keep them busy.

The papers and news channels were still reporting and analysing the events of the previous day. Some commentators were stirring up criticism of the police and the Celebrity Crime Squad in particular. They were saying that someone should be held accountable for allowing a murderer to gain access to a police interview room.

My name kept cropping up because they'd discovered that I was the only detective who'd had a conversation with him. Some anti-establishment activists were even calling for me to be suspended. But I had too much on my plate to let it get to me. I knew the flak would be flying for weeks, possibly months, and that I'd eventually have to face a grilling as part of an internal inquiry.

But right now I needed to stay focused on an investigation that was hurtling forward like an express train.

And I didn't dare lose sight of the fact that my main objective was to find Helen Troy, given that there was a slim possibility she was still alive.

PART 3

Chapter 1

In the dream Helen was back at home in her own bed. She was safe and secure and felt comforted by the gentle heartbeat of her beloved cat, Biscuit.

As usual he was lying next to her on top of the duvet, his breathing the only sound in the room.

She reached out and stroked him, running her fingers through his soft fur and wondering how she would cope if at some point in the future he wasn't there.

She couldn't imagine loving Biscuit any more than she did. He was her baby, her most trusted companion. He kept her grounded at a time in her life of momentous change.

She was surrounded by people who just wanted to exploit her. She had no real friends her own age anymore. Those who resented her success had stopped calling. The others she just wasn't able to squeeze into her busy schedule.

But Biscuit was always there for her. He didn't care that she was rich and spoilt and more demanding than she used to be. He didn't criticise her choice of lovers or give her disapproving looks when she got drunk or snorted coke.

Biscuit simply loved her despite the person she had become. And in return for that she would always treat him as her most prized possession.

He would never be hungry or lonely or unsafe. She would indulge him and protect him as though he were her own flesh and blood.

In the dream she continued to stroke Biscuit but suddenly something was different. She couldn't feel the beat of his heart or hear the sound of his breathing.

Instead she heard herself crying and felt a heavy weight pressing down on her chest.

Then a cold shiver squirmed through her body and her eyes snapped open.

The dream had ended abruptly and she was plunged back into the horrific nightmare from which she had briefly escaped.

*

She was chained to a single bed in a small room with white-painted walls. Next to the bed there was a bucket into which she'd been told to shit, piss and vomit. It was half full already and gave off a diabolical smell that made her gag repeatedly.

She had no idea how long she had been here or what they were planning to do to her. But the fear of what was to come filled her mind with an almost paralysing dread.

She was lying on her back staring up at the ceiling. The dream had receded and it its place was a dark, hideous reality. She raised her arm and looked at her left wrist – just to make sure it was still attached to the metal restraining cuff. It was. Clipped to the cuff was a chain about 6ft long that was secured at the other end to the frame of the bed. It wasn't possible to remove it. She'd tried.

Her wrist was sore and swollen and she knew it wouldn't be long before the cuff cut through the skin, making it hurt even more.

She experienced an explosive pain in her arm every time she shifted her body. But she couldn't just lie still for hours on end. It was bad enough that she could only move away from the bed as far as the chain allowed. It was just long enough to enable her to reach the bucket and the small mirror that was stuck to the wall to the left of the bed.

This was where she had found herself when she had first woken up from a drug-induced sleep. The bed itself wasn't uncomfortable. The mattress was soft, and there were two pillows, an under-sheet and a duvet.

The room was lit by a single, unshaded bulb suspended from the ceiling. The man who had been bringing her food and drinks had told her it would be left on because the curtains would stay closed across the only window in the room. And they were thick, lined curtains that kept out the light, making it impossible for her to know if it was day or night.

Her watch had been taken from her, along with her jewellery and her clothes. Thankfully they had stripped her while she'd been sedated. She was now wearing a grey, two-piece track suit but no underwear. She tried not to think about what might have happened to her while she was unconscious.

She eased herself up into a sitting position and looked around. The man must have come again while she'd been sleeping. He had left a bottle of water and a bunch of bananas on the bedside table. The last time he'd brought her a cup of tea and a pre-packed ham sandwich.

But the man never said much and ignored all her questions. However, he did tell her in a strong Eastern European accent that she could scream as much as she wanted because nobody would hear her.

'You're in a house in the middle of nowhere,' he said, and those dark, almost black eyes made her flinch. 'You won't be here for long. Soon you will be taken to a place that is much more comfortable. So be patient. There's nothing you can do about your situation. You have no choice but to accept it.'

Her situation!

He'd made it sound like being kidnapped and imprisoned in a strange room was no big deal.

The memories of exactly what had happened to her were vague and fragmented. But she did clearly remember the moment she emerged from the club toilets and came face to face with the two men wearing black balaclavas.

She had tried to fight them off but they'd been too strong and aggressive. She'd been helpless as they dragged her into the alley behind the club and then into the back of a van.

And that was where she had been forced to lie face down while one of the men sat astride her. She'd felt a needle being inserted into the side of her neck and then almost at once a wave of blackness had engulfed her.

She had remained unconscious until she'd woken up in this room. And God only knew how long ago that was. It felt like she had been here for days. She hadn't washed or cleaned her teeth. Her eyes were beaten red from crying and her throat was sore from screaming and shouting.

The man had entered the room on only two occasions. The first time he had brought the bucket, a toilet roll and a lukewarm cup of coffee. The second time he'd brought the tea and sandwich.

She knew he wasn't staying in the house because before he came and after he went away again she heard a car outside. So she assumed she was alone and that very few people knew she was here.

She had wondered at first why the man hadn't beaten or raped her. There was no way she'd be able to stop him doing whatever he wanted to her.

But then it had occurred to her that since she had been kidnapped the man and his accomplices were probably waiting for a ransom to be paid.

It seemed to be the only explanation, and it meant there was still a chance that she would eventually be freed.

She had lots of money after all, and she knew there were people out there who would pay large sums of cash to secure her release.

Leon Serova was one of them. Alexander Orlov was another. Both men would be beside themselves with worry. She knew that they both thought the world of her.

Leon was her lover and she adored him. Alexander was like an attentive uncle who was helping her with her career. It was Alexander who had introduced her to Leon back when they were partners before the launch of the magazine. It was a shame they had fallen out.

Neither man had been prepared to tell her what had caused the rift, but it was obviously pretty serious because they'd spent months slagging each other off.

Alexander had tried to encourage her not to continue seeing Leon, claiming the man was a worthless adulterer who could do a lot of damage to her reputation and her career.

Leon, for his part, had told her that Alexander had only befriended her because he wanted to exploit her talents through the magazine and his publishing company.

'He's not the genial gentlemen he wants people to think he is,' Leon had said. 'He's a vindictive, power-obsessed individual who will drop you as a friend as soon as you stop earning money for him.'

However, she was confident that the pair would put their differences aside and join forces to do whatever it took to secure her freedom.

The trouble was she knew that however much they tried they might not succeed, despite the fact that they were two of the wealthiest men in the country.

She was at the mercy of men who were far more ruthless. Men who had been prepared to take a huge risk by seizing her inside a busy nightclub.

There was no guarantee they would let her go, no matter how much money they were given. Perhaps they had already decided to kill her regardless of whether a ransom was paid.

Or maybe they were planning to keep her imprisoned – either here in this pokey room or somewhere else – for weeks or months to come.

That was why dark thoughts continued to chase through her mind and a relentless panic throbbed inside her.

She had no control over what would happen next.

Chapter 2

I didn't get home until just before midnight. By then my head was bursting with facts about the other four women who were missing.

I'd spent hours surfing the net and reading reports emailed to us by police in France, Germany, Italy and Russia.

It was apparent that none of the other investigating teams had suspected the cases might be connected. Each one was treated in isolation.

The 'Targets' file on Kulik's computer therefore caused widespread alarm. Interpol reacted by agreeing to set up a unit to investigate. It would also coordinate input from the various forces.

In Russia the Ministry of Internal Affairs opened up a dialogue with the Foreign Office in London. They were in a flap not just because two of the missing women were Russian, but also because those believed to be responsible were also Russian.

They were given all the information we had on Kulik, Anton Drach and others whose names had come up. They were also given a detailed description of the man who had murdered Mike Dennis.

The official at the Foreign Office who was liaising with them told Lattimer they'd promised him their full cooperation. But of that I was sceptical. I couldn't believe they would tell us everything they knew about Anton Drach and the Russian mafia's activities across Europe.

Drach and his mob had friends in the Russian police and the Kremlin. They also had strong ties with the powerful oligarchs living in London. So it was therefore hard to see how the authorities in Moscow would want to provide information that might cause them huge embarrassment and ignite diplomatic tensions.

Unsurprisingly I struggled to go to sleep as my mind tried to grapple with too many thoughts. It didn't help that whenever I closed my eyes the events of the past couple of days flashed before me in a series of vivid and disturbing images.

When I did eventually drop off there was no respite. I had a dream in which Helen Troy was lying on a mortuary slab, her naked body battered and bruised.

But her eyes were open and she was talking to me through blood red lips – asking why I hadn't been able to save her.

Chapter 3

I arrived at Caxton Street the following morning to find that news of the latest development had already been leaked to the media.

A newspaper reporter in France got tipped off by a police contact. Questions were asked and the story spread. Inevitably it was picked up by one of the news agencies and from there it went viral.

Nobody on my team was surprised. It's hard enough to keep things under wraps within the Met. When other police forces get involved you just know that someone somewhere will let slip or call a newspaper to earn a quick buck.

'Make no mistake it will add to the pressure we're under,' I said when the morning meeting got under way. 'But I don't want it to distract us. Let the press office worry about the media. None of you should talk to the papers or the TV people. Just concentrate on the job at hand.'

But it wasn't going to be easy. I knew that. We were working under the ferocious glare of publicity.

We were being watched, judged and criticised by the press, the public and our superiors.

In such circumstances it's easy to succumb to desperation and paranoia; to rush to conclusions and to make silly mistakes.

I had seen it happen before on the big, high-profile cases, and I didn't want it to happen to us.

The scale of the investigation was now beyond anything any of us had ever worked on. That in itself was enough to cause some members of the team to doubt their own abilities, including me.

I was angry with myself because I still couldn't make sense of what was going on. Plus, under my command the investigation had lurched from one dramatic low point to the next.

Surely, I thought, it was time for the tide to turn in our favour.

*

By lunchtime a lot had happened. Paul Rhodes, along with Russell and Clara Pike, had appeared before magistrates and were remanded in custody.

And 25 more people, all associates of Ivan Kulik and Anton Drach, had been interviewed. But they all claimed not to know anything about Helen Troy and the other women, or where Drach could be found.

Meanwhile, we still hadn't found Drach's employee Viktor Franko, the Ukrainian whose prints were found on the Mercedes.

We'd been to his flat in Lambeth where he lived with his young wife Nadia and their five-year-old son.

She claimed that she hadn't seen him since this morning when he left to go to work.

She'd been taken in for further questioning while a forensic team had moved into the flat. I was praying they'd turn up something useful.

We needed some solid evidence that would tie all the strands together, and provide answers to a string of crucial questions.

I kept telling the troops that we were making headway, which was why Mike Dennis had been murdered and Drach had dropped out of sight.

But what I didn't need to tell them was that we might well have cracked the case by now if we hadn't managed to lose our two main suspects.

Chapter 4

We did get a breakthrough in the middle of the afternoon. It came from Joe Deakin at the National Crime Agency. He rang in response to the description we'd circulated of Mike Dennis's killer.

'The blond hair and the gold tooth rang a bell,' he said. 'So I've spent a bit of time searching back through our files and talking to our contacts in Russia.'

'I'm all ears, Joe,' I said.

'Well, the description matches that of a guy named Dmitri Kaplan, who first appeared on our radar three years ago. It was during an investigation into people trafficking. We'd arrested some Serbian sleazeball who became a key witness. During questioning he told us he was fearful for his life because the traffickers had employed the services of a contract killer from Russia named Kaplan. So I ran a check and sure enough Dmitri Kaplan showed up.'

'That's a bloody result. Tell me more.'

'Well until five years ago Kaplan was working as a detective for the Moscow police department. But he went on the run after he stabbed a fellow officer to death in a fight. Turns out Kaplan was corrupt and had been in league with the Russian mafia. He fled the country and has been operating in Europe ever since as a gun for hire.'

'Can this Serbian guy identify him from the CCTV stills we've put out?' I asked.

'That's why I held off ringing you until now, Sam. I got someone to take a print to the guy in Belmarsh Prison where he's currently residing. He said he was pretty sure the man in the photo and Kaplan are one and the same.'

*

I wasted no time putting Kaplan's name out there. I asked a couple of detectives to build a profile of him and to carry out an extensive search online.

One of them came back to me within the hour to say Russian police had confirmed what Deakin had told me.

They had also sent us a head-and-shoulders photograph of Dmitri Kaplan. I was handed a printed copy and immediately recognised him as the man who had posed as Dennis's lawyer.

His hair was darker in the picture and he wasn't showing his gold tooth, but there was no mistaking it was him.

They'd found no reference to him on the web, but he was known to several organised crime agencies. He was on a list of men and women who were believed to be operating in Europe as contract killers. The agencies knew why he had fled Russia. They said that while working as a detective in Moscow he'd had a reputation for being brutal as well as corrupt.

What intelligence they'd gathered on him since then had come purely from within the criminal fraternity. There'd been rumours, gossip and claims that he was responsible for a string of gang-related killings.

But he'd never been arrested and his whereabouts were not known.

*

Contract killers are two a penny in this day and age. The world is full of people who are prepared to murder for money.

People like Dmitri Kaplan. To them life is cheap, and they are oblivious to the consequences of their actions.

Kaplan was among those operating in the big league. It sounded like he was a natural born killer, the kind who enjoy their work and find regular employment with criminal gangs, mad dictators and clandestine government agencies. Some operate on exclusive retainers, while others don't care who they work for so long as they're paid well.

And by all accounts the Russian mafia are among the biggest payers. It's one of the terror tactics they employ to instil fear in rival mobs. They want it known that if you cross them you can expect a visit from a seasoned pro who will carry out the contract no matter what kind of resistance he or she comes up against.

The hit on Mike Dennis was a case in point. He'd been in one of the safest places in London – an interview room inside a police building. And yet Dmitri Kaplan had walked in and strangled him.

Just as impressive was the fact that Kaplan had been given no time to plan and prepare for the murder. No one knew Dennis was there until he made the call, purportedly to his lawyer. Whoever he called must have contacted Kaplan right away and instructed him to head over to Caxton Street and use his initiative to get close to Dennis.

That told me he was an exceptionally resourceful individual and as cool as a cucumber under pressure.

'It probably also means that he's based himself here in London,' Lattimer said when I discussed my thoughts with him in his office. 'And I'd wager that he's on Anton Drach's payroll.'

'Makes sense,' I said. 'The Russians always stick together. They only ever trust each other.'

'So what's your reading of the situation, Sam? Has this bloke been let loose as part of a damage-limitation exercise?'

'It seems likely. Killing Mike Dennis sends out a clear message to anyone tempted to talk to us about what is going on.'

'So do you reckon they're in a panic?'

I nodded. 'I think they were on a roll and Helen Troy's kidnapping was their latest success. But letting Jennifer Booth run away was a costly mistake. Because it was caught on camera things started to spiral out of control for them. The Mercedes led us to Ivan Kulik and he led us to Mike Dennis. Now we also know about the other women.'

'And we have another name as well,' Lattimer said. 'Dmitri Kaplan. How do you think he'll react when we release it at the next press conference?'

I shrugged. 'I should imagine they've been expecting it since the CCTV clips were put out there. But I doubt it will stop him being a threat. He probably has a bunch of aliases and disguises for when the going gets tough. If he is living here it's almost certainly under a different name anyway.'

'Well, at least it's a positive development to pass on to the media,' he said. 'The other stuff is reflecting badly on us and I know I'm in for a rough ride at the presser.'

'Is that why you don't want me there, guv? Not that I'm complaining.'

'You've guessed it, Sam. You'll be put on the spot over Mike Dennis's murder, and it wouldn't be fair. Besides, I'm sharing the platform with the Deputy Commissioner. He wants to harp on about how we're working closely with our partners in Europe.'

'Do you intend to reveal how we came by the information about the other women?'

'The DC thinks we should. It's partly so we can make it known that the man shot dead by the police officer was involved in the kidnappings.'

'What about the text messages between Kulik and Dennis?'

'Again, we're going to talk about them because it should help counter some of the flak that's flying around. We want the public to know that Dennis wasn't an entirely innocent victim.'

There was a knock on his office door, which was pushed open. When I turned I was surprised to see Doug Ellroy standing where with a concerned look on his face.

'Sorry to disturb you gents, but something has happened and I think you should be across it,' he said.

'Well, get to it, man,' Lattimer responded.

'There's been a shooting over the river in Southwark, sir. One of those shot has been identified by the first response team as Anton Drach.'

Chapter 5

The terraced house was in an unremarkable inner-city street just east of Waterloo station.

Doug and I arrived to find the road blocked by police vehicles and an ambulance. We had to flash our ID cards to get beyond the incident tape.

The air buzzed and crackled with radio chatter and I felt my body tense as I approached the house. I was dreading what we'd find. We'd left Caxton Street in a rush, before the details had filtered through. All we knew for sure was that four people had been shot and one of them was Anton Drach, who had been described as being in a critical condition. But that was 20 minutes ago and I was hoping desperately that he was still alive.

Before mounting the steps to the front door, we donned forensic overalls and shoe covers. And we were warned that the victims were still in the house so to brace ourselves.

As we entered the house I immediately started searching for the face of authority. But what greeted me was a scene of utter carnage. There were two bodies lying on the floor in the large, square entrance hall.

They were both fully dressed males in their 20s or 30s. One was sprawled out on his back and it looked as though half his face had been blown away. The other was slumped against the stairs with a wound to his chest that was still oozing blood. There were also scattered droplets of blood over the walls and stair carpet.

I realised in an instant that neither of the dead men was Anton Drach, which came as a relief. But the relief was short-lived. As we stepped carefully across the hall and into the living room we saw two paramedics trying to resuscitate a third man.

I couldn't see his face from where I stood but I could see the pool of blood on the floorboards all around him.

'Hello, Sam,' said a voice to my right.

I turned towards the familiar face of DI Donna Reid, a member of the Murder Investigation Team. We had worked together years ago but I hadn't seen her in a while. She had a thin face, with prematurely grey hair and a Home Counties accent.

'I was told to expect you,' she said. 'But I didn't expect you to get here this quickly.'

There was no time for small talk so I asked her if she was in charge.

'I am until the boss gets here,' she said. 'And as you can see for yourself this is a bad one.' She gestured towards the man on the floor. 'He's the only survivor. A bullet to his lower abdomen. He's in a bad way, but the paramedics think he might pull through. The other three are dead.'

I opened my mouth to speak but Reid pre-empted what I was going to say.

'I'm afraid Anton Drach didn't make it, Sam. They tried to save him but he died just after I got here.'

I didn't try to mask my disappointment.

'Fuck it. Where is he?'

'In the kitchen. He took two bullets in the chest.'

At that moment a couple more paramedics came rushing into the room with a stretcher.

DI Reid took me by the arm and steered me through a door into the kitchen.

A scene-of-crime officer was kneeling beside Drach's body. He, too, was sprawled on his back, and the white T-shirt he was wearing was drenched in blood. His pockmarked face was the one I'd become familiar with from the photos I'd seen. But he was shorter than I'd imagined him to be, and his arms were covered in intricate tattoos.

A hollow feeling opened up in my stomach as I stared down at him and I felt like being sick.

It just didn't seem possible that we had lost yet another suspect. Drach was the man I'd come to believe would be able to answer all our questions – the gang leader who had engineered the abduction of Helen Troy and the other women.

I watched as the SOCO picked up a revolver that had been lying on the floor next to Drach.

'We already know that's not the murder weapon,' DI Reid said. 'One shot has been fired and the bullet slammed into the wall over there.'

I followed her gaze and saw a hole in the tiles just to the left of the fridge.

'It looks as though Drach tried to defend himself against the killer,' she said. 'But he wasn't quick enough.'

'Why do you think this was the work of only one person? I asked.

'Because the man next door who called in after hearing a shot also saw a guy exiting the front door before running away along the street.'

'And he only heard one shot?'

She nodded. 'That's right. Which suggests to me that the killer used a gun with a silencer attached.'

My mind raced through the possibilities and after a few moments I said, 'Has the neighbour given you a description of who ran off?'

'Indeed he has.'

'Then let me guess,' I said. 'The guy has blond hair and was quite tall.'

She lifted her brow. 'Are you saying you actually know who he is?'

'I'm 99 per cent sure,' I said. 'His name is – or was – Dmitri Kaplan. And this is what he does for a living.'

Chapter 6

I was in no doubt that Kaplan was responsible for the bloodbath. He had beaten us to Drach and had yet again displayed an incredible degree of resourcefulness.

It had probably taken him less than a minute to shoot all four men. There were no signs of forced entry so it looked as if they had let him in.

It seemed he had then walked from room to room shooting them the moment they appeared. Or perhaps he'd stayed for a while chatting before deciding to take them out.

'It's possible the one who's still breathing was shot last,' DI Reid said. 'Kaplan might have been rushing to finish the job and didn't check to make sure he was dead.'

The survivor was now on his way to the hospital in an ambulance and DI Reid had been handed a wallet that had been taken from his pocket. She sifted through it and took out a driving licence.

'His name's Viktor Franko,' she said.

I scrunched up my brow. 'I don't believe it. He's the Ukrainian we've been looking for.'

I explained that his prints had turned up on Kulik's Mercedes.

'We believe he must have been in the car when Jennifer Booth escaped from it,' I said.

I didn't need to elaborate because Reid had been following the events closely.

'Where are they taking him?' I said.

She shrugged. 'You need to check. But it's probably the emergency unit at St Thomas' Hospital.'

'Okay, well I don't want it to get out that there's a survivor. Let it be known that all four men are dead.'

'I'll need to get authorisation for that, Sam.'

'You've just got it – from me. I'll also get it cleared higher up the chain. So don't worry about it.'

I rang Lattimer straight away and caught him just as he was leaving the press conference.

I told him about the Ukrainian and asked him to send a protection unit to the hospital right away.

'And slam a news black-out on it, guv. I don't want anyone to know that Franko is alive.'

He said he would sort it and I said I'd ring him back in a while and asked DI Reid to talk me through what else she had.

She said her team had carried out a search of the house, including the four upstairs bedrooms.

'None of the beds is made up, and there are no personal possessions in any of the wardrobes and cupboards,' she said. 'According to the neighbours it's empty most of the time. These four guys suddenly showed up this afternoon.'

She then introduced me to a detective named Scott who was the crime scene manager. He had a collection of evidence bags containing the personal effects taken from the pockets of the victims, including wallets and mobile phones.

I didn't recognise the names of the other two, but they sounded Russian or Ukrainian.

All their mobile phones were password-protected so I would have to wait to get inside them.

Drach's jacket had been found draped over a chair in the kitchen. Inside the officers had found a folded photograph showing a man and a woman sitting at a table outside a restaurant. The woman I didn't recognise but the man was Leon Serova. I suspected that this was the same photograph that had come into the possession of the NCA and Alexander Orlov.

I showed it to Doug and said: 'That must be Drach's wife. Deakin told me there was a picture in circulation of the two of them together.'

'Which means Drach knew about the affair,' Doug said.

'Looks that way. I wonder if he'd been planning to do anything about it.'

That was just one of the questions that this latest bloody development had thrown up. But there were at least two other questions that had me really confused.

Why, if Anton Drach and his outfit were behind the kidnappings, had he been targeted by Dmitri Kaplan?

And who the hell had ordered Kaplan to carry out the brutal massacre?

Chapter 7

Helen was sitting up on the bed with her arms wrapped around herself. She hadn't moved for what seemed like hours.

The room was stiflingly hot and under the tracksuit her body was damp with sweat.

She had been trying to fill her mind with positive thoughts. Burrowing in the past was the only way to beat back the terror that had all but consumed her.

She imagined herself back on the stage at the Brit Awards, when she realised that she had finally made it. The reaction of the audience to her rendition of *Somewhere Over The Rainbow* had infused her with a sense of self-worth, as had the praise and attention that had been heaped upon her these past couple of years.

True, her success had led to the break-up of her relationship with Paul. And she'd been forced to endure his abuse and stalking episodes.

But if she hadn't become a celebrity she would never have met Leon. To her their affair was like a fairytale. He was the handsome prince who had stolen her heart and shared with her his years of experience as a lover.

He had told her he planned to leave his wife so that they could have a proper, open relationship. And she believed him, despite the warnings from Alexander that Leon was a serial adulterer with a perverted passion for women half his age.

Helen saw Leon for what he was – a kind and generous man whose immense wealth had failed to make him happy.

She had been looking forward to spending last Saturday night with him at his house. She'd intended to give him a real birthday treat in bed. Instead his special day had been ruined and she could imagine him pacing up and down inside the Tequila Club, frantic with worry.

Suddenly, involuntarily, her mind returned to the present and the gruesome reality of her predicament.

She didn't understand why she was still here, chained to a bed in a hot, stuffy room. Stinging tears blurred everything around her and her stomach roiled with anxiety.

She felt dirty and hungry. She had eaten the three bananas the man had left on the bedside table, but that was ages ago and he hadn't returned.

She wondered how long she'd survive if he never came back. Would it be days or weeks? It occurred to her that anything might happen to him. The man could be killed in a road accident or stabbed to death by one of his fellow criminals. And if he was the only person who knew where she was then she'd be left to rot.

No one will hear your screams, he had told her, and those words still echoed inside her head, filling every waking moment with fear and dread.

There was still some water in the plastic bottle on the bedside table. She picked it up and took a sip, shuddering as she swallowed.

Then she forced herself to get up off the bed. Her joints ached and she felt dizzy. But that was to be expected, she supposed, since her insides were awash with sedatives.

The chain attached to her wrist rattled as she shuffled over to the mirror on the wall. It was the first time she had dared to look at herself, and she was shocked at the sight of the person who stared back at her.

She was sure that few people would have recognised her as Helen Troy, the beautiful and talented singing superstar.

'Oh, my God!'

The words tumbled out of her mouth and her heart leapt into her chest.

She looked terrible. Her hair hung in rat tails and her skin was a sickly pallor and smeared with mascara. Her pupils were hugely dilated and the bags beneath her eyes were the colour of milky coffee. She had chapped lips from where she'd been constantly passing her tongue over them.

So transfixed was she by her own reflection that at first she didn't hear the car's engine outside. When she did hear it her breath trembled in her throat.

The man was back and for a moment hope surged. Had he returned to tell her that a ransom had been paid and she would soon be free to go?

She heard a car door slam shut so she turned away from the mirror and got back on the bed. Her thoughts raced chaotically as she waited for him to come into the room. At the same time panic throbbed inside her.

She wiped the tears from her eyes and took long, deep breaths to help control her nerves.

She heard the key in the lock and the door was pushed open. The man entered the room and stared down at her. He was wearing a black polo sweater, black trousers and dark, wire-rimmed glasses. And he was carrying a leather bag.

'It's time to leave here,' he said, placing the bag on the floor. 'But first you need to have a shower and put on some clean clothes. I'm sure you're ready for that.'

He gave a thin smile and she caught a glimpse of what looked like a gold tooth in his mouth.

Then he brushed a hand through his wavy blond hair and took a key from his pocket before approaching the bed.

Chapter 8

Dmitri Kaplan was suddenly the most wanted man in London. Over two days he had added five kills to his murderous tally.

Every police officer in the Met was on the lookout for him, and security was being stepped up at railway stations and airports.

We released more information about him to the media, along with the photo we had received from the Russians.

The front page headline on the Evening Standard dubbed him the 'Gold-toothed Assassin.' In the story it said police were still withholding details about the massacre in Southwark but it was believed four people had been shot dead.

There was fevered speculation that the murders, and the killing of Mike Dennis, were the start of a bloody turf war between rival gangs.

'This has been brewing for a long time,' intoned Gordon Cain, the BBC's most respected crime reporter. 'In recent years the Russian mafia have expanded their operations in the UK where they believe mass immigration has created a range of new business opportunities. They've moved into areas previously run by Chinese, Romanian and Chechen gangs.

'In London, the Russians now dominate the high-end prostitution rackets and Anton Drach, one of the men shot in Southwark, was believed to have been in control. He's also linked to the kidnapping of the singer Helen Troy on Saturday night.

'Sources within the police have told me they fear she was abducted, along with other female celebrities across Europe, so that they could be sold on or rented out to wealthy individuals. If that is true, then it's without doubt a new and despicable development in the vile trade of human trafficking and sex slavery.'

I had no idea who Cain had been speaking to but what he was saying wasn't far off the mark. It was certainly conceivable that Helen Troy had fallen victim to a ghastly sex racket where rich men paid a premium so they could have their way with some of the world's most desirable women.

Anton Drach already had a potential customer base here in London with the oligarchs who'd been hiring girls through his escort agency.

I wondered if any of them had used their considerable wealth to acquire women who would otherwise be unattainable.

Chapter 9

Once I had confirmation that Viktor Franko had been taken by ambulance to St Thomas' Hospital I left Doug at the house of horror in Southwark and headed over there.

It was less than a mile away but it was slow going because of roadworks and heavy traffic.

What I had witnessed in the house had left me feeling cold and unbalanced. But then no amount of on-the-job experience can prepare you for the grisly aftermath of a bloody massacre. It didn't matter that the victims probably deserved to die, or that the world was a better place without them.

It was still hard to take, and harder still to push the images to the back of my mind. I tried to, though, by bringing my thoughts to bear on where this left us.

Anton Drach was dead, along with two men who would surely turn out to have been members of the Russian mafia. It was another unexpected setback for us. But at least there remained a glimmer of hope because the 'Gold-Toothed Assassin' had made a mistake. He had failed to finish off one of his victims.

Viktor Franko was by all accounts lucky to be alive. I would soon find out how badly hurt he was and if he was expected to survive for longer than a few hours.

He had been shot in the lower abdomen, one of the most vulnerable parts of the human body. Serious damage can be done to the intestines and essential arteries.

If he died then we might never find out why he and the others had been in that house. Or why Dmitri Kaplan had come gunning for them.

St Thomas' Hospital is situated across the river from the Palace of Westminster. I got there just before six, parked up, and made my way to the intensive care unit.

There I learned that the Ukrainian had already undergone surgery and was recovering in a private room.

A jowly-faced doctor put me in the picture. He said Franko was serious, but not critical.

'We got to him in time,' he told me. 'The bullet shattered part of his pelvic bone structure, then passed through his bladder before exiting his body. It missed his femoral and iliac arteries and the lower part of his spinal column. A lot will need to be done, but he's very lucky to be alive.'

'When can I talk to him?'

'Well he won't be coming round for several hours. But when he does there's no reason he shouldn't be able to speak to you.'

'Can I see him?'

The doctor summoned a nurse and told her to take me to Franko's room. Her name was Janet and she had silver hair that was dragged back into a ponytail at the nape of her neck.

Two armed police officers were on guard outside the room. They both looked like they knew what they were doing, and I was pleased when they demanded to see my ID before allowing me inside.

It was a small room with a single bed and a huge array of tubes, wires and monitoring equipment. The smell of iodine was thick in the air.

Viktor Franko was attached to a drip and to two noisy computers. On a small screen, pulsing letters and numbers displayed his vital signs.

What I could see of his face beneath an oxygen mask was gaunt and pale, and the tendons in his neck were taut. He had bushy eyebrows and both his arms were covered in tattoos. I wondered if they identified him to those in the know as being part of the Russian mafia.

The nurse assured me he would remain under close supervision, and I told her I wanted to hang around until he regained consciousness.

'It could be a long wait, Inspector Quinn,' she said. 'There's a room along the corridor. It's comfortable and there's a coffee and snack machine.'

I thanked her and followed her out. I told the two PCs not to move under any circumstances.

'Take it in turns to go to the loo,' I said. 'If anyone turns up to see him who isn't one of us then raise the alarm.'

I helped myself to a coffee as soon as I entered the waiting room. It was weak and tepid but it hit the spot.

A restless energy burned through me, so I paced the floor instead of sitting down on one of the hard, moulded chairs.

Outside the evening was drawing in and the sky was dark and low. I caught sight of my reflection in the window. My eyes were sagging with exhaustion and it seemed like my cheeks were hollowed out.

The case was wearing me down. Every time we moved forward we were getting knocked back.

Viktor Franko was now a key witness as well as a major suspect. To lose him too just didn't bear thinking about. That was why I couldn't leave. I needed to talk to him the moment he woke up. I didn't want to give him time to demand a lawyer or convince his doctor that he was too ill to be interviewed.

I called Lattimer and updated him.

He said: 'We've checked out the two other men found dead at the house. They were both on the books of Drach's security firm and are linked to the Russian mafia. One was arrested three months ago after a Polish prossy claimed he beat her up. But we had to let him go after she withdrew her statement and said he was the wrong guy.'

We talked for a bit. He told me that DI Reid's boss at MIT would be reporting into us on the murders. We would then have an open line into their investigation. It had also been made clear that I would be the one to interview Viktor Franko when he came round.

'I'll get Doug Ellroy to join you at the hospital,' Lattimer said. 'And for your information I've arranged for two more armed officers to be stationed in reception.'

'That's good.'

'So let me know if and when Franko is talking.'

'I will. Meantime can I ask a favour, guv?'

'Sure. What is it?'

'Will you send a big bunch of flowers to Anna? Being here has reminded me that I forgot to do it.'

Chapter 10

The house she had been imprisoned in was so very ordinary. That was the thought that struck Helen as she emerged from the bedroom.

She stood on an upstairs landing that was well lit. The walls were painted magnolia and there was an industrial grey carpet.

The man with the gold tooth had used his key to remove the chain from her wrist. Now he pointed towards a closed door at the end of the landing.

'The bathroom,' he said. 'Go and use the shower.'

He handed her the leather bag he had brought with him.

'Everything you need is in there, including a towel and clean clothes.'

'Where are you taking me?' she asked him.

He put a finger to his lips. 'No questions. Just do as I tell you. And be grateful that you are alive.'

'But who are you?'

'There's no need for you to know that. Now go and clean yourself up or I will do it for you.'

He had a cruel face, she realised. It was the first time she had seen it clearly because her eyes weren't brimming with tears.

She guessed he was in his early 40s. His hair was thick and shiny. He had a narrow mouth and smooth, tight skin. His nose was slightly crooked and his cheekbones looked odd because they were too pronounced. She couldn't see his eyes behind the tinted glasses, but she knew he was giving her a hard stare, and it chilled her to the bone because it felt like he was looking inside her head.

'Please tell me what this is about,' she pleaded with him. 'Why am I here? Is it money you want?'

She was rambling, falling over her words, her voice crackling with fear.

'This is your last chance,' he said, his tone more threatening. 'Go into the bathroom and sort yourself out. I haven't got time to mess around. You have ten minutes. And don't lock the door. If you do I'll kick it down.'

She was in no position to argue. She knew that. She felt the air lock in her chest and the panic start to build again.

Holding the bag, she walked along the landing to the bathroom, the carpet soft and springy under her bare feet.

Once inside she closed the door behind her and pulled the cord to turn on the light. There was a bath tub with a separate walk-in shower cubicle, plus a toilet pan and sink. It was a matching suite and looked quite modern.

The first thing she did was drop her tracksuit bottoms, sit on the toilet and urinate. It was a blessed relief after having to use the bucket.

Then she set about unpacking the bag. Inside there was a hair and body shower gel, a pair of rubber flip flops, a toothbrush and tube of toothpaste, a small brown towel, and a beige one-piece tracksuit, but no underwear.

She laid it all out on the tiled floor and stared at it for a long time. Her mind was in total disarray. She wanted to believe that the worst was over, that her terrible ordeal was finally coming to an end. Why else would the man want her cleaned up if not to exchange her for a ransom?

But she also feared it might be too good to be true. After all, her captor had offered little encouragement other than to say he was taking her to a place that was more comfortable.

And suddenly that seemed ominous rather than reassuring.

Chapter 11

She was tempted to linger under the shower. The water felt so good, and the power jets blasted some of the life back into her.

But Gold Tooth had told her she had ten minutes and she didn't want him storming into the bathroom while she was naked.

So she quickly washed her hair and body, then got out and towelled herself dry. She brushed her teeth and slipped into the tracksuit, which looked and felt brand new.

She glanced at herself in the mirror above the sink. Her face was flushed from the heat of the shower and her hair hung limp and damp. The whites of her eyes were yellowed and patterned with broken veins. But at least she no longer looked like the walking dead.

She slipped her feet into the flip flops which fitted perfectly. Then she took a couple of deep rasping breaths and tried to ignore the nerves that fluttered in her stomach.

She opened the door and stepped back out onto the landing. She expected Gold Tooth to be standing in the same position with a stern look on his face and his arms folded. But he wasn't there. The landing was empty.

She didn't know what to make of it until she heard someone speaking downstairs. She felt a stab of alarm. Christ, she thought, it never occurred to her that he might not be alone.

She moved to the top of the stairs and strained to listen, but the words were indistinct. She couldn't even tell if there was more than one voice.

She looked down into the hall at the bottom of the stairs. There was no movement, but she did feel a cool draught on her face, which made her think that the front door was open.

She gulped more air into her heaving chest and started down the stairs. When she reached the bottom, she saw that the front door was indeed open, and Gold Tooth was standing on the step outside. He was talking into a mobile phone and he had his back to her.

Her eyes darted fearfully around. There was no one else in sight. The hall was empty of both people and furniture. There was a door just ahead to her right, and to her left the hall continued deeper into the house.

Her mind seized on the fact that Gold Tooth wasn't aware that she was behind him. He was too wrapped up in his phone conversation.

She moved instinctively, without thinking and without knowing what she was going to do. She stepped backwards along the hall away from the front door. A quick glance over her shoulder revealed an archway leading to a kitchen.

She decided to creep in there in the hope that she'd find a back door that wasn't locked, or perhaps a weapon she could use to protect herself.

But just then she saw the man take the phone away from his ear and start to turn.

She was lucky. There was an alcove beneath the stairs and she swiftly stepped into it. She held her breath, felt the blood pounding through her veins.

Then she heard the tread of his shoes on the stairs. She peered out, saw that he had left the front door open.

She knew that it would take him mere seconds to discover that she had vacated the bathroom. Therefore she couldn't afford to hesitate.

The front door gaped open, imploring her to go for it. Before she did she kicked off the cumbersome flip flops. Then she made a desperate dash towards the door.

She expected him to shout or grab at her from behind. But he didn't, and she was along the hall and out through the door in what seemed like the blink of an eye.

Chapter 12

Viktor Franko's wife Nadia was brought to the hospital under police escort to visit her husband. She was allowed into the room briefly and broke down in tears at his bedside.

Nurse Janet arranged for me to speak to the woman afterwards in an administration office. By then several other people were using the waiting room so there was no privacy.

Nadia Franko was in her late 20s and with only a basic command of English. She had pixie-like features and cropped brown hair, and was wearing a light sweater and jeans.

I was aware that she had already been interviewed formally and that her home had been searched. She was reluctant to talk but I did manage to get her to answer a few questions.

No, she did not know why Viktor had been at the house in Southwark. No, he most definitely was not a member of the Russian mafia. Yes, she did know that he worked as a so-called security consultant for Anton Drach, but he did not talk to her much about his job.

'Viktor is good husband and father,' she said. 'He provides for us. He no longer involved with criminals.'

She insisted she had no idea why he'd been shot. She also said he'd been at home with her on Saturday night when Helen Troy was kidnapped. But from the way she hesitated I got the impression that she was lying.

She was taken away after the doctor assured her that her husband wasn't about to die. The officers escorting her said that she and her child would be spending the night in protective custody.

I was allowed to stay in the office after telling the nurse that I needed to make and receive some important phone calls while I waited for Franko to wake up.

Doug arrived with a Big Mac and a cold drink. By this time my body was crying out for sustenance so it went down a treat.

He also brought me an update from DI Donna Reid.

'They've unlocked the phones belonging to all four victims,' he said, referring to his notepad. 'It turns out they all received the same text message this morning. It was short and to the point and said: '*Need to meet up. Safe house at two. Be there*'. And it was signed off DK.'

'So DK is probably Dmitri Kaplan.'

Doug nodded. 'Problem is the message came from an untraceable pay-as-you-go number. The number and the initials are in each of the victims' contact lists.'

'Sounds like Kaplan lured them to the house so he could take them out.'

'Indeed it does.'

'This untraceable number. Is it the same as the one that Mike Dennis rang from Caxton Street when he said he was calling his lawyer?'

'No. I checked. It's different.'

'So someone must have decided it wasn't enough just to kill Dennis. To play safe all those involved in the kidnapping had to be got rid of.'

'It's a drastic move, guv.'

'Maybe not from their point of view if they fear being exposed.'

'I suppose not,' Doug said. 'But if Kaplan finds out that Franko is still alive then he may drop by.'

'Well, if he does we'll be ready for him. No way am I losing another suspect.'

Chapter 13

Helen ran out of the house like a panicked deer, wincing as she felt the sharp gravel against the soles of her feet.

She paused for only a split second to get her bearings and decide where she was going.

It was dark and dry and the air was crisp. Right in front of her a car was parked with its boot open. Beyond it was a wall of trees and bushes.

They were the only details she had time to take in before she veered off to the left and sprinted along the driveway which sloped downwards away from the house.

Cold air rushed into her lungs, and every cell in her body was shaking, like static beneath her skin.

She was conscious of a crescent moon hanging high and white in the sky above her. It was thanks to its vaporous glow that she could see where she was going.

There were trees either side of the driveway, shadows shifting among the trunks.

Gold Tooth called out behind her and she heard the anger in his voice. It spurred her on, forcing her to ignore the sharp pain that pulsed from the bottoms of her feet and up through her entire body.

She had no sense of the distance she had covered. It was probably less than 40 yards. But she was already burning up inside, and her legs felt heavy and weak.

Suddenly she realised that the driveway was coming to an end. Ahead was a road. Or more likely some remote country lane because there were no cars, no lights, no people.

Fuck it, she thought. I'm in the middle of bloody nowhere, deep in the English countryside. There might not be any sign of life for miles around.

Gravel turned to tarmac under her feet as she hit the road. She swung to the left, her breath short and rapid. As she ran, her face was contorted by pain and exhaustion.

She wanted to look around, to see how close he was, but she knew it would slow her down. She couldn't hear him, but he was there and she didn't understand why he hadn't caught up with her.

Maybe he hadn't actually seen her fleeing down the driveway, or thought she had plunged into the shelter of the trees. Perhaps it was because he was out of condition despite his athletic physique.

Helen was thankful now that she had subjected herself to a strict keep-fit regime over the past two years. The almost daily gym sessions, the jogging for miles – they had given her stamina and muscle mass. She was sure that was why she was able to push through the pain barrier and stay on her feet.

But she was beginning to flag, and she had to use her arms to try to pump up speed.

Her eyes were filled with tears and her vision was unfocused, and because of that she almost missed seeing the light blinking through the trees to her right.

A house. It had to be. Isolated just like the one she had fled from. But how far away was it? And how could she get to it?

The answer to the second question immediately presented itself. The entrance to another driveway, with a sign on a pole displaying the name of the property.

She turned into it without slowing and was relieved that the surface was tarmac and not gravel.

A frisson of hope stirred inside her as the house came into view. Two storeys. Detached. Light bleeding through two of the ground floor windows.

A sob exploded in her throat when she spotted a small car, a Fiat 500, parked in front of the house.

As she approached the pebble-dash façade, she prayed that Gold Tooth had gone off in a different direction or had lost sight of her in the dark.

A moment later her breath roared in her ears as she came to a stop outside the front door. She slumped against the frame, wheezing and sobbing, and feeling like she had been drained of every last ounce of energy.

She groped for the buzzer and pressed it. Then she turned to look back the way she'd come, fearful that Gold Tooth would appear out of the darkness to pounce on her.

But nothing stirred in the moon's eerie glow.

A sound reached her from inside the house. A woman's voice.

'Yes? Who is it?'

Helen had to get her breath back before she could respond. The delay caused the woman to ask the same question again, only this time much louder.

'Oh God, please let me in,' Helen said, her face up against the door. 'I need your help.'

'Who are you?'

'My name's Helen. There's a man and he's after me.'

'You should call the police then.'

'I can't. I don't have a phone. Please, please open the door.'

She should have expected this. People who live in isolated homes are inevitably reluctant to throw open their doors to strangers, especially after dark.

'Look, you must help me. Please. I was kidnapped, but I got away. It's the truth. I promise. Now I need to contact the police.'

No response. Helen felt a sickening wave of despair rush through her. Surely this can't be happening, she thought. If this woman didn't help her then she didn't know what she would do.

She was about to start banging her fists against the door when it opened as far as the chain lock would allow.

The woman's face appeared. She had to be in her 70s, with frizzy grey hair that tumbled to her shoulders. Her small frame was shrouded in a beige dressing gown, and her rheumy eyes bulged at the sight of Helen.

'Where have you come from?' she asked.

Helen leaned closer. 'Another house. Along the road. Please let me in. I need to call the police.'

The woman scrunched up her face and came to a decision.

'Very well,' she said. 'I believe you.'

The chain was removed and the door pulled open. Helen stumbled inside and started to cry the moment the door was shut behind her. She'd made it. The relief hit her full on like a tsunami. The woman reached out and put a hand on her shoulder.

'You look dreadful my dear. Are you hurt?'

Helen tried to speak, but choked on her own tears and started coughing.

'I'm Lucinda,' the woman said. 'I live here by myself. That's why I have to be careful.'

She held on to Helen's arm and steered her along a short corridor into a small cosy living room with rustic furniture. The layout was unusual, with a wooden staircase situated at one end of the room. At the other a television was on and showing what looked like a movie.

'Sit down my dear,' the woman said, and Helen realised that she probably didn't recognise her. 'I'll make you a cup of tea.'

'There's no time,' Helen said, finding her voice. 'Your phone. Please.'

Lucinda stepped over to a table next to the sofa. A house phone rested on it. She lifted the receiver out of its cradle, but then dropped it on the carpet because her hands were shaking.

As she bent down to pick it up there were several loud thumps on the front door.

Helen froze. It was Gold Tooth. Had to be. He had been behind her after all.

Lucinda lifted the phone and straightened up. Her jaw dropped as she stared beyond Helen towards the hall. She was clearly petrified.

The doorbell sounded then and Gold Tooth started shouting.

'Open up. I know you're in there.'

Neither woman could move, such was the degree of terror that consumed them. Helen struggled to breathe as bile rushed into her mouth. She managed to lift her arm, point to the phone.

'Dial 999' she said. 'Now.'

The poor confused woman looked at the receiver in her hand, as though unaware she had been holding it. At the same time Gold Tooth stopped shouting and silence descended on the room.

'Do it,' Helen yelled. 'Or give the phone to me.'

Her words galvanised Lucinda into action. She started to tap out a number on the phone.

But she didn't get far because just then the window to her left caved in and her face exploded.

Chapter 14

Blood and brain matter showered the room. Some of it landed on Helen's tracksuit like a spray of crimson paint.

She stared in horrified disbelief as the old woman came crashing down on top of a glass coffee table that shattered under the weight.

Helen screamed and felt a cold blast of terror sweep through her body.

Lucinda's head landed on the carpet only a couple of feet from where she stood. The old lady's face was a bloody mess, and it didn't take a great leap of the imagination to realise it had been destroyed by a bullet fired through the window.

Helen was in such a state of shock that she didn't register the sound of more breaking glass, or see Gold Tooth climbing through the window. She became aware of his presence only when he seized her arm and thrust the hot muzzle of a revolver under her chin.

'You're to blame for what just happened,' he shouted at her. 'You should not have run away.'

A part of her wanted him to pull the trigger. To end the nightmare once and for all and to assuage the guilt that had erupted inside her.

Instead, he withdrew the gun, which she noticed had a silencer attached to the barrel, and used his free hand to slap her hard around the face.

The impact sent her stumbling backwards. She lost her balance and dropped onto the sofa.

'Is there anyone else in the house?' he demanded to know.

She looked up at him. He had removed his dark glasses and his brown eyes were wide and threatening.

'Well is there?' he yelled.

She shook her head. That in itself was a huge effort.

He looked around, then at his watch. He seemed remarkably calm, she thought, for someone who had just committed a brutal, senseless murder.

She watched him thrust the gun into his belt. It seemed like it was happening in slow motion. Like it was part of some horrendous dream.

'You'll have to stay here while I go and get the car,' he said.

His words sank in but she didn't fully comprehend their meaning.

He grabbed her again, wrenched her to her feet. Then he dragged her out of the living room and into the adjoining kitchen. She didn't resist. She couldn't. It felt like her mind had been detached from her body.

In the kitchen he started opening and shutting drawers until he found what he was looking for – a ball of string and a tea towel. Then he hauled her back into the living room and pushed her onto the bottom step of the stairs. He used the string to tie her wrists together and secure her to a banister. Then he tied her feet and wrapped the towel around her face so she couldn't speak or cry out.

'That should keep you out of trouble until I get back.'

Before walking out of the house he checked the other rooms, including those upstairs, and then stamped on Lucinda's phone, leaving it in bits.

When he was gone, Helen looked at Lucinda's lifeless body and said sorry over and over again. The poor woman is dead because of me, she told herself. Even if I survive this the guilt is going to blight the rest of my life.

Something on the TV drew her attention away from the wretched corpse. The BBC ten o'clock news was showing a video clip of the kidnappers dragging her away from the Tequila Club and bundling her into the white van.

Then it cut to a photograph of her lying on a carpet with blood around her head. A caption beneath it claimed that she was dead.

More images were to follow, along with more shocking revelations. She learned that Mike Dennis had been strangled and four other men shot dead by a man they were calling the 'Gold-Toothed Assassin'.

The news reader said that other female celebrities – including the actress Jennifer Booth – had also been kidnapped, by men belonging to the Russian mafia.

Helen gasped when she heard that her ex-boyfriend had appeared in court charged with causing criminal damage to her home. And that he'd had help from Clara the cleaner and her husband.

She also learned that her dear friend Alexander Orlov had offered a £1million reward for her safe return.

But that nobody had so far demanded a ransom.

Chapter 15

It was just after ten o'clock and Viktor Franko was still out for the count.

I'd sent Doug home to try to get some sleep and be with his family. It didn't really matter to me where I spent the evening since I'd be by myself anyway.

And at least the office I had commandeered had a television. So I sat watching the BBC news while drinking copious amounts of coffee.

There was plenty to hold my attention, including some more information on the 'Gold-Toothed Assassin', courtesy of the Beeb's industrious crime correspondent, Gordon Cain. He had managed to interview Dmitri Kaplan's father via Skype from his home in Moscow.

Mr Kaplan, who was in his late 60s, said he had disowned his son some years ago because he had brought disgrace on their family. In broken English, he described Dmitri as a callous murderer and sociopath.

'He was always bad, even as small boy. They should never have let him join the police. He enjoy hurting people.'

Cain had also obtained a copy of a confidential report produced by the Moscow police department after Kaplan fled the country.

The author, a senior official within the department, revealed that they had been suspicious of Kaplan's corrupt activities long before he murdered a colleague who was threatening to expose him.

'According to the report, Kaplan was also about to be questioned about the murder of a man who was going to give evidence against several high-flying Russian businessmen suspected of colluding with mafia gangs,' Cain said. 'The man was strangled with a belt at his home just outside Moscow. Kaplan was one of the detectives working on the case.'

It was an angle that was sure to be followed up, fuelling further the media hysteria surrounding the so-called 'Gold-Toothed Assassin'.

The more I learned about the man the more fearful I was that he would strike again. I wondered if there were others within Anton Drach's inner circle who had been targeted. Or was Kaplan's killing spree over?

On the TV, Cain was now talking about the massacre in Southwark over video footage of the house. He said police still hadn't released details of the dead but it was believed the number of victims totalled four.

'What I can report is that within the Met there is increasing concern over the investigation's lack of progress,' Cain said. 'It's believed to be one of the reasons the Commissioner has decided to set up a task force.'

I shook my head and clucked my tongue. As if I didn't feel bad enough already.

'Detective Inspector Quinn?'

I hadn't noticed the door open and the nurse enter the room. It wasn't Janet. She had already gone home. The night nurse was a young Asian woman with a warm smile and big eyes.

'I've been told to let you know that Mr Franko is awake,' she said. 'He's been told you're here and he wants to speak to you.'

*

The oxygen mask had been removed from the Ukrainian's face. I noticed that he had a flat nose and a large scar across his left cheek.

His eyes were open and they followed me as I stepped up to the bed.

The doctor I had seen earlier was still on duty. He told me that his patient had been awake for ten minutes and had responded well to surgery.

'But he is still very tired, Inspector. He asked me what happened to the other men who were with him in that house. After I told him they were killed he insisted on talking to you.'

The doctor retreated from the bedside and stepped out of the room.

'I'm Detective Chief Inspector Quinn,' I said to Franko. 'I'm investigating the kidnapping of Helen Troy and a number of other women. I'm also eager to find the man who shot you and murdered the men you were with, including your boss Anton Drach.'

He stared up at me, his breathing ragged. Deep lines encircled his eyes and phlegm rattled in his throat as he spoke.

'You have to protect my wife and son,' he said. 'They will be in danger.'

'What makes you think that?'

'Because I am alive. And I shouldn't be.'

'Your wife came to see you earlier,' I said. 'She's in protective custody at the moment.'

'Then keep her safe. I beg you. She and my son are all I have.'

His eyes were liquid and his voice was low and hoarse.

'There's only so much we can do,' I said.

'What do you mean?'

I shrugged. 'We know you were involved in the kidnappings. We found your fingerprints on Ivan Kulik's car. We also have you on CCTV chasing Jennifer Booth to her death on the motorway.' He didn't deny that he was the one with Kulik, so I pressed on. 'And I have no doubt that more evidence will emerge that will link you to other crimes, including the murder of Mike Dennis.'

'I had nothing to do with that,' he said. 'It was Kaplan.'

'You mean the man who came for you?'

He gave a slight nod and blinked a couple of times.

'We know that Dmitri Kaplan is a very dangerous man,' I said. 'And I can understand why you fear for your wife and son. But we don't know where he is and as long as he's out there somewhere, then you and your family are at risk.'

'But you have to protect them.'

'We don't have to do anything, Mr Franko. Not unless you help us, of course. Then we'll do whatever it takes to keep you all safe and secure.'

He squeezed his eyes shut for several seconds. When he opened them he shifted his gaze from me and stared at the ceiling.

'You're in very serious trouble, Mr Franko,' I said. 'But then you know that don't you? And you must also be aware that the best thing you can do now is to tell us all you know. You've got nothing to gain by holding back. If you cooperate I promise I'll do what I can to make things easier for your family.'

He continued to stare at the ceiling as the beeping of the machine filled the silence. I let him think it through, knowing that he was at his most vulnerable, and therefore more open to persuasion.

When I realised that I still hadn't managed to convince him to come clean, I said, 'Look there's just you and me in this room. You haven't been cautioned and whatever you tell me you can go back on later. A good lawyer will know that this conversation can't be used against you in court. But if I'm to find Kaplan and protect your family I need to know stuff. Do you understand?'

I waited, knowing I'd just provided him with a get-out clause. But I didn't care. Right now I needed answers.

After about half a minute he turned towards me again and said: 'What is it you want to know?'

'Everything. Start with why Helen Troy and the other women were abducted.'

He drew a breath, licked his dry lips, 'They were kidnapped to order on behalf of a man who fixates on famous young women he's met or seen on television and in movies.'

My mouth dropped open. I was so shocked that my throat contracted and I had difficulty asking the next question.

'Who is this man?' I said.

'I don't know. Drach was the only one who had contact with him. We were only ever told that he was rich and very influential.'

'So Drach never mentioned a name?'

'No. He only ever referred to him as the client.'

'So where does Dmitri Kaplan fit into it?'

He swallowed. 'That's obvious. He works as an enforcer and hatchet man for the client and must have been told to kill everyone who knows what's been going on.'

Chapter 16

As Helen sat tied to the stairs her mind was awash with shock.

She struggled to comprehend what she had seen and heard on the television. The news reader had moved on to another subject, but Helen was no longer listening. Her eyes were closed and she was trying to process the information.

There had been no ransom demand and an online photo had been posted to try to convince people that she was dead.

Other women – including the actress Jennifer Booth – had also been kidnapped.

Mike Dennis had been strangled.

And the man who had just shot dead a defenceless old lady was on a murderous rampage.

Holy Shit!

The faint glimmer of hope that had flared up inside her was now extinguished. Gold Tooth was not planning to exchange her for a ransom. That, it seemed, had never been his intention.

So what was he going to do with her? And what had he done to Jennifer Booth and the others?

Helen opened her eyes and her unsteady gaze was drawn to Lucinda's body. It made her flinch. There was so much blood. It was spread all over the room, on the walls, the carpet, the furniture. There were even blood spatters on the ceiling.

She felt nauseous, and once again the cold finger of fear moved along her spine.

The fact that her life had been blasted to hell because she was a celebrity was not lost on her. She should have listened to the people who had told her she needed to be more security conscious. She should never have put her trust in Clara Pike on the basis of a positive recommendation from the previous owners of her house. She should have had her checked out or contracted a big established cleaning company instead.

And she should have told the police about Paul's abusive and threatening messages, and his stalking. She had sensed that he was working up a head of steam but had chosen to ignore it, telling herself that he wouldn't do anything bad just to get back at her.

But she had been wrong, just as she'd been wrong to have insisted on only having one bodyguard and not upgrading the surveillance system around the house.

The world, she now realised, is a dangerous place – especially for those people who draw attention to themselves by becoming rich and famous.

*

Gold Tooth returned after 20 minutes. When he came in she was still feeling totally shell-shocked from what she'd seen and heard on the television.

Her heart was booming in her ears and hot tears of fear and shock rolled down her face.

She watched, wide-eyed, as he searched for the bullet that had killed Lucinda. He obviously didn't want the police to find it.

'What are you going to do to me?' she screamed out and he didn't even bother to turn towards her.

Panic surged through her and she tried to untangle her hands from the string that bound them to the banister. But it was too tight and she was too weak.

Gold Tooth quickly determined that his bullet had come out the back of the old lady's skull and was wedged in the wall. He used a penknife to pick it out, then wiped it clean on a cushion before dropping it in his pocket.

He then used the same knife to cut the string and free Helen's hands.

'If you try to run away again I won't hesitate to kill you,' he said.

He pulled her up and she cried out because the soles of her feet were raw and painful.

'You only have to walk as far as the car,' he said.

She jerked her arm free of his grip. 'I know what you've done,' she said accusingly. 'And I know about the other women. I just saw it all on the news.'

His eyes flashed towards the television where a young man was now presenting a weather forecast and warning of showers to come.

Then Gold Tooth turned back to her and said: 'You would have found out soon enough. It makes no difference to anything.'

'They're saying you killed four men today,' she said. 'You're a fucking monster.'

He simply shrugged his shoulders and this prompted a fierce reaction from Helen. She screamed out and aimed a punch at his face. But he saw it coming and moved his head so she missed him by a mile.

He grabbed her arm and yanked it up behind her back.

'Don't be stupid,' he said. 'You're no match for me and you'll only get hurt.'

He pushed her face against the wall and a stabbing pain ripped through her nose and forehead.

'Oh God, help me,' she yelled. 'I don't want to die.'

Her despair had reached a new peak because she now knew for certain that no one was coming to save her. She was alone and helpless, and her captor was a ruthless psychopath.

Out of the corner of her eye she was able to see him pull a syringe from his pocket. She flinched as he plunged the needle into the side of her neck.

'That should calm you down,' he said.

Having done it he pulled her across the living room into the hallway. She tried to break away but he held on firmly to her arm and she couldn't loosen his grip.

As they moved towards the front door she felt herself becoming light-headed. Once outside on the driveway, he pushed her towards what looked like a grey Volvo.

'Tell me why you did it,' Helen shouted. 'Why did you kill those men? And Mike Dennis? Why did you do it?'

He reached the car and opened the boot. Then he looked at her and shrugged again.

'If you must know I did it to protect the man I work for – the same man you are about to meet.'

'What man?'

'You'll soon see.'

'But why are you taking me to him?'

His lips parted in a rictus grin. 'Because he's chosen you to be his latest sex slave.'

Helen was too shocked to react immediately. Her mouth fell open and her head spun as the sedative kicked in. She stared at him but his face went quickly out of focus. She opened her mouth to speak but the words wouldn't form in her throat.

'Get in the boot,' he demanded.

She wasn't able to respond. Instead she closed her eyes and felt herself falling as the blackness enveloped her like a shroud.

Chapter 17

Viktor Franko continued to open up to me. There was a faraway look in his eyes, and he was clearly uncomfortable, but he seemed determined to tell me what he knew.

His voice was weak and there were long pauses as he struggled to get his thoughts together. But for a man who had undergone surgery only a short time ago, he was remarkably coherent.

'Drach got only a small group of us involved in the kidnappings,' he said. 'There was me, Kulik and two others. When the client identified a woman he wanted us to abduct he called Drach and we spent at least two weeks working up a plan. No expense was spared. Drach was paid £1million each time and we shared it between us.'

I could barely believe what I was hearing. The mystery man had spent £6million so that he could enslave half a dozen women. But, of course, they were not ordinary women. They were celebrities. Young, beautiful and talented. Women who were considered unattainable.

'So were you involved in kidnapping all six women?' I said.

Franko nodded. 'I was.'

'And how did it work with those in other countries?'

'We flew there, all expenses paid, and watched the target for several days,' he said. 'Each kidnap was carried out with military precision. After we seized a target she was handed over to Dmitri Kaplan. He was across everything and flew to each country independently. He oversaw the operations alongside Drach and he then arranged transport for them to the UK, probably on a private jet.'

'So where did you take Helen after she was abducted?'

'We delivered her to a house just west of London, in Berkshire, where Kaplan was waiting.'

'Is this the home of the man you knew as the client?'

'He may well own it, but he doesn't live there. It's small and nothing special. She would have been moved on from there.'

'Do you know where she was taken?'

'I don't. I swear.'

'Okay. So you delivered the women to Kaplan. But that wasn't the last you saw of them was it?'

For the first time a look of guilt came over his face.

'After the client was finished with the women we had to go back to the house in Berkshire to pick them up,' he said. 'They were always in a bad way because the client is into sexual masochism. He did bad things to them.'

I thought about the cuts and bruises on Jennifer Booth's body and my heart missed a beat.

'Is that why Jennifer was in the Mercedes with you and Kulik?' I said. 'Had you just picked her up?'

Another barely perceptible nod.

'She gave us the slip. After that the whole thing started to unravel. According to Drach it caused the client to panic.'

'So where were you taking her?'

He hesitated before responding, and when he did his voice dropped to a whisper. 'Burgess Wood, near Marlow,' he said. 'There's a concealed well there that goes deep into the ground. We were going to put her in it with the others.'

I felt my stomach flip over.

'Are you saying that you dumped the bodies of the first four victims in a fucking well?' I said.

He swallowed. 'Drach told us we had to. He said they would never be found. So we piled earth and rocks on top of each one.'

'Please tell me you didn't bury them alive.'

He moved his head from side to side. 'Kulik shot them first, in the back of the head. I never had the stomach for it.'

I took a deep breath and counted to ten in my head. It was the only way I was able to stop myself from smashing a fist into Franko's face.

Chapter 18

The effects of the sedative were short-lived. Helen was still in the boot of Gold Tooth's car when she slowly regained consciousness. But she still felt dizzy and disoriented, and there was a throbbing pain in her head.

It was too dark to see anything, and after fumbling around for a minute or so she realised there was no way out.

She could hear the muffled groan of the engine and she could feel the car moving. She could also feel the fear squirming around inside her like a living thing.

What Gold Tooth had said to her before she passed out was still fresh in her mind.

'He's chosen you to be his latest sex slave.'

The man sounded like a vile monster and she was about to be delivered to him on a plate. How sick was that?

But there was nothing she could do about it. Her only chance of escape had come and gone. She was trapped in a never-ending nightmare.

The faces of the other women who had been kidnapped flashed in her mind. Their photographs had appeared only briefly on the news and yet she felt she knew them. Jennifer Booth's death had been tragic, but she wanted to believe that the others were still alive. In her heart, though, she knew that was unlikely. At least one of the women had disappeared two whole years ago.

The only one she had ever heard of was Jennifer Booth, having seen one of the films she'd starred in. Helen recalled how well she'd played the part of a young mother whose world falls apart when her husband leaves her.

Helen also remembered when the news broke about her disappearance in Spain. Everyone believed she had drowned whilst swimming in the sea near her villa. But the truth was far more awful. For two months she had been held captive until, according to the news, she had managed to run away, only to be cut down by a lorry.

Two months. Jesus.

Helen did not even try to imagine what the poor girl had gone through during that time. She didn't dare because now it was her turn to suffer the same gruesome fate.

*

She felt the car come to a stop. The engine was turned off and she heard a door open and shut.

A second later the boot sprang open and she had to shield her eyes against the light that flooded in.

'We're here,' Gold Tooth said.

He took hold of her arm and helped her out. Her head spun and her heart started beating furiously.

After he closed the boot she saw that he had removed his leather jacket and glasses. The sleeves of his black sweater were rolled up, exposing arms entwined with tattoos.

They were in a large garage with space enough for two cars. The door was already closed and a long florescent light hummed above them.

'Where am I?' Helen said, feeling groggy and confused.

'You've been in this property before,' he said. 'Only not this part.'

He gripped her arm tightly and pulled her towards a door with a security pad on the wall next to it. He spoke as he tapped in a code.

'This is the private entrance to a converted basement that very few people know exists,' he said. 'It'll be your home for the foreseeable future.'

The door clicked open and he pushed her into a short carpeted corridor. At the other end of it was a lift. He led her up to it and pressed the button. The door slid open.

'Step in,' he said.

Her mind was screaming at her to resist. To attack him with all the strength she could muster and do whatever she could to get away.

But she was too weak, too dazed, to do anything other than comply.

So she stepped into the lift. There were just three buttons on the inside panel and they were marked U, G and D. Gold Tooth pressed D, and she didn't need to be told that they were going down.

The lift didn't make a sound, but perhaps she just couldn't hear it because her pulse was pounding in her ears.

She turned to her captor and said: 'You don't have to do this. It's wrong. Please let me go. I'm rich and I can make sure you'll be rewarded.'

His expression remained impassive. 'I'm being well rewarded already,' he said. 'The man I work for has been very generous these past few years. In fact I have just one more job to do for him later tonight and then I'm retiring. Things have suddenly got too risky for me. It's time to enjoy the fruits of my labours.'

They locked eyes and Helen couldn't help but wonder what made this man tick. He seemed completely at peace with himself despite what he did. His eyes were like glass balls that had been pressed into the sockets. There was no sign of emotion in them. They were just windows into a dark soul.

The lift stopped and the door opened. Gold Tooth nudged her forward into a room that was in darkness.

But as she stepped into it the lights suddenly came on and she was confronted with a sight that took her fear to a new level.

This was no ordinary room. It was a purpose-built torture chamber, complete with black walls and a red shag-pile carpet.

It was perhaps 20sq ft and filled with equipment that was designed to cause pain.

Chains hung from the ceiling. Whips and paddle beaters were lined up on shelves along a wall. On another wall hung an array of fetish and bondage equipment including leather straps, collars, cuffs, body harnesses and leg spreaders.

There was a table covered with masks, dildos, vibrators and a variety of sex toys for inserting into every orifice on the human body.

But the centrepiece was a large scary object in the middle of the room. Helen had seen pictures of such things on the internet. It was called a cage bed and it consisted of a black metal frame over a firm mattress covered in red leather. It had head and foot boards with head, wrist and ankle holes, and beneath the mattress was a cage large enough to accommodate a person lying down.

Vomit rose in her throat and she thought she might collapse. She probably would have if Gold Tooth hadn't been holding onto her.

'Welcome to the best-equipped dungeon in the whole of London.'

It was a moment before she realised that it wasn't him speaking. The voice had come from over to the left where a door had been eased open.

At first her heart jumped at the sight of the man who was so familiar to her.

But just as quickly hope turned to despair as she realised that he hadn't come to her rescue.

'It's good to see you again, Helen,' he said. 'And it's such a privilege to have you here. However, I think it's only fair to tell you that I intend to make your stay as unpleasant for you as possible.'

Chapter 19

'Is Helen Troy alive?'

I was surprised it had taken me so long to ask that particular question, and I suspected it was because I dreaded hearing the answer.

But after what Franko had told me about how four of the other women had been murdered and thrown into a well, I needed to know.

He didn't respond immediately, though. By now he was struggling to speak and his eyes were half-closed. We were losing him to the drugs that had been pumped into his body.

But I was reluctant to call the doctor in because I knew he would probably make me abort the interview. So I asked the question again, and this time Franko said: 'The truth is I don't know. The last time I saw her was at the house in Berkshire. We took her there straight after dumping the van.'

'So who was with you?'

'Drach and Kulik. We were the ones who snatched her.'

'And you left her there with Kaplan?'

'That's right.'

'But what about the photograph of her that was posted online? The caption that went with it said she was dead.'

'It was staged,' he said. 'She'd been sedated.'

'And the blood on the carpet?'

'It was ketchup.'

I felt both surprised and relieved. It meant that there was still hope.

'So who took the picture?'

'Drach took it before we left the house, but it was the client's idea because he wanted the world to think that she was dead.'

'Why?'

'It was part of a plan he had to pin the blame for Helen's disappearance on someone he had a serious grudge against.'

'Who was that?'

'Leon Serova. He's part-owner of the Tequila Club. That was why we were told to seize Helen from there even though we knew we'd be caught on CCTV cameras going in and out.'

'That doesn't make sense,' I said.

'Well, it did to the client. The thinking was that if it happened there, Serova would be under a cloud of suspicion because he'd invited her to his party.'

'And how did you convince Mike Dennis to help out?'

'That was easy. Mike had been on Drach's payroll for years.'

I shook my head. 'But I still don't get it. Why did Drach go along with this when it made what you were doing far more risky?'

'Because he also had a compelling reason for punishing Serova.'

'What reason?'

'The client told him that Serova had had an affair with his wife during trips to Moscow.'

Franko closed his eyes then and I realised he was about to go to sleep. I seized his arm and shook it. But at that precise moment the doctor came back into the room and saw me telling Franko to stay awake.

'That's enough, Inspector,' he said. 'My patient needs to rest. You'll have to come back tomorrow.'

But I wasn't about to give up that easily. There were still too many loose ends.

'Tell me how they intended to put the blame on Serova,' I said, raising my voice. 'What was the plan?'

His eyes flicked open again and he tried his best to focus on my face.

'I really must insist that you leave the room immediately,' the doctor said. 'This is completely out of order.'

I ignored him and said to Franko: 'Answer the bloody question and I'll leave you alone.'

Franko started speaking but his voice was so low that I had to lean over the bed until my face was only inches from his.

'The camera that was used to take the picture of Helen,' he whispered. 'They were going to plant it on Serova, along with a note confessing to kidnapping and killing Helen.'

'But how could they have done that without Serova knowing?'

'Simple. Drach was going to kill him first – and then make it look like he'd committed suicide.'

The doctor ushered me out of the room then while threatening to complain to my superiors about my behaviour.

But I wasn't unduly concerned. The Ukrainian had given me more information than I could possibly have hoped for considering his condition.

And I was glad now that I'd got him to talk even though much of what he'd said we wouldn't be able to use against him.

I believed what he'd told me about not knowing the identity of the man who had paid them to kidnap Helen and the other women, the man he referred to as 'the client'.

But there were enough clues to the man's identity in everything else Franko had said, clues that pointed to an individual who had cleverly managed to distance himself from what had happened.

As I rushed out of the hospital I took out my phone and called Lattimer.

'Get a team together,' I said. 'I know who's behind it. And I think that Helen Troy might still be alive.'

Chapter 20

Helen had always considered Alexander Orlov a friend as well as a business partner. It was her agent, Abigail Trainer, who had brought them together.

Abigail had seen an opportunity to secure a massive amount of publicity through Orlov's magazine and publishing interests. And from the start things had gone well.

The column she wrote for the magazine about the showbiz world had proved hugely popular and her ghost-written biography was all set to be published later in the year. Plus, of course, there was the £100,000 she was paid for performing at the event to mark the magazine's launch.

The man himself had always been charming and polite. They'd met on perhaps 20 occasions over 11 months, usually at functions and parties, including two at his home in Belgravia, of which the custom-built torture chamber in the basement was obviously a part.

She would never have believed him to be anything other than a decent man. He had always had an easy, approachable manner. It was something that surprised her given the fact that he was a Russian oligarch and one of the richest men in Britain.

He was also known for being a philanthropist as well as a hard-nosed businessman who ran companies all over Europe.

Sure, whenever she had seen him on social occasions he'd had a stunning woman on his arm, no doubt hired through an agency.

At no time had he given her the impression that he was a sexual masochist.

But now as he stood before her he looked like a total stranger – as well as a repulsive little perv.

His short, portly body was wrapped in a bright red Japanese kimono with a dragon motif on the front. His hands were behind his back and his head was tilted slightly to one side. His legs and feet were bare and so she assumed that he was naked underneath. The thought turned her stomach.

'I can see you are surprised to see me, Helen,' he said, 'but that is to be expected. It's the first time that someone who has been a friend has become one of my slaves.'

His words sent her hurtling back into a state of shock. She knew that she had no choice now but to abandon all hope. There was nowhere to run and nowhere to hide. And there was no point begging for mercy because it would only satisfy and excite him.

'Dmitri called me from the car to tell me what happened this evening,' he said. 'It's a shame about the old lady. But there can be no denying that you are responsible for her death, and therefore deserve to be punished. So you should remember that when we get going.'

His lips curled back in a malicious smile and he waved his hand to indicate the room.

'This is where the fun takes place. You'll be here until I grow tired of you. You'll be fed and watered and able to use the bathroom. You should be aware that the entire basement is soundproofed. No one is allowed down here without my say so, and that includes my housekeeper and bodyguards who are completely oblivious as to what goes on here.

'I will see you most days but when I'm not around you will have access to a television with a remote control to keep you occupied.'

She stared at him, incredulous. The banality of his words made what he was saying all the more chilling.

'I know from conversations we've had when you've been a touch inebriated that you're not into the rough stuff,' he said. 'But if you've read *Fifty Shades of Grey* you'll have some idea what to expect.'

She was breathing hard now, but she couldn't seem to get enough oxygen. Every muscle in her body was tense, and she felt overwhelmed by a gut-wrenching wave of fear.

He stepped forward so that he was standing just a few feet away from her. She could smell alcohol on his breath as he continued to speak.

'You are one of the chosen few, Helen. As you have probably guessed or been told I have a thing for stunning young celebrities like yourself. The more famous the better. The kick it gives me is beyond description. But I have to be very selective because if too many go missing there'll be an outcry and the rest of them will take their own security far more seriously.

'Right now it's relatively easy to abduct those young self-obsessed stars who inhabit the world of music, television and the movies. You just have to know the right people and have enough money to pay them.

'And that's what's great about having more money than I could ever spend, Helen. It means that there is very little that I can't do and can't have. I never have to be bored. I can fulfil my most outrageous fantasies and get away with the most heinous of crimes.'

He brought his arms round from behind his back. She saw something glint in his right hand. It was a syringe!

Helen jumped back and cried out, but at the same time Gold Tooth grabbed her from behind. She thrashed her head around, kicked out with her feet. But he held her in a vice-like grip so she couldn't move.

'You can't do this,' she yelled. 'It's insane. You're insane.'

Orlov licked his plump lips with a sharp, pink tongue. There was a look of childlike excitement on his face.

'Don't fight it, Helen. It's pointless. I'm going to inject you with a dose of propofol. You probably know it as the drug that Michael Jackson overdosed on. But I'll give you just enough to render you unconscious in about 20 seconds. And the good thing about it is that you will only be out for about ten minutes, and when you wake up you won't have an anaesthetic hangover. So you'll know exactly what I'm doing to you.'

Gold Tooth twisted her head to the right and she felt the needle go in. Within seconds she could feel herself go limp, the world turning to liquid around her.

The last thing she heard before she passed out was the sound of her own screaming.

Chapter 21

I was sure I was right. If not, then I was about to trigger an almighty diplomatic storm.

As I raced across London towards Belgravia, my heart was galloping, and the face of Alexander Orlov was cartwheeling through my head.

Based on what the Ukrainian had told me, I was convinced that the billionaire oligarch was the man he had described as 'the client'.

For starters, Orlov could afford to fork out a staggering £6million to satisfy his cravings. He would have been able to fly those kidnapped in Europe back to the UK in his private jet, which was presumably what he did with Jennifer Booth.

Plus, he had known Anton Drach and had admitted renting girls from the gangster's escort agency to use as 'hostesses' at parties and events.

But what really led me to believe that he was our man was the fact that the so-called client had a grudge against Serova.

Orlov had told me that Serova had tried to force him out of the magazine business. Then in retaliation he had blackmailed Serova by threatening to tell Drach that Serova was banging the gangster's wife.

But it obviously wasn't enough – which was why he must have decided to set Serova up with Drach's cooperation.

If it had all worked out it would have been a dream scenario. Orlov would have procured another celebrity victim. The photograph of Helen, along with Serova's fake confession, would have convinced the world she was dead. And Serova's apparent suicide would have sated Orlov's hunger for revenge.

To top it off, Orlov himself would never have come under suspicion. He'd have been free to keep Helen as his sex slave for as long as he wanted. He had already pulled a masterstroke by offering a £1million reward for Helen's safe return, knowing that it would never have to be paid out.

It was doubtless why he had also arranged for Helen to join him in the South of France the day after she was kidnapped.

I wondered how long his sights had been set on Helen, and if his hatred of Serova became more passionate because of the latter's affair with the singer.

It was all circumstantial, of course, but for me it was enough to justify a police raid on his £40million home.

A response team was already on its way there, and Lattimer had launched a full blown probe into Orlov's business and personal affairs.

If he was indeed the man ultimately responsible for the string of kidnappings and murders, then he was about to discover that even all his wealth and power would not be enough to protect him now.

Chapter 22

Helen woke up to find herself naked and damp with sweat. She was lying on her back on the cage bed and she could barely move.

Her wrists and ankles were spread wide and trapped in the head and foot boards.

She started to shake, and her breath came faster as she tried to fight back the panic.

'Hello again.'

It was Orlov and he was standing next to the bed with a cruel smile on his face. She stared at him with utter loathing. Her saliva was drying up, and when she tried to swallow, she gagged.

'Try to relax,' he said, as though addressing a patient. 'You never know, you might actually enjoy what is about to happen to you.'

He took off his kimono and let it fall to the floor. His bloated body was pale and hairy. His skin sagged and looked too big for him, and his half erect penis was small and unimpressive.

'Feel free to make as much noise as you want,' he said. 'The slave you replaced – dear little Jennifer – was a real screamer, which is why I kept her here for so long. But the bitch caused me grief when she ran away. That's why I need to make the most of you, Helen. It's likely you'll be my last high-profile submissive for some while.'

She tried to speak but her terror-stricken throat refused to comply. She felt done in. Defeated. She wanted to let go and die because she knew it was the only way to escape this nightmare.

'We are totally alone now,' Orlov went on. 'Dmitri has gone to perform one last task for me. He's going to kill your lover Leon and make it look like suicide. After that the world will think that Leon was responsible for your disappearance.

'How does that make you feel, Helen? Your lover has only a short time to live. But it serves him right. He should never have crossed me. And he should not have lured you into his bed just to make me angry.'

There were tears in her eyes now and she struggled to focus on his features. She had just as much trouble understanding what he was saying.

'I want you to try to appreciate what this is going to be like for me,' he said. 'I get enormous pleasure from dominating women and causing them pain and humiliation. There are many women out there who are prepared to submit themselves to me. That's how it works most of the time.

'But to be able to do what I do to someone who is beautiful, famous and idolised by countless numbers of people – well that is something else again. I can't describe what a power kick it is. And how immensely gratifying.'

She tried to shut out the agony by thinking about what life had been like before she was plunged into this hellish nightmare. She pictured her mother, her cat, the trappings of success. She recalled how wonderful it was to make love to Leon and how she'd had the world at her feet.

But she couldn't hold on to the images or the thoughts. They slipped away as soon as she felt the hot liquid pooling beneath her buttocks. Dear God, she had pissed herself!

Orlov, seeing this, gave a moan of satisfaction.

'That's what I like to watch, Helen, the manifestation of fear. There's nothing quite so intoxicating.'

She started screaming and crying then even though she knew that nobody other than Orlov was going to hear her. The tears burned tracks down her temples onto the mattress and clogged up her throat.

'I've done enough talking,' he said. 'It's now time to have some fun before I go to bed. And don't worry. I've got a whole bunch of sedatives and pain killers on hand to make sure you'll be able to get a good night's sleep in your cage.'

She lifted her head, still crying, and watched him step silently over to the table and pick up a short chain with small metal attachments at either end.

'We'll start with the nipple clamps,' he said. 'And then I think I'll give you a taste of Doc Johnson. And to heighten the experience for both of us I'll set it to music.'

He picked up a remote control device from on the table and pushed a button.

Helen flattened her head against the mattress and closed her eyes as music filled the room.

Then she heard her own voice singing the cover version she'd recorded of her favourite song – *Somewhere Over The Rainbow*.

Chapter 23

I beat the response team to Orlov's house by mere seconds. They screamed into the street, sirens wailing, just as I was jumping out of my car.

By the time I'd mounted the steps and was pushing the buzzer, several armed officers were behind me. The man who answered the door had the kind of face that only a mother could love. He looked like a boxer who had lost too many fights.

His mouth fell open as I stepped aside to let the officers pile in.

I thought for a moment that he was going to try to stop them. But, sensibly, he moved out of the way and said in a distinct Russian accent, 'Hey what is this? You cannot just come inside without permission. This is a private residence.'

I held up my ID and asked him if Orlov was in.

'I ... I don't know,' he responded.

'You're one of his bodyguards aren't you? Of course you fucking well know.'

I was about to lose it with him when a woman's voice came from further along the hall. It was Lena, the housekeeper I'd met on my first visit here. She was shouting at the officers who were charging from one room to another calling out Orlov's name. I pushed past the bodyguard and went up to her. Her face was white with shock.

'The owner of the house,' I said. 'Where is he?'

She cleared her throat. 'Mr Orlov isn't here.'

'Then tell me where he is.'

She hesitated, and that told me she knew and was lying.

'If I have to ask you again I'll place you under arrest for obstructing the police,' I said. 'Now where is he?'

The look on her face changed from one of shock to panic.

'He ... he's in the basement flat,' she said.

'Then take me there.'

'But I can't. We ... we're not allowed. Nobody is.'

'What's that supposed to mean?'

'It's Mr Orlov's private place. He goes there to be alone.'

221

'Is that right? Well there's a chance he might not be alone right now.'

After another brief hesitation, she said: 'There are two entrances. One around the back through the garage and another via a lift from Mr Orlov's bedroom.'

'Take me to his room,' I said.

She was about to move when an officer called down from the top of the stairs.

'There's a private lift up here, sir. But you need a code to access it.'

Lena responded with alacrity to that by insisting that she didn't have the code.

'Well, somebody must have it,' I said.

I swung round and jabbed a finger at the bodyguard, who was still standing just inside the front door and looking confused.

'What's your name?'

'Gregory,'

'Then Gregory you need to understand that this is part of a major investigation into a series of murders and kidnappings. I have to talk to your boss Orlov as a matter of urgency.'

'Then I will call him and get him to come see you.'

'Will he already be aware that we're here?'

He shook his head. 'It's my job to alert him if he has any visitors. I have not had time to do that.'

'Then I don't want you to. But I do want you to give me the code so that we can get into the lift and drop in on him.'

'But I haven't—'

I held up my hand to stop him. 'Don't piss me off by telling me that you don't have it. That's bullshit. You provide security for him so you'll know everything about this house.'

'But—'

'No buts, Gregory. You need to know that if we aren't given access to the basement in the next minute then we'll just shoot our way in and do a lot of damage at the same time. Then afterwards I'll make sure you're deported from the country. Understood?'

That did it.

'The code is 4–7–6–2,' he said. 'Once inside the lift you will have to press the D button.'

'Will Orlov know we're on our way down?'

'Not unless he is standing in front of the lift.'

Chapter 24

She had never known such pain. It was sharp and intense, and it spread from her nipples across her entire chest.

Orlov had applied the metal clamps with delicate precision. Now he was standing back touching himself as he watched her writhing in agony.

Her face was red and distorted and tears glistened in her eyes.

Orlov began humming along to the song that continued to play in the background. *Somewhere Over The Rainbow*. She was actually listening to her own voice as she was being abused. It was sick, grotesque, surreal.

'You have a beautiful body, Helen,' he said. 'It will look even better by the time I have finished with it.'

The pain was so bad now she could barely draw breath. Her head was pulsing, lights dancing in front of her eyes.

And still he continued to hum and rub himself and grin like he had just hit the jackpot.

Then suddenly he went to the table again and came back holding the biggest dildo that Helen had even seen. It was black and shiny and must have been eight or more inches long.

'Meet Doc Johnson,' he said, holding it up for her to see. 'If anything was designed to make your eyes water then it was this baby.'

The sight of it could not make her feel any worse than she did.

She shut her eyes and attempted to withdraw into herself. But her senses failed to respond and she heard him panting like a dog on heat as he approached the bed again.

She tried to prepare herself for what was to come. Her stomach muscles tensed up. Then she felt his warm, sticky hand on her thigh and a flash of white exploded in her skull.

'Just imagine it's a real black cock,' he said. 'And it's going to rip into you like a pile driver.'

She braced herself for the moment of penetration. But it didn't come. Instead she felt Orlov step back and her own singing was drowned out by a sudden riot of shouting and cursing.

Chapter 25

There was me and two armed officers. As soon as the lift door opened we stormed out – and then reacted immediately to the scene before us.

The other two did the shouting while I tried to make sense of what I was seeing.

The room was like a dungeon filled with BDSM equipment. In the middle of it was a cage with a bed on top. A naked man was standing next to the bed and a naked woman was lying on top of it.

I recognised Alexander Orlov straight away. As he swung round towards us the look on his face was priceless.

He was holding a large black dildo, which he dropped on the floor as he raised his arms in the air.

'Stay where you are and don't move,' yelled one of the officers.

That was when the woman turned her head and I realised who it was.

'Helen!'

I blurted her name involuntarily as I rushed across the room.

The sight of the clamps on her nipples and her terrified expression made me go cold inside. I yelled for the officers to call an ambulance as well as back-up.

'You're safe now,' I said to Helen. 'We've got you.'

I took off my jacket and placed it over her body before gently removing the clamps. Then, as she sobbed uncontrollably, I freed her legs and wrists from the boards before helping her sit up. I spotted a blanket inside the cage so I picked it up and draped it around her shoulders.

While this was happening, Orlov was being cuffed and made to sit on the floor. His flabby body was trembling and he was rambling to himself in Russian.

It was hard to believe that he was the same smart and articulate billionaire I'd met just two days ago in this very house.

'I know everything,' I said, stepping over to him. 'One of Drach's men has told me what you've been doing. I even know where the bodies of the other women are buried.'

He looked up at me, and despite his situation there was a defiant glint in his eyes.

It struck me then that here was a man whose obscene wealth had made him believe that he could do what he wanted; that he was untouchable. It would probably take a while for him to grasp the fact that his time was up.

'Where is Dmitri Kaplan?' I said.

He took a deep breath through his nose and his bare chest expanded. Then the faint trace of a smile touched his mouth.

'He's on one last errand for me,' he said. 'Then he plans to disappear for good with my blessing.'

The anger raged inside me like a storm.

'Tell me where he is you bastard,' I said. 'Or so help me I'll—'

'You'll what, Inspector? Beat me up? I don't think so. If you lay a finger on me I will make sure you lose your job.'

I decided to ignore his threat and seize him by the throat. But as I was reaching towards him, Helen's voice stopped me.

'Kaplan is going to kill Leon,' she said. 'Leon Serova.'

I looked at her.

'How do you know?'

She pointed at Orlov. 'He told me after he sent him to do it. They want to make it to look like suicide.'

It hadn't occurred to me that with all that was happening, Orlov would still go through with the plan he had hatched with Drach.

'How long ago was this?' I said.

'I'm not sure. After Kaplan brought me here earlier I was sedated. When I woke up, he was gone.'

I turned back to Orlov, who now had an ugly grin on his face.

'Serova is going to get exactly what he deserves,' he said. 'You can't save him.'

I wasn't prepared to waste time trying to get the information out of him. He had nothing to gain now by telling me where the killing would take place.

I took out my phone and called the ops room, told them to send units to Serova's house. Then I got them to give me his mobile number and I punched it into my own.

The call went through, thank God. It rang once, twice, three times. When it was answered, I was relieved it wasn't a recorded message.

'Hello.'

'Is that you, Mr Serova?'

'Yes. Who is this?'

'It's DCI Quinn,' I said. 'Are you at home?'

'Why do you want to know that?'

'Because your life is in danger.'

I heard him catch his breath.

'Please tell me where you are,' I said. 'I need to know.'

'I've just arrived at an industrial estate in Pimlico.'

'Why are you there?'

'Alexander Orlov called me earlier. Told me to meet him here at midnight and insisted I come alone. He said he had information about Helen Troy's whereabouts and he wanted to share it with me.'

I looked at my watch. It was dead on midnight.

'Well it's a trap,' I said. 'A man named Dmitri Kaplan has been sent by Orlov to kill you. You need to leave right away.'

He didn't respond for perhaps three seconds. Then he said, 'I think it's too late, Inspector. There's a man and he's walking towards me. I can see it's not Alexander.'

'Are you in your car?'

'No. I'm standing next to it. There's no time to—'

He didn't get to finish the sentence and I heard what I took to be his phone being dropped on the ground.

It was followed by the unmistakable sound of two loud gunshots.

Chapter 26

We used the signal from Serova's mobile phone to triangulate its position.

Before heading for the industrial estate in the response vehicle I told Helen that she would be taken care of.

'You're in good hands,' I said. 'I'll meet up with you again as soon as I can.'

I didn't tell her what I had just heard on the phone because she was already in a terrible state.

'Thank you so much, Inspector,' she said when I patted her shoulder. 'I really didn't think anyone would come for me.'

'It looks like we got here just in time,' I said.

She gulped back a sob. 'He told me he was going to keep me here as his slave. He was going to hurt me.'

I looked across at the pathetic slob as he was hauled to his feet so they could cover him with a bright red kimono.

'We'll he can't hurt you now, Helen. And he'll never be able to hurt anyone again.'

*

Twenty minutes later we arrived at the industrial estate in the response vehicle.

Two patrol cars had beaten us to it and were parked in a car park behind what looked like an empty warehouse.

I could see why Orlov and Kaplan had chosen it as the perfect place in which to trap their victim. It was dark and quiet, and there was no fence or wall to keep people out.

I saw a sleek black Bentley parked between the patrol cars and I assumed it had belonged to Serova. Then I saw his body sprawled on the ground a few feet away from it.

Only when I got up close I was shocked to discover that it wasn't *his* body.

The man lying dead on the tarmac with two bullets in his chest was Dmitri Kaplan. His gold tooth sparkled under the beam of a torch that was shone down on his face.

'The man who shot him is over there,' one of the officers said. 'He claims it was self-defence. We've recovered the revolver.'

Leon Serova was leaning up against one of the patrol cars. He'd been cuffed and had bloodstains on the front of his white shirt.

I told an officer to remove the cuffs and said that the dead man was a paid assassin who had lured Serova here to kill him. I then told Serova that I heard the shots being fired over the phone.

'He came at me with the gun in his hand,' he said. 'But I managed to grab his arm and there was a struggle. I got hold of the gun and just pulled the trigger in blind panic.'

I knew instinctively that he was lying, and not just because of the way he refused to make eye-contact with me. I just didn't think that Kaplan, a seasoned professional, would have been that careless. Plus, what I'd heard over the phone hadn't sounded like a struggle.

I took his arm and edged him away from the others. When we were out of earshot, I said: 'What really happened here, Mr Serova?'

Now he did look into my eyes but his expression was furtive.

'I just told you,' he said.

I shook my head. 'I'm afraid I don't believe you. And I'll wager that the gun you shot him with will not be the same one that he used on his other victims.'

'But you know I was defending myself, Inspector. You even called to tell me it was a trap.'

'And I know that to be a fact,' I said. 'Orlov admitted that he sent Kaplan to get you.'

'So what is the problem?'

'There's no problem, Mr Serova. It's just that I want to be sure of the facts.'

'So why do you think I am not being truthful?'

'For one thing you're a man who is used to going everywhere with bodyguards. So I can't imagine that you would rush off for a midnight rendezvous with a man you know to be your enemy without ensuring you had some form of protection – such as a gun.'

'It's illegal to be in possession of a firearm in this country, Inspector. We both know that.'

'And isn't that why you've come up with this story?' I said. 'You don't want us to know that you were armed yourself, and that you caught him unawares as he approached you and shot him twice before he had time to produce his own gun?'

He thought about it for a long moment, then chose his words carefully before replying.

'Would it really make a difference if that was what happened?' he said. 'It would still be self-defence, and a known assassin would have failed in his attempt to claim another victim. And surely it would be unfair if I were then to face the serious charge of possessing a gun.'

We stared at each other for a long time and I realised that I agreed with what he'd just said. Of course he had broken the law by arming himself with an illegal gun. But if he hadn't done so then he'd be lying dead on the ground and Kaplan would be free to carry on killing. And there would be no guarantee that he would ever stand trial for the savage crimes he'd committed.

'Okay, Mr Serova,' I said, coming to a decision. 'I'll accept your account of what happened here and I won't express any more doubts. But I do want an assurance that Kaplan's weapon will never turn up or fall into the wrong hands.'

He nodded and there was the merest shadow of a smile. 'There's no chance of that, Inspector. I give you my word.'

Chapter 27

Before leaving the scene I learned that Kaplan had parked his car on a service road behind another warehouse. Inside there were motor insurance documents with another name on them.

The name would later prove to be one of his aliases, and the address given would turn out to be a house in Clapham where Kaplan had lived for the past few years.

I was also shown two items of evidence that were found in his pockets. The first was a digital camera and on it was the photograph of Helen Troy that was posted on the internet. The second was a typed-up note which read:

'I fell in love with Helen Troy, but the bitch was going to end our affair. I therefore arranged for her to be abducted. I intended to keep her locked up until she realised she could not live without me. But she said she would always hate me. So I killed her and buried her body. Now I can't live with myself and I accept that I will face my punishment in hell – Leon Serova.'

As suicide notes go it was totally unbelievable. But that probably hadn't mattered to Orlov when he wrote it. Without any evidence to the contrary those words would have been enough to convince everyone that Serova had killed his lover.

And Orlov would have ensured that her body was never found.

*

Needless to say I didn't get to bed that night. And as the new day began I was in for another surprise.

Helen told one of the detectives about the elderly woman named Lucinda who had been shot by Kaplan.

It took us a couple of hours to trace her and for a unit to arrive at her house and discover her body. Shortly after, using directions Helen had provided, another unit found the house where she and the other kidnap victims had been kept.

While I was at the hospital with Helen, Lattimer called with information he'd gathered about Kaplan.

'We now know how he ended up working for Orlov,' he said. 'There was a big corruption case in Russia involving several businessmen. The main witness against them was strangled and the case was dropped. Kaplan was one of the detectives involved and police suspected he committed the murder.'

'The BBC have been running that story,' I said, recalling Gordon Cain's report.

'That's right. But they don't know that Orlov was one of the businessmen who got off.'

'So he probably paid Kaplan to do it and when Kaplan fled Russia he came to London and looked up his old pal.'

'I guarantee that's what happened, and even if Orlov won't confirm it there's bound to be some kind of paper trail.'

It was all coming together at last and I was pleased, of course. But at the same time I didn't feel like celebrating. Too many bad things had happened and too many people were dead. And once again my faith in humanity had taken a huge knock.

But at least Helen Troy was alive, and saving her had been my main objective all along.

As I sat with her in the hospital, however, I could tell that what she had been through had left her emotionally depleted. The scars she'd suffered weren't visible, but they were there inside her head. And I seriously doubted that she would ever fully recover from the damage that had been done to her mind.

Chapter 28

Helen experienced a strange mixture of emotions as she told Detective Inspector Quinn what had happened to her. There was relief, guilt, shock and even a sense of euphoria.

But she knew in her heart that it was going to take time for her to come to terms with what had happened to her.

Would she ever be able to get her life back together? Would she ever have the confidence to sing again in front of an audience?

She wasn't at all sure that it was going to be possible to get back to where she had been before she was kidnapped.

And that included her relationship with Leon Serova. She was pleased that he had managed to survive the attempt on his life. And she was delighted that Gold Tooth was now dead. But it was too early to say whether or not they might get back together. After all, he would serve as a constant reminder of what had happened to her, and surely that would make it harder for her to move on.

Detective Inspector Quinn was a good listener and she liked him a lot. She knew that if it hadn't been for him, she would have spent weeks or months as Orlov's sex slave before he killed her.

'I'd like to thank you again, Inspector,' she told him. 'And please thank everyone else who helped you to find me, including the detective who was shot. I hope she recovers fully.'

There was one thing the detective didn't tell her before he departed – and that was that her cat Biscuit was dead. Instead he left it to her mother to break the news when she arrived at the hospital.

Her mind flashed back to the dream she'd had whilst chained to the bed at the house in the country. She remembered how she was stroking Biscuit and then suddenly realised that he had stopped breathing.

The memory was yet another stab of pain to her heart, and it stayed with her until she finally cried herself to sleep in her mother's arms.

EPILOGUE

A week later, on the same day that Alexander Orlov was committed for trial on charges of kidnapping and conspiracy to murder, Viktor Franko was deemed well enough to leave his hospital bed.

He took us to the hidden well in the Berkshire wood where he and his accomplices had buried the bodies of the four young women.

It took two days to recover the remains, and these were sent back to the countries from where the women had come.

Their funerals all took place on the same day nine days later, along with Jennifer Booth's funeral.

Each funeral became a worldwide media event and was attended by thousands of fans as well as family and friends.

I watched the coverage on the television and felt overwhelmed by a deep and profound sadness.

But I took some comfort in the knowledge that at least one of Orlov's victims was still alive – and that he himself would end his days in prison.

Printed by Amazon Italia Logistica S.r.l.
Torrazza Piemonte (TO), Italy